TEAM CHU
AND THE EPIC
HERO QUEST

PRAISE FOR *TEAM CHU AND THE BATTLE OF BLACKWOOD ARENA*

★ "Dao is a bright voice in middle grade fiction . . . A fresh title that weaves elements of sports stories and sci-fi with realism and beautifully developed characters."
—*School Library Journal*, starred review

"Through the siblings' alternating perspectives and respective internal struggle . . . Dao delves into the Chus' intergenerational dynamics, pressures, and expectations. A rousing adventure and heartwarming series opener."
—*Publishers Weekly*

"Chapters alternate between sports-loving Clip's voice and academically inclined Sadie's point of view as the siblings unravel the mystery in the most challenging—and imaginative—game of laser tag they've ever played. Young gamers, and readers who enjoy rooting for a strong sibling relationship full of competition and support, will revel in this fun, fast-paced adventure."
—*Booklist*

"An action-packed tale of sibling rivalry where thrills and challenges highlight the importance of family and teamwork. This book will delight readers with its fast pace and captivating worlds. Dao has once again crafted a must-read story full of immersive adventure."
—Adrianna Cuevas, author of Pura Belpré Honor Book
The Total Eclipse of Nestor Lopez* and *Cuba in My Pocket

"Laser tag has never been cooler! Both a wild, rollicking adventure and a sweet and nuanced sibling story, Julie C. Dao's middle grade debut is first on the leaderboard for me."

—E. L. Shen, author of *The Comeback*

"Julie Dao delivers a thrilling, pulse pounding joy ride of an adventure brimming over with humor and heart. Readers will love following bickering siblings Sadie and Clip into their wildly imaginative and sinister game of laser tag that will test their skills, their nerve, and their love for each other. Team Chu forever!"

—Samira Ahmed, *New York Times*-bestselling author of *Internment*

"An epically cool adventure that combines fantasy, virtual reality, and competitive sibling rivalry. *Team Chu and the Battle of Blackwood Arena* is fast-paced and bursting with richly designed gaming worlds that you'll wish were real. It's vivid, thrilling, and so much fun."

—Akemi Dawn Bowman, author of the William C. Morris Award finalist *Starfish* and the Infinity Courts series

"The perfect balance of heart and action that will have young readers racing to that last page—and then screaming for the next book."

—Scott Reintgen, Indie-bestselling author of the Nyxia Triad series

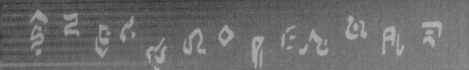

TEAM CHU
AND THE EPIC
HERO QUEST

JULIE C. DAO

FARRAR STRAUS GIROUX
NEW YORK

Farrar Straus Giroux Books for Young Readers
An imprint of Macmillan Publishing Group, LLC
120 Broadway, New York, NY 10271 • mackids.com

Our books may be purchased in bulk for promotional, educational, or
business use. Please contact your local bookseller or the Macmillan
Corporate and Premium Sales Department at (800) 221-7945 ext. 5442 or
by email at MacmillanSpecialMarkets@macmillan.com.

Library of Congress Cataloging-in-Publication Data is available.

First edition, 2023
Book design by Aurora Parlagreco
Printed in the United States of America by Lakeside Book Company,
Harrisonburg, Virginia

ISBN 978-0-374-38881-2
10 9 8 7 6 5 4 3 2 1

**TO EVERY KID WHO'S EVER WANTED
TO BE THE HERO OF AN EPIC FANTASY:**

This one's for you!

TEAM CHU AND THE EPIC HERO QUEST

CHAPTER ONE
JEREMY

"GOOD AFTERNOON, FOLKS, THIS IS YOUR CAPTAIN speaking," a man says over the plane intercom. "We will be landing in Dublin in fifteen minutes. Weather on the ground is cloudy with a chance of light showers, and it is 13 degrees Celsius or about 55 degrees Fahrenheit. On behalf of the crew, thank you for flying with us and have a wonderful day."

I lean into the aisle to watch the flight attendants collect people's used cups and napkins, but my mom yanks me back. "Be careful, Jeremy! I don't want you getting clipped by a cart."

"I'm okay. They're still twenty rows away." I take in her wide, panicked eyes and the sheen of sweat covering her dark brown skin. "Are *you* okay, Mom?"

She closes her eyes. "I will be once we land."

"It'll be sooner than you think," Dad reassures her. His face is pressed against the tiny window and all I can see is the back of his head with the cloud of tight black curls we share. "Wow, it's so lush and green down there. Want to take a look, Jer?"

"Yeah!" I say eagerly, and he leans back in his seat so I can see past him and Mom. As the plane tilts sideways, I spot buildings and houses scattered across an emerald-green land striped with roadways. "Whoa, Mom, you gotta see this! It's not scary, I promise."

"I'll take your word for it." Mom hugs our dark gray pit bull mix, who is sitting calmly on her lap. "Chickpea and I will keep our eyes shut until the plane lands, won't we, girl?" But our dog's soft hazel eyes are glued to the window, fascinated, and Dad and I grin at each other.

"I think Chickpea's excited for Ireland, too," I say, rubbing my dog's floppy Yoda ears, and she turns to lick my face. "You know what? I'm glad you guys are all here."

Mom squeezes my knee. "We're glad, too, honey."

"Are you kidding?" Dad exclaims. "We wouldn't miss your big TV debut for anything. I'm just sorry it's taken so long for us to go on a family vacation."

"It's cool. You guys have been busy lately," I say.

The truth is, my parents are *always* busy. Dad is the chief of surgery at our local hospital and Mom works at a cancer research clinic. Most of the time, I'm home alone with Ruth, our housekeeper, which is why we adopted Chickpea at the local shelter. I knew she was going to be my best friend the second I saw her goofy puppy face and white-dipped paws that look like they're wearing socks. I don't mind hanging out with her and Ruth, but getting to go to Ireland with my parents? And for the *awesome* reason of being on a TV show? You just can't beat that.

A flight attendant passes by, beaming at Chickpea. "What a well-behaved dog you have there," he says, and she wags her tail politely. "She's been so quiet the whole trip."

Mom smiles. "Chickpea's my security blanket. I'm not great with planes."

"You're not alone, ma'am. You should ask your doctor about nausea wristbands."

"She *is* a doctor," I call after him, as he continues down the aisle.

My best friend, Sadie Chu, who's sitting across from us with her mom, shushes me. "Jer! Don't use the D-word with *them* around," she says, pointing to her grandparents in front of her. She's mostly kidding, because her grandpa is watching a movie with his headphones on and her grandma is napping. Grandpa and Grandma Tran, as I call them, really want Sadie and her brother,

Clip, to go to medical school someday. They hint about it all the time, even though Sadie's only going to be in the sixth grade this fall, like me, and Clip is starting the seventh grade. According to Sadie, they've wanted to have a doctor in the family ever since they left Vietnam fifty years ago . . . but it hasn't happened yet.

"Sorry!" I say, grinning. I close my tray table and slide my graphic novel into my lap. The cover shows three warriors battling an orc. It's one of two copies I own of *War of Gods and Men: The Saga*. I always buy two of every book so I can keep one in mint condition and read or lend out the other one. The book I'm holding is obviously the read-and-lend copy. On this plane trip alone, it's been passed between rows 28, 29, and 30 at least a dozen times.

"Thanks for letting me borrow that, by the way. I reread the section about the mages, and so did Iggy." Sadie leans over and pokes Iggy Morales, a big seventh-grade kid with dark hair and glasses who plays soccer with Clip. Both boys are in the row in front of me with Iggy's dad. "Hey, Iggy, did you memorize the names of all the mage kingdoms?"

Iggy nods. "Oh yeah. I studied hard!"

Clip raises himself up in his seat to look back at us. He's the total opposite of his sister. Sadie is short, skinny, and a bookworm like me, while Clip is tall, athletic, and a front-runner for captain of Saybrook Middle School's boys' soccer team—and he won't let you forget it. "But you already know all about the mages," he tells Iggy. "You're a Level 115 Silver Mage."

"That's only in the game," Iggy points out. "We're about to actually *live* the game."

Two dark blond heads pop up in the row in front of *them*. Caroline and Derek Marshall are twins and going into the seventh grade with Iggy and Clip, and they borrowed my book before our plane even took off from Boston. Caroline's mouth moves, but I can't hear her.

"She says she knows more about the War of the Orc Kings now than the US Civil War," Clip says. "And Derek studied the warlocks' poems in case they show up in a puzzle."

Usually, I'm the only one who *really* gets excited about this stuff. Give me a wizard, a dragon, and an epic quest, and I'm on board. But seeing how equally hyped my friends are about the show makes me happy. "Just think, guys: The child hero of Pantaera could be on the plane right now," I say, and Clip passes my words on to the twins. Sadie leans over and gives me a jellyfish, our special fist bump where we wiggle our fingers like tentacles as we pull away.

Mom and Dad are staring at me in amusement.

"I know you've been explaining to me and Dad for months," my mom says. "But I'm still amazed by everything you just said. Orcs? Warlocks? *Child hero*?"

"I know, Mom, it's a lot to take in." I get ready to launch into another rundown of the story. Or as Sadie likes to call it, another one of my lectures.

But Dad jumps in before I can get going. "Hold on, let me see if I get this right. So, *War of Gods and Men* is that online video game you kids play, and now they've turned it into a TV show. The game takes place in a fantasy world called Pantaera, and orcs and warlocks are some of the magical beings that live there."

"Show-off," Mom jokes.

"Hold on, I got more!" Dad pushes his glasses up his broad nose. "Evil forces are trying to take over Pantaera, and according to a prophecy, three human heroes will save the day: an adult, a teenager, and a child, to represent the three stages of a hero's journey. How'd I do?"

"You get an A-plus, Dad!" I tell him proudly. "The show's gonna have three seasons: one for adult contestants, one for teens, and one for kids my age. Each winner will be named one of the Pantaereon, which is a trio of legendary heroes. That's what we're going to try out for." I point to myself, the Chu siblings, the Marshall twins, and Iggy. "We won spots on the show—"

"Thanks to your epic laser tag victory," Mom finishes. "I know *that* part, at least!"

Two months ago, at the beginning of summer vacation, the Blackwood Gaming Arena opened up in our town with an intense virtual-reality version of laser tag. My friends and I beat the entire game, and the owners of the arena happened to have connections to the *War of Gods and Men* franchise, so the grand prize was a spot on the TV show. Since the six of us won the laser tag tournament together, we *all* got spots.

"So there'll be actors and a set, but it's a competition where you kids climb and run and do obstacle courses?" Mom asks, elbowing Dad. "Sounds like those

Nickelodeon game shows we watched back in the dark ages, like *Legends of the Hidden Temple*."

Dad winces. "It wasn't *that* long ago, hon, but yes. Climbing and obstacle courses sound pretty physical, though, Jer Bear. Think you'll be up for all of that?"

Mom elbows him again. "Nathan!"

"I know you'll be great, of course," my dad adds quickly, smiling at me. "You're good at everything you do. I just meant that you hate gym class, is all."

"Well, this won't be like gym class. It'll be fun, and I bet—" Mom breaks off when the plane makes a sudden dip, and goes back to hugging Chickpea with her eyes squeezed shut.

Within minutes, the wheels hit the tarmac and we're speeding toward our airport gate. The second the plane comes to a complete stop and the seat belt sign turns off, everyone is on their feet, stretching, yawning, and grabbing stuff from the overhead bins.

I stay in my seat, looking down at my book.

It's true, what Dad said: I do hate gym. I've never been the kind of kid who liked going outside and throwing a ball around. Every time we have to run a mile in PE, I end up walking most of it, and I always get picked last for teams because I fall on my face a lot. Once, when we were doing a gymnastics unit, I got stuck on the uneven bars and my teacher had to help me down. I'm just not good at physical stuff. I'd rather curl up with Chickpea and play *War of Gods and Men*. In the game, I'm fast and strong and run around saving the world. But in real life? Not so much. I already know this show is gonna be way harder for me than it is for my friends.

The feeling only gets stronger when Derek pops up from his seat and announces, "Me and Caroline have been rock climbing *nonstop*, so we can scale any goblin castles they have."

"That's why I paid for that gym membership add-on? So you two could practice scaling castles?" jokes Mr. Marshall, the twins' dad.

"At least that was at the gym," Mrs. Chu tells him. "Every night, we've had to listen to Sadie run up and down the stairs and Clip pounding the floor in his room as he does barfees."

"They're called *burpees*, Mom!" Clip groans.

Mr. Morales snorts and ruffles Iggy's hair. "You guys think you've got it bad? My whole household has become a health food zone since this one decided he's no longer eating trans fats or red meat. You know how hard it is to give up empanadillas and pasteles?"

I'm almost drooling at the memory of dinner at Iggy's house, when his parents cooked us some amazing Puerto

Rican food, but Iggy claps his hands over his ears. "Dad, *please*, you're not supposed to mention those until the show's done," he says. "Then we can eat whatever."

"Yes, the kids have been working hard," Grandpa Tran chimes in, looking at Sadie and Clip. "If only Clip worked as hard at school, though. So many Bs on his report card."

Sadie looks delighted, since school is the one thing her brother can't beat her at. But before she can come up with any snappy remarks, Clip says loudly, "Okay, from now on, no talking about school allowed. It's August, we've got less than two weeks of summer vacation left, and we're about to get famous on a TV show. We need to *focus*."

When the plane door finally opens, everyone shuffles out with their bags. Mom leads the way with Chickpea on her leash, chatting with Mrs. Chu. I notice she and Dad were awfully quiet when the other parents were talking about their kids' workout routines—probably because *my* version of intense exercise is playing Wii Tennis in the basement.

Sadie glances at me, sensing my worry. "The show's gotta have brainy challenges, too, Jer, and you're better at puzzles and riddles than any of us."

I perk up. "Yeah, I do like those!"

It's Saturday afternoon and Dublin Airport is packed. After what seems like forever, we get through customs, collect our stuff at baggage claim, and head downstairs to catch our bus.

"Three more hours on a coach bus, after we just spent five hours on a plane," Derek grumbles, as we ride the escalator down. "Why can't the producers just film right here in Dublin? Why do we have to drive across the entire country of Ireland?"

Caroline gives her brother a withering look. "Because we need to get to the countryside out west, where it'll feel more like being in an epic fantasy. Right, Jer?"

"Right!" I agree. "There are cliffs and forests where we're going. Clarebriar Castle, where the show's being filmed, is five hundred years old and has lots of cool history."

Sadie claps. "I can't believe we get to stay there! And I'm glad we have a long bus ride. That's three more hours to study up and figure out what we might need to know for the show."

"Good point," Derek concedes.

On the ground floor, we head through a set of automatic doors to a parking lot full of buses. Dad and Mr. Marshall open a folder full of information from the TV producers, searching for the name of our ride, but

I've already spotted it. "Look!" I say, pointing to the long silver bus. A woman is standing in front of it, holding a big sign that says "To the Land of Pantaera."

Derek and Caroline cheer, Iggy and Clip high-five each other, Sadie squeals and hugs me, and all of the grown-ups laugh.

"We're going," I say, grinning so hard my face hurts. "We're really going to Pantaera."

CHAPTER TWO
JEREMY

"HELLO THERE!" THE LADY SAYS. SHE'S SHORT AND pale, with curly red hair, and speaks with a soft Irish accent. "You must all be with me, since you aren't asking me where on earth Pantaera is, like everyone else passing by. Of course, I have to tell them Pantaera is not on Earth at all!"

"I'm sure that clears things up," Caroline jokes.

"My name is Maureen, and I'll be driving you to the set. Names, please?" We tell her, and she checks us off on a clipboard. "Great! You're the last people to arrive. I drove two contestants and their families yesterday, and two others landed in Dublin an hour ago. They're on the bus, waiting." Maureen catches sight of our dog, and her voice goes up about three octaves. "Is this Chickpea?! You are listed here as a very special passenger, you adorable thing!"

Chickpea surges forward at the sound of her name, whacking us all with her happy tail.

Maureen pets my dog's head, then directs us to a big storage compartment near the bus wheel. "Everyone, store your things in here and pick out your seats, and then I'll do a *very* brief introduction," she says. "You will be having lunch with the producers at the hotel when we arrive, and they'll have all the information you need. Sound good?"

"Sounds good," everyone choruses.

Mom hands me Chickpea's leash and a poop bag. "Jer, honey, can you take her to go potty while Dad and I handle the bags?"

"Sure, Mom." As I take the dog, I hear Dad say to Maureen, "We'd like to visit the Aran Islands if Jeremy's done filming early. Do you recommend renting a car to get to the boat or . . ."

My shoulders slump as I walk Chickpea over to a patch of grass. Dad's been saying stuff like that ever since I found out I was going to be on the show. "If Jeremy's done filming early," or "Climbing and obstacle courses sound pretty physical," or "Think you'll be up for all of that?" He clearly doesn't think I have a shot at winning, and I don't, either. I want to believe I *could*, even if I'm not fast, strong, or athletic . . . but then I remember how I always trip or fall in gym class. It feels like a box has been drawn around me, and I can't figure out how to break out of it.

I sigh.

"What's weighing you down, young man?" a voice asks.

I turn to see an elderly man on a bench nearby. He has pale skin, a gray beard, and light blue eyes that match his robe and tall cone-shaped hat. He looks like he decided to dress like Gandalf the Grey, the wizard from the Lord of the Rings, but only made half the effort, since he's also wearing ratty old flip-flops over white socks and holding a Starbucks cup. A big black cat is on the pavement between his feet, staring at Chickpea, who's busy sniffing the grass.

"Um, I'm fine. Thanks for asking," I say politely.

In fantasy books, wizards' eyes are always described as *keen*. I never really knew what that meant, but I feel like I do now. The man watches me like he knows everything about me. "Are you certain?" he asks. "You look a bit upset to me. Go on now. What's eating you?"

I shrug. "Not much. Just . . . just people not believing in me."

"Is that so? And why do you need people to believe in you?"

"Because it feels good, I guess?"

The wizard looks thoughtful. "Isn't it enough to believe in yourself?" he asks, crossing his legs. His flip-flop almost whacks the black cat. I watch nervously as it hisses and moves toward Chickpea, who still hasn't noticed it. My dog weirdly *loves* cats—at the shelter, they told us that she might have lived with some once—but I don't know how this cat feels about dogs. It doesn't come any closer to us, though, but sits nearby with its amber eyes narrowed. "Ah, maybe that's the problem, then," the old man adds, when I don't answer his question right away. "You don't believe in yourself."

I shift my weight. "Sure, I do."

"No. And that's why you'll always search for it in others. A quest, I'm afraid, that will never fulfill you." The wizard leans forward. "To me, you look like a capable and intelligent young man. You clearly have a fire inside of you, but it will die out if you don't feed it."

Chickpea chooses that moment to take a big poop on the grass.

But the old man doesn't miss a beat, his pale eyes still locked on mine. "Feed that fire, my young friend. Tell yourself you are enough, and you can do anything your heart desires."

Goose bumps form on my arms. I know we're at an airport, and my dog is pooping, and the wizard is drinking a fancy latte, but I feel like I'm a character in a book. Like a wise old mentor just told me my whole life is about to change. "I thank you, sir, and bid you good day," I say grandly, because that's what a character would say. (I've *always* wanted to talk like that.)

He gives me a toothy smile and toasts me with his Starbucks cup.

"Jer! Let's get a move on, son!" Dad hollers.

I turn toward him and call, "One sec!" But when I look back, the wizard is gone. He must have run *really* fast back inside the airport. "What a weird guy," I mutter. His big black cat is still there, though, and Chickpea has noticed it at last. Her tail goes about a hundred miles an hour as I clean up after her. "Come on, girl, we gotta go," I say, leading her back to the bus.

We find the grown-ups sitting up front near Maureen. The kids are all in the back, where there's a funny little bathroom you have to climb down some steps to reach.

"What took you so long, honey?" Mom asks me.

"I was chatting with a wizard," I say, and everyone immediately looks out the bus windows. "I mean, a guy dressed like a wizard. He's gone now, but it was cool."

"Was he a part of the show?" Sadie suggests. "Like an actor, maybe?"

Maureen frowns. "All of the actors are already on set.

Filming starts tonight, as soon as you get to the castle. He couldn't have been part of our show."

"What did he say to you?" Clip asks.

I hesitate. For some reason, I want to keep the wizard's words to myself. They were kind of personal, after all. "Just, uh, some inspirational stuff. It was nice."

Suddenly, Chickpea's tail starts wagging again. Coming up the aisle toward us—slowly and confidently, like it owns the whole bus—is the black cat we saw outside.

"Hey, that's the wizard's cat!" I say. "It followed us."

"Awww, it's so cute!" Iggy says, and the cat looks at him and meows. "Hey, little guy."

"No, no, no. Off the bus," says Maureen, shaking her head at the cat. "You're not on the passenger list, kitty. We don't take stowaways here."

"Jeremy, be careful," Mom calls, but she doesn't need to worry. The cat just stands still, letting Chickpea sniff it and rolling its amber eyes like it's saying, "Ugh, *dogs.*" After a moment, it lifts a paw, like it's saying, "Okay, enough." Chickpea backs away at once and hops onto the empty seat beside Derek, plunking her head on his knees for a nap.

Maureen approaches the cat, but it jumps onto Iggy's chest, purring. Iggy strokes the soft black fur and pleads, "Can he come? He and Chickpea are good. They won't fight!"

Derek raises his eyebrows at me. "Doesn't he belong to that wizard, though?"

I shrug. "The wizard left him behind, so maybe not."

"Iggy, you are not taking that cat with us," Mr. Morales calls from the front of the bus. "You and Marta already have two at home. Bring it outside and let it go."

"Please, Dad!" Iggy begs, his arms tightening around the cat. "I'll let him go when we get to the hotel, I promise. I can't take him on the show anyway."

"Well, he does look comfortable," Maureen says doubtfully, as the cat starts purring even more loudly against Iggy's chest. "Okay, it's fine with me. But keep an eye on him, all right?"

I take a seat next to Sadie and notice two new kids behind her. One is a white girl with brown hair and freckles, and she's small and skinny like Sadie. The other is a dark-skinned boy who is even broader in the shoulders than Iggy, and he's wearing a hockey jersey. *Great, another athlete*, I think, my heart sinking. I shake their hands and introduce myself.

"Elizabeth Baker, but call me Lizard," the girl says, orange braces glinting on her teeth.

"I'm George Quinn Jr." The boy grins at me. "I thought I was gonna have to be the only token Black kid in medieval Europe, but I'm glad I was wrong!"

I laugh. "I know. It's hard to find us in fantasy books, even though we were definitely in Europe. I mean, England controlled one-fifth of the globe and people came from all over!"

"You're brainy," George says, giving me an appreciative nod. "I like that. That'll be important in this competition, maybe even more than being athletic."

"You think?" Lizard and Clip say together, looking doubtful.

"What makes you say that?" I ask hopefully.

"Well, look at the message of the Lord of the Rings," George says. "The most heroic people aren't always the ones swinging swords or becoming kings, right? You could even argue that Sam, who's a tiny hobbit gardener, is the hero of the whole story."

Sadie nudges me, smiling, and I get the overwhelming

urge to hug George. Between what he and the wizard told me, I'm starting to feel a lot better.

"So how did you two get on the show?" Caroline asks the new kids.

"I won a mini-golf tournament in my town," George says. "I made it in under the wire, 'cause I'm the maximum age, thirteen. My parents are jazzed! They're even bigger *War of Gods and Men* fans than I am. They run an online forum for players over thirty, and they've been trying to recruit all of your parents since you guys came on the bus."

"I won a triathlon at my elementary school," Lizard explains. "We ran a mile, biked a mile, and swam a hundred yards to raise money for breast cancer, which my mom survived. That's why I did it. But it was cool to win a spot on this show, too."

I deflate again. Does *everyone* here have to be more athletic than me?

"A triathlon, huh?" Clip looks impressed. He's been sizing George up since we started talking, but now he checks Lizard out, too. "You said elementary school? How old are you?"

"I just turned eleven last month. I'm the youngest on the show. I'm a little worried, though," she adds, "since I haven't played the game much. I don't know a ton about it."

"That's okay, Jeremy here is a walking encyclopedia of Pantaera," Sadie says, patting my shoulder. "He knows more about it than anyone, probably even the game designers."

The Marshall twins nod in agreement and my cheeks grow warm, but Clip says, "That's impossible. Jer does know a ton about the game, but not more than the designers. When *I'm* a video game designer, I'll make sure I know my world like the back of my hand."

"Oh, you want to make games someday?" George asks. "Cool!"

Clip shrugs, trying and failing to look casual. "That's the dream."

"Isn't becoming a game designer hard, though?" Sadie jokes, poking her brother. "You might need to actually work sometime, instead of sleeping in and watching TV."

He swats her hand away, scowling. "I know that."

At the front of the bus, Maureen claps her hands for attention. "Okay, everyone! Listen up, please. We have a three-hour ride to county Mayo. Or should I say . . . Pantaera?"

Everyone cheers, and the kids are the loudest of all.

"We are going to the village of Clarebriar, where the families will stay at the hotel for the duration of this trip, all expenses paid by the show," Maureen says, and this time, the grown-ups cheer the loudest. "It's a lovely place, with shops, restaurants, cafés, and even a museum. Best of all, it's only twenty minutes to Clarebriar Castle, where the filming will take place. But before I take the contestants to the castle, everyone will enjoy luncheon at the hotel, where the producers have planned an official welcome and introduction."

Mrs. Chu raises her hand. "The kids won't be staying at the hotel with us, right?"

"Right. The producers want to make this experience as immersive as possible, so the contestants will be staying on the grounds of the castle itself," Maureen explains. "They won't have access to modern technology, like computers or mobile phones, and they will dress and eat and live as medieval fantasy warriors would. However, I am happy to confirm that there will be modern plumbing and heating in their accommodations."

"Phew! I was worried they'd make us use chamber pots," Iggy mutters.

My dad raises his hand. "The kids won't keep in touch with us during the show, then?"

Maureen nods. "Correct. But there will be shuttles to take you to the castle, where you can secretly watch the filming anytime you like. Any contestant who is eliminated will of course return to their families at once. Okay, I'm sure you have a million more questions, but let's save those for the luncheon. What do you all think? Shall we hit the road?"

There's another chorus of loud cheers, and Maureen takes her place in the driver's seat.

Sadie throws her arms around me. "It's happening, Jer!"

I hug her back, forgetting my worries for the time being. All my life, I've read about heroes in epic fantasy books, and for the next week or so, my friends and I will actually get to try to *be* those heroes. "Pantaera, here we come!" I shout.

CHAPTER THREE
SADIE

"SADIE, ARE YOU GONNA BE GLUED TO YOUR PHONE the whole time?" Clip asks.

"No," I say, snapping photos of everything. "Maureen said we won't have our cell phones on set, remember? I mean, *mobile* phones. That's what they call them in Ireland."

"What do you guys think about George and Lizard?" Jeremy asks.

"I like them. They seem nice," I say.

Clip snorts. "Who cares about *nice*? They're our competition." He looks over at George, who's helping his parents with their suitcases. George is a copy of Mr. Quinn, minus the beard, and they're even wearing the same jersey. "That kid is a three-season athlete. Soccer, football, and ice hockey. He's going to be my biggest threat on this show."

We haven't even started filming yet, and my brother already assumes he's going to be one of the finalists. "*Your* biggest threat?" I repeat, annoyed.

He flaps a hand. "I meant in general."

"Did you guys catch all the movie and book references he made?" Jeremy asks, biting his lip. "He's sporty *and* cool *and* a fantasy nerd. George is the perfect contestant."

"Like I said, you know way more about *War of Gods and Men* than anyone," I reassure him. "And Lizard is just as big of a threat, even if she's the youngest. She *did* win that triathlon."

Clip crosses his arms. "So she says."

We glance at Lizard. She's standing in front of the hotel doors with her mom, who is fun and pretty and seems to have hit it off with *our* mom. As I watch, Lizard straightens the avocado-printed bandanna on her mother's bald head before they take a few selfies together.

Jeremy fidgets with his backpack straps. He seems to have gotten more and more nervous the closer we get to filming. I keep telling him it can't be all jumping and running and climbing. The competition could favor brainy kids, like George said, and I hope he's right. I definitely think of myself as more bookish than athletic.

I go back to capturing our surroundings on my phone. The Kearney Hotel sits on a hill overlooking the village of Clarebriar. It has a great view of the cobblestone streets, houses, and shops below, which have colorful wooden shutters and thatched roofs. In the distance, the misty cliffs drop off to the North Atlantic Ocean, where a few boats with white sails bob in the harbor. The air is clean and cool and smells like salty seawater.

"Sadie!" Grandma says loudly. "Make sure you go to the bathroom, ha? Don't hold it in. It's not healthy. I didn't see you go on that bus."

"Grandma, please lower your voice!" I beg, as Clip cackles at my embarrassment.

"Why lower voice? Who cares? Everyone pees and poops, even your friend's cute doggie," she says, pointing at Chickpea, who is currently demonstrating on the hotel lawn.

Meanwhile, our grandpa is digging through his bag. "Clip! Where did I put my memory card?" he asks. "I need to make sure I can record your show."

"It's going to be on TV, Grandpa," Clip points out. "They have cameras to film it."

"Yes, but it's not the same! They won't zoom in on only you and Sadie!"

Mom shoots us a look of sympathy and wrangles our grandparents into the hotel. We enter a beautiful lobby with deep-red carpets and an antique chandelier. To one side of the front desk is a whiteboard that says: "Pantaera Luncheon, Magnolia Ballroom. 14:00."

Derek frowns. "Jer, what's fourteen o'clock again?"

"It's not fourteen o'clock. It's two p.m.," Jeremy explains. "You have to subtract twelve. That's how they write the afternoon and evening hours in Ireland and the UK."

"Kids, why don't you go find the Magnolia Ballroom?" Dr. Thomas suggests, as she leads Chickpea through the lobby. "We'll meet you there after we check in."

Iggy and his dad are already at the front desk, where the big black cat is walking back and forth and rubbing its face on the computers and phones. Everyone behind the desk is going, "Awww!" as Iggy tells them, looking misty-eyed, "Please find him a good home, okay? He hitched a ride with me from the airport and I wish I could keep him."

"Let him go, son," Mr. Morales says. "They'll take care of him."

Iggy hugs the cat. "Goodbye forever, Tuba," he says in a shaky voice, then joins the rest of us leaving the lobby. Clip and Caroline put their arms over his shoulders comfortingly.

"Tuba?" I whisper, and Jeremy looks just as confused.

Derek explains to us in a low voice. "Iggy texted his

sister about the cat. Marta wanted to name him Tuna, but autocorrect changed it to *Tuba*, and they thought that was funny, so they kept it. They were hoping their dad would let them adopt him, but no luck."

"Poor Iggy," Jeremy says sympathetically.

The Magnolia Ballroom is huge, with floor-to-ceiling windows and lots of round tables and chairs. A buffet station stands near the front, covered in silver platters that smell amazing. I hear my friends' stomachs rumbling along with mine, like we're some kind of hungry orchestra.

At the sight of all the food, Iggy's chin wobbles like he's about to cry for real. "I smell gravy, but I'm still eating only fruits and veggies for the show," he says.

"Dude, we're practically *on* the show right now," Clip points out. "Eat whatever you want. And who knows what they're gonna feed us at the castle?"

Someone laughs. "Oh, they'll feed you well, I promise."

We turn to see three people coming in behind us. The man who spoke is Mom and Dad's age and Asian, with kind eyes behind wire-rimmed glasses. The other two are white; one is an older man with a gray mustache and the other is a blond woman in an old-fashioned velvet dress.

The man in glasses shakes our hands. "I'm Redmond

Nguyen, but you can call me Red. I'm an executive producer on the show, and these are my colleagues, Andy and Bess."

"Nguyen?" I repeat. "Are you Vietnamese American, too?"

His eyes twinkle at me. "Sure am. You must be Sadie Chu, and that's your brother, Clip, and your friend Jeremy Thomas. And you two are the twins, Derek and Caroline Marshall, and the fruits-and-veggies guy is Iggy Morales. Mardella told me all about you guys and your epic laser tag victory," he adds, laughing at our surprised faces. Mardella is one of the owners of the Blackwood Gaming Arena, and her son, Tom, played on our laser tag team back in June.

"Are the Blackwoods here?" Caroline asks eagerly.

Red chuckles. "I've been sworn to secrecy, but let's just say you might see some familiar faces hidden among the extras on set. Ours included. You'll have to look hard, though."

"Perk of the job, getting to be on-screen," Bess jokes, curtsying in her long velvet dress.

Both Clip and Jeremy are staring at Red with their mouths open and eyes like saucers.

"It's *such* an honor to meet the original creator of Pantaera," Jer says, his face glowing. "I was hoping to get your autograph at New York Comic Con, but your line was ridiculous!"

"Thanks, Jeremy. It's an honor to meet you guys, too," Red says kindly. He scans the rest of our group. "Aha, you guys must be George Quinn and Lizard Baker. And over here are the final two competitors! Let me introduce Krisztina Kurso and Molly Wan."

Two girls enter the ballroom with their families. Krisztina is a white, heavyset girl with strawberry-blond hair and a Star Wars T-shirt. Molly is short, with her jet-black hair dyed blond at the tips and eyes that size up me and Clip, the only other Asian contestants in the room. Behind them are all of the grown-ups in *our* group, so the space suddenly feels crowded.

"Okay, looks like everybody's here!" Red says, and after more introductions, he directs us to the buffet. "Everyone, grab some food and we'll get started. I'll make it quick, I promise. I know the adults must be tired, and the competitors are dying to get up to the castle."

The kids don't need to be asked twice. As we rush to grab plates, I hear Grandma loudly asking Red if he's married and which part of Vietnam his ancestors are from.

While waiting in line, I film a five-second video of the buffet with my phone, then upload it on TikTok with a simple caption: "Excited to be in Ireland for a family vacay!"

"Family vacay?" Caroline asks. She's looking at TikTok on her phone, too, and just saw my update. "You're here to be on TV, Sadie! Don't be shy! Let your followers know."

I blush. Some days, I can't believe that she and Derek are *my* friends now, too, not just Clip's, and that she's following me on social media. The twins are really, really cool and popular. "I, uh, don't want to get in trouble for posting too many details about the show. You know, confidentiality and stuff. And I don't want kids at school to know."

"Why not?" Caroline asks curiously. "Clip's told *everyone*."

My big brother has a mouth the size of Texas, so of course the whole school knows about him, Iggy, and the Marshalls competing. "It's fine for him, 'cause everyone at school likes him," I say. "No matter what he's into, kids will think he's cool. But for me—"

"You're cool, too, Sadie," she interrupts.

"Thanks," I say shyly. "But, um, it's different for me."

Caroline plops a baked potato onto her plate. "Why?"

I take a clean plate. "I guess 'cause I'm starting sixth grade and it'll be my first year at the middle school," I tell her. "It's, like, a fresh start. I want to try new things, like write for the school paper or even do a sport. I don't want kids to just know me as 'that girl who pretends she's in a fantasy world,' 'cause then that might be all they ever know me for."

"I get it. But—" Caroline breaks off when her dad comes over to say something to her.

I notice Molly Wan at my elbow, listening to our conversation. "Hi," I say, smiling at her. "I know Red just introduced us, but I'm Sadie and that's my brother, Clip, behind you."

"Check it out," Clip says, laughing and pointing to the three of us. "If we formed a team on this show, we could be Asia versus the rest of the world."

I laugh at the joke, but Molly doesn't. "Are you guys Chinese, too?" she asks.

"Nope, we're Vietnamese like Red," I say.

"Oh." Something about her tone rubs me the wrong way. She scoops green beans and baked chicken onto her plate. "Too bad *War of Gods and Men* has nothing to do with Vietnam. It's too small. Writers always prefer to use China as inspiration."

Jeremy, who's behind Clip, overhears her. "Actually, that's wrong," he says cheerfully. "Part of the Kingdom of Verdigris is inspired by Vietnam. The Dao dynasty rules there."

"There's also a Nguyen dynasty, isn't there?" I ask.

He nods. "Yep. They were the kings of Verdigris before the Battle of the Seven Warriors. They had almost total control of oceanic trade at one time."

Molly laughs in a mean way. "Wow, you guys sure know a lot about a place that doesn't even exist," she says, looking us up and down. "I just know the basics and that's more than enough for me, but I'm glad for *you*."

My stomach tightens. Her reaction is exactly why I didn't tell the kids at school about this show. "I think knowledge of Pantaera will be important for the competition," I say, annoyed. "How'd you hear about this show, anyway, if you're not a fan of the game?"

"They were advertising the competition in my town, so my friends and I applied and *I* got chosen." Molly flips the bleached tips of her hair over one shoulder. "We had to write a short essay, and I'm *really* talented at writing. That's how Kris got picked from her town, too."

The redhead in the Star Wars shirt nods from the opposite side of the buffet table, where she's grabbing bread and butter. "I wanna get published before I turn thirteen," she tells us.

"Why?" Jeremy asks.

Kris shrugs. "Because it's impressive. The younger

a writer is, the better. My mom's a literary agent—that's somebody who helps you get your book out to publishers—and she says I'll get a lot of attention if I publish a novel before I even hit the eighth grade."

"Well, I have eight million followers on that website Awesome Novel Land," Molly says quickly. "I posted a story about a girl who meets a hot vampire in biology class. It's very, very original."

Kris raises an eyebrow. "But that sounds a lot like—"

"It's different," Molly interrupts her. "It's got hundreds of millions of reads!"

"Do you think it's a good idea to post your story there, though?" Kris asks. "That's eight million people who might steal your idea. My mom says, legally, that you . . ."

My friends and I hurry away with our food as Kris keeps talking and Molly's face grows bright red. "Looks like rivalries are starting already and we're not even on set yet," I mutter.

We sit with Iggy and Derek. Iggy's eyes are closed as he chews on a piece of chicken dipped in thick, salty gravy, and Derek has already inhaled everything on his plate.

I open a ketchup packet a little too aggressively, and it splatters all over my chicken. "I can't believe that girl Molly thinks we're silly for knowing so much about Pantaera," I fume. "There's nothing wrong with having background information!"

"She's just jealous," Jeremy says, dumping pepper all over his mashed potatoes. "We're going to have fun on this show 'cause we care about it, unlike her."

I sigh and start eating. I wish I could be more like Jer and not care about what people think of me . . . but I *do* care. It's not that I mind liking geeky stuff, like epic fantasy and reading about other worlds. But the kids at school seem to like labels, and I don't want to get stuck with one before I even have a chance to figure out what else I like.

Maybe this is a sign. Maybe I should keep more of my excitement for this show inside and cover up my geek- iness. At least, until I find out what (and *who*) I really want to be.

CHAPTER FOUR
SADIE

RED BOUNCES ON HIS TOES LIKE HE'S AN EXCITED contestant, and not the producer of the show. "Okay! As promised, I will keep this short and sweet," he says, over the clinking of silverware and noisy slurping (mostly from Clip and Iggy). "Welcome, heroes and families! I am thrilled to launch the junior version of *War of Gods and Men*, the TV show. Our parent company, JCD Universal, cast a very wide net to find contestants from all over the US through essay contests, triathlons, mini-golf tournaments, and even laser tag," he adds, his dark eyes twinkling at our table. "This is going to be the most epic series ever to hit television!"

Everyone cheers and claps.

"As fantasy fans know, three is a magical number," Red continues. "So I'm pleased to announce that we've already secretly filmed the first two seasons of the show and crowned an adult hero and a teen hero. And I believe that this third and final season—in which we search for the youngest member of the Pantaereon—will be the most magical of them all!"

The room bursts into applause again.

"I can't believe they've found two heroes already!" Jeremy says excitedly.

"My team and I wrote an original storyline just for this show, so even if you've been playing the video game for years, everything will be brand-new to you." Red's face grows serious. "This will be an epic fantasy come to life. On the first season of the show, ten adult warriors battled it out in the Kingdom of Verdigris, in the treacherous western deserts of Pantaera. Only one of them was found truly worthy of the title of *hero*."

Next to me, Jeremy shivers with anticipation. Even Clip has stopped chewing to listen.

"On the second season, ten courageous teenagers competed in the Kingdom of Malachite, in the icy wastes of eastern Pantaera. Again, only one emerged victorious." Red looks each of us in the eye. "Now, the ten of *you* have been called forth to the northern forests and windswept peaks of the Kingdom of Celadon. You've been summoned by the Keeper of Fortunes, an immortal being with the power to see through all of time. Will you answer her call?"

"Yeah!" Jeremy, Lizard, and George shout, and the rest of us echo them.

"Pantaera is on the brink of war," Red says softly. "It is a world of secret agendas, rulers grappling for power, and gods who move kings and queens like chess pieces on a board that only they can see." The room has gone silent. He has this intense way of storytelling that reels you in, and I see everyone listening with rapt attention. Grandma isn't even scolding Grandpa for letting his food get cold. "Once, the magical beings of Pantaera lived in harmony, but greed and conflict have weakened and divided them. Now, the Forgotten Queen and her forces are gathering near the borders, waiting for the chance to strike. To swoop in and seize Pantaera for her own."

I shiver. I could *almost* believe this is real. I peek at Molly. For someone who made fun of us for knowing so much about Pantaera, she looks just as caught up in the story as anyone else.

"Friends, we must fight to save the beauty, magic, and goodness of Pantaera," Red says. "An ancient prophecy tells of three seemingly ordinary humans who hold within them the souls of champions. They will be the Pantaereon, destined to save this land from the Forgotten

Queen. Two of them have already been found. Will one of you be the third and final hero?"

This time, nobody hesitates. All of the kids shout, "Yeah!"

The grown-ups smile and whisper to each other.

Red nods. "This week, you will undergo a series of ten challenges to prove that you have the five most important qualities of a hero: courage, determination, humility, intelligence, and strength. Each task will take place in a unique setting and be hosted by a different magical being. And that's all I will say for now. Soon, the games will begin!"

Everyone bursts into cheers and applause once more.

"This is going to be *incredible*!" Jeremy exclaims, his eyes shining.

"I'm so excited!" Derek says. "Guys, I bet laser tag gave us good practice for this show."

"Oh yeah, I think we've got this one in the bag," Clip says smugly. "The winner's definitely gonna be someone from our group."

At the front of the room, Red announces, "Okay, I can take a few questions now."

Iggy's hand flies up. "Who is the Forgotten Queen again, and why was she forgotten?"

"It's a long story. But here's the short version: She was

a princess of Pantaera, next in line to rule the Kingdom of Malachite. But her father saw the greed in her ruthless heart and gave the throne to her younger brother instead. She left to form an army, and now she wants to take back what she believes is hers." Red looks around and sees my hand. "Question, Sadie?"

Everybody looks at me, and my cheeks grow hot and I fidget under the attention. "Um, you said there's an adult hero and a teen hero already. Will we get to meet them?"

"Yes. The final episode will see the Pantaereon come together: adult, teen, and child."

Mr. Morales raises his hand. "Why do the heroes have to be outsiders? I mean, why can't one of Pantaera's own people save the world?"

"Because it's a TV show and they need contestants," another parent jokes.

Everyone laughs.

"Well, *yes*," Red says, grinning. "But also, many of the magical beings of Pantaera want power. An outsider will fight out of the goodness of their heart. Not for land, status, or rewards."

Clip, whose hand was raised high, drops it and turns bright pink.

Red notices. "Clip, did you have a question?"

"Um . . . I was gonna ask about the prize for winning

the show," he says sheepishly, and everyone laughs again. Mom shakes her head in amusement.

"That's a great question," Red says kindly. "The winner will receive a two-day trip to LA, all expenses paid for them and a parent or guardian, to join me on the set of *War of Gods and Men*, the *movie*! That's right, folks, we are branching out into Hollywood!" He has to yell the last sentence because everyone starts talking loudly and excitedly.

"Whaaaaaat, there's gonna be a *movie*?!" Iggy shouts.

"We are *so* dressing up for the midnight premiere," Derek says to Clip and Caroline.

Jeremy is practically dancing in his seat. "They're finally making a movie! I've only been dying to see one for *years*!" he declares. "Can you believe it, Sadie?"

I shake my head, laughing. I'm the only one in our group of friends who doesn't play the video game, but their excitement is contagious.

"Can't wait to see you in LA!" Clip calls to Red, who grins and gives him a thumbs-up. I roll my eyes and Derek gives my brother a playful punch in the arm. "What, guys? It would be awesome for me to spend two whole days on set with Red. If I want to be a game designer when I grow up, I need to pick his brain about writing *War of Gods and Men*, right?"

"It's not *that*. It's the fact that you automatically assume you're gonna win," I say.

Clip smirks. "Who says I won't?"

I make a show of looking around at all of the other contestants. "Um, the other nine kids who are competing against you and have just as much of a chance as you do?"

"Uh-oh," Derek whispers loudly to Caroline. "The Chu-pocalypse is launching again."

"I thought laser tag cured them of it," she whispers back, just as loudly.

Clip is the sporty one in our family, and for some reason, he thinks this makes him the clear winner of any game we play. He and I fight a lot because I think he's an arrogant bighead, and he thinks I'm slow and weak. When we played laser tag this summer, though, I showed him I was tougher than he thought, and he showed *me* that he could be a good leader sometimes. He had even started to respect me. But now that it's every kid for themselves on this show, I guess he's back to assuming that he'll be the best and I'll get eliminated right away.

I clench my jaw. *We'll see about that.*

Bess waves her hands for silence. "Hi, everyone, I'm Bess Fitzgerald, co–executive producer, with a few more details. The kids will stay on the grounds of Clarebriar

Castle. Most belongings, including phones, will be taken and stored securely. You can keep toiletries and medications, but the idea is for you to be immersed in the world of Pantaera. There will be microphones, lights, and cameras, but those will be as subtle as possible and cleverly hidden."

"How are they going to hide an entire camera crew?" Iggy mutters, and we all shrug.

"Families can go to the castle to watch the filming, but they'll also be hidden," Bess continues. "The kids will be guided by actors who have a loose script and will improvise as needed. Each challenge is designed to eliminate one or two contestants, who will then return to their families here at the Kearney Hotel. They'll get to watch the filming, too, but they're no longer a part of the show. That about covers it, right, Red? Any final questions?"

Mr. Marshall raises his hand. "If all three seasons of the show are being prerecorded, when will they start streaming on TV?"

"We're aiming for next winter, right before the school holidays," Bess answers.

"The winner has to be kept a secret for a whole year?" asks a red-haired woman who must be Kris's mom. "So they don't spoil the show for their classmates?"

"Correct," Red says. "You all signed nondisclosure

forms when your kids accepted their spots on the show. We want to keep it fun and suspenseful for viewers."

Clip snickers. "Sounds like a pretty tall order."

"Yeah, especially for you," I say, and he sticks his tongue out at me. Out of all of us, he would 100 percent have the hardest time keeping quiet about an epic victory.

Jeremy's dad raises his hand. "Will there be medical staff on-site in case of injuries?"

I notice Jeremy slumping in his seat. "Your dad's a doctor. He has to ask that. It doesn't mean he thinks you'll get hurt," I whisper to him, and he nods, but doesn't look convinced.

"There is medical staff, but rest assured, we will take every precaution to prevent injury." When no one else raises a hand, Red grins. "Okay, heroes, time to bid your families farewell! In fifteen minutes, your adventure begins. Are you ready?"

"Yeah!" all the kids say.

He cups a hand to his ear. "Sorry, what?"

"YEAH!" we scream, and then everyone gets up and starts talking at once.

Grandma grabs Clip and kisses his cheeks, while Grandpa says, "Bà ngoại and Ông ngoại are so proud of you. You're going to be a hero." They fuss over him like the old-fashioned Vietnamese grandparents they are. They've always paid special attention to Clip because he's a boy. Mom told me they did the same thing with her brother, Jack, when she was growing up.

Mom smiles like she knows everything I'm thinking and squeezes me tight. "You're going to be a hero, too, Sadie. Dad and I can't wait to watch you kick orc butt. He'll be here tomorrow! His boss is letting him leave early to catch his flight."

"Great," I say, hugging her back. Over her shoulder, I see Molly at the next table, watching us. "Ugh, what's her problem?"

"Who?" Mom asks. Quickly, I fill her in on what Molly said. "Oh, honey, don't let that bother you. She might just be nervous about not knowing Pantaera as well as you and Jer do. And she might have zeroed in on you because you're the only other Asian girl in the competition."

"But why not try to be *friends*, instead of enemies?" I ask, but before Mom can answer, it's my turn to be showered with my grandparents' attention.

"Don't make weird faces. I'll be zooming in on you the whole time," Grandpa warns.

Grandma kisses me. "Don't run too fast and hurt yourself. And did you go—"

"I'm going to the bathroom right now," I interrupt her,

to prevent more loud poop talk in front of the producers. "I mean the loo. That's what they call it in Ireland!"

Everyone finishes saying goodbye, and the other kids go out to the lobby while I head to the loo. I notice Molly sticking close behind me and try to shake off my annoyance. Maybe she *is* just nervous, like Mom said, or even thinks I'm her competition the way Clip thinks George is his. "Are you excited? I wonder if our first challenge is tonight," I say, trying to be nice.

She shrugs. "Why is your grandpa recording you if the show's going to be on TV? And what do *baaa whyyy* and *ummm whyyy* mean?" Clearly, she was listening to my family talk.

"Grandpa wants to try out his new camera. And bà ngoại and ông ngoại are Vietnamese for the grandma and grandpa on your mom's side. The ones on your dad's side are different—"

"We have different names for grandparents in Mandarin, too," she interrupts me. "You guys copied a lot of our traditions. And our food, too."

I raise an eyebrow. "*Copied*? China and Vietnam are right next to each other, so they have a lot of stuff in common. Plus, Vietnam was ruled by China for centuries."

"I know you're a big geek, but you don't need to teach

me about history," Molly snaps. "*I* was actually born in China. Were *you* even born in Vietnam?"

There it is. The word *geek*, which I know she was itching to use earlier. "My brother and I were born in the US," I say icily. "Hey, what's your deal? You haven't been very nice to me."

Her face goes red and she cuts in front of me, slamming the bathroom door behind her.

"What is with her?" I mutter, exasperated, as I go into the other bathroom.

A few minutes later, when we join the other kids in the lobby, we find them all talking excitedly. Jeremy grabs my arm and says, "Sadie! We just saw the wizard!"

"What?" I ask, surprised. "The one you met at the airport?"

He points at some armchairs. "He was sitting right there! He said hi to us!"

"He was so *weird*," Caroline declares. "Yet cool and nice at the same time!"

"Dude, who wears socks with flip-flops?" Iggy asks.

"Hey, don't question wizard fashion," George jokes.

Lizard holds up her tiny hand. "He gave me a high-five!" she brags, then looks down at her palm in awe. "Maybe I have magic powers now or something."

"Well, he mostly looked at *me* when he was talking,"

Clip brags. "What if he's the one who's gonna give us our challenges and decide who the winner is?"

"What did he say?" I ask, feeling a twinge of disappointment that I missed the first actor we'll meet on the show. "Anything interesting?"

"Just that we look like a fun group," Jeremy says. "He pretended he didn't know what competition we were talking about, but he felt sure we would do our very best no matter what."

The hotel manager comes over to us, smiling. "Hi there. Do you all need help with something? The wagons are waiting outside to take you to the set of your show."

"We're fine, thanks," Derek tells him. "We were just chatting with the wizard."

The man raises his eyebrows. "Wizard?"

"You know, the guy who was sitting here," says Kris, pointing to the armchairs. "He had a tall pointy hat and a Starbucks cup. You were looking right at him, weren't you?"

"No, I was looking at you kids and wondering if you were confused about where to go. I haven't seen anyone sitting in these chairs all day, let alone somebody in a wizard costume."

We look at each other, surprised by the man's response. But then Clip laughs and says, "Wow! I guess

Red and the other producers got the hotel staff in on the show, too! Nice."

But the manager still looks confused. Maybe he's just a good actor.

"Come on, guys, let's go!" my brother says, leading the way outside.

We push through the doors and get ready to begin our adventure.

CHAPTER FIVE
CLIP

WHEN WE STEP OUTSIDE, IT'S CLEAR WHAT THE producers meant about this being *immersive*. (I had to ask Jer what the word meant, and he said it means we'll feel like we're really in Pantaera. I didn't ask Sadie, obviously. She would just give me a mean look and tell me to read more.)

Two horse-drawn wagons are waiting for us in front of the hotel, each of them piled high with hay. The drivers wear dark green clothes, like Robin Hood, and one of them even has a cap with a red feather. He lifts it and says, in an old-timey English accent, "Good morrow, brave heroes! Five of you to each wagon, please. Take a seat and we shall be on our way. Your possessions are already on board. We had, er, a spot of trouble with a trunk that popped open."

"Did it have Mickey Mouse on it?" Lizard asks.

The man raises his eyebrows. "Mic . . . key Mouse? I do not know what that is, madam."

"How do you not know—" Lizard stops, then gives him an exaggerated wink and a nod. "Ohhh, gotcha. Disney World doesn't exist in Pantaera. Well, I bet it's my trunk anyway." She clambers onto the first wagon, followed by the two girls whose names I've already forgotten.

Quickly, I push Iggy and the twins toward the other wagon.

George taps my shoulder. "Hey, Clip, do you mind if I ride with you guys?"

"Sure thing," I say. I was planning to keep a close eye on him this week anyway. I knew he would be tough competition the second I heard he was an athlete like me. We're even the same height, though he's got a little more muscle than I do.

Caroline bats her eyelashes at him. "You can sit between me and Derek."

I plop down on a hay bale across from them and wait for Iggy to join us. He's staring back at the hotel with one foot on the wagon. "Ig, are you okay?" I ask.

"That's funny, I thought I just saw Tuba," he says. "But it couldn't have been him. The hotel staff wouldn't just chuck him out the side door . . . would they?"

"Of course not," I say, as patiently as I can. Iggy has always loved cats, but I've never seen him so obsessed with one. "Don't worry. They promised to find him a good home."

He sighs and takes a seat beside me. "Yeah, you're right."

Derek leans back, relaxing. "Hayrides are the best. Remember the one we took through the Haunted Acre Wood? Iggy punched a zombie and almost got thrown out of the park."

"It was a reflex! He was in my personal space!" Iggy protests.

I snicker. "And Caroline ate a bad sno-cone and threw up on the Ferris wheel."

Caroline aims a light kick at my shins. "I did *not*!" she argues. "I gagged because the sno-cone tasted like old broccoli. And hey, maybe we should cool it. Remember, there are cameras and microphones hidden everywhere."

"Oh yeah. You're right." I sit up straight and smooth my hair, even though I can't see where any cameras could be. Then again, the producers *did* say they would be concealed well.

George crosses his arms. "So, Clip, you sounded excited about winning that trip to LA to hang with Red."

His eyes get big. "Hey, what if you guys ended up writing a game together?"

"Yeah, whatever. That might be fun," I say, trying to keep my voice casual.

It's always been my dream to write video games. But whenever I mention it, Mom and Dad say it's a lot of work (like I don't already know), and Sadie chimes in with "You don't even like writing for school!"—as if doing an essay about the branches of US government is even *close* to building a fantasy world. It stinks that my family isn't supportive. They think I'm too lazy, so I've learned to keep my goal close to my chest. I pretend it doesn't mean as much to me as it does. But if I get to spend time with Red in LA and pitch my ideas to him, maybe they'll finally get it. And who knows? Red might like me and let me work with him someday.

All I have to do is win this show. It's not like it'll be *hard*. I'll probably have to, like, climb some walls, jump over hurdles, and run from a few orcs. Easy peasy, lemon squeezy!

"Everyone ready?" The driver snaps the reins, and the horses turn off the cobblestone street onto a narrow, grassy path. A light rain begins to fall, and the air gets humid and warm.

"I wish I brought my workout shorts," I say. "I wonder what clothes we'll compete in."

"A suit of armor?" Derek suggests.

George points at the driver. "Or maybe they'll give us a Robin Hood getup like his."

"Hey, I thought he looked like Robin Hood, too!" I say, and he grins at me. I start to grin back but settle for a calm smile. He seems cool and nice and has already won everyone else over (especially Caroline, who clearly thinks he's cute), but I can't forget that he's my rival. I'm here to win, not make friends. I've got enough of those at home.

What I *don't* have is a major win on network television . . . yet.

I picture the season finale and imagine standing in front of a cheering crowd as a king crowns me the child hero. No, wait . . . maybe a princess will crown me. A really hot princess.

"How far away is the castle?" Caroline asks the driver. "Is it a big tourist destination?"

"We will be there in twenty minutes, madam, and I do not know the word *tourist*," he says seriously, and Derek and I smirk at each other. This actor sure is into his role. "The Castle of the North Wind is beautiful. It's been passed down in the king's family for generations, and I hope it will be for generations more . . . provided we can keep our land safe."

"Which king is this?" I ask.

"King Rothbart VII. A good and gracious monarch, though he is so young. Many people doubted that a man of eighteen would rule us well, but I was not one of them."

Derek raises his eyebrows. "Eighteen? Wow, he's only six years older than us!"

"Five years older than George. You're thirteen, right?" The way Caroline flutters her lashes reminds me of when Uncle Jack gets dust in his contact lens and is trying to blink it out.

George nods, not seeming to notice her googly eyes. "Are we staying in the castle?"

"No, I'm afraid not," the driver says. "The castle is for the king and his family, but as honored guests, you shall have comfortable lodgings on the grounds."

The wagon enters a deep, dense forest, with ancient-looking trees that bend over the path like they're watching us pass by. There's no sun today, so it feels even gloomier in the woods, with the branches blocking out any light from the cloudy gray sky.

"This place is spooky," Iggy mutters.

The driver glances over his shoulder. "Listen carefully. We are entering the Witchwood, a dark and treacherous place. The witches here are not always friendly to trespassers. I would have taken the long way around, but the Captain of the Guard insisted that I bring you to training as soon as possible. Whilst here, you must remain as quiet as you can. Do you understand?"

I want to laugh at his scared tone. This is literally a guy in a Robin Hood costume, driving five kids through a park in Ireland. If I looked to the left, I'd probably see a Starbucks.

But everyone else looks as serious as he sounds, and Derek answers, "We understand."

It's a little eerie riding in complete silence, with nothing but the crunch of leaves under the wagon wheels. From time to time, we hear the loud crack of branches breaking somewhere deep in the woods. My friends seem uneasy. Caroline and Iggy jump every time we hear a sound, and Derek keeps scanning the trees like he's waiting for someone to leap out at us.

George is keeping his cool, though, so I do the same. I don't even bother to check out the surroundings. Nothing scares Clip Chu, and I have to show everyone that right off the bat.

Another branch breaks nearby, and then there's the unmistakable rustling of fabric.

"What was that?" Caroline squeaks.

Everyone turns to look, even George and me. I catch

sight of a long black cloak slipping through the trees like smoke. It vanishes into the shadows before I get a good look.

"We're not alone," Derek murmurs, like someone in a horror movie.

"Relax, guys," I say, because Caroline and Iggy look genuinely freaked out. "It's okay."

"Quiet, please!" the driver warns.

I peer at the wagon in front of us. The other driver and the two girls whose names I can't remember are all facing front. I spy Sadie's ponytail swinging as she studies the trees. The only faces I can see belong to Jeremy and Lizard, and I can't decide which of them looks more excited and happy, even though we're supposed to be traveling through a forest of murderous witches. Lizard's mouth is wide-open with awe, and Jeremy is smiling from ear to ear.

"Guys! Look!" George whispers, pointing at trees carved with strange drawings. They look like stick figures or some kind of ancient language.

"Witch's runes," Iggy says. "I read about them in Jeremy's book."

Other trees have old-fashioned mirrors hanging from them. They're cracked and stained, and I can't help shuddering at how jagged and weird our reflections look. Suddenly, there's a flash of color in a giant silver mirror as we pass by. For a brief moment, we see the head of a woman with long, jet-black hair and pale skin. She's wearing a tall, sharp crown made of daggers and a dark veil that covers almost her entire face, except for her grinning, bright red mouth. I can almost hear her laughing in the silence, low and sinister and dangerous.

Iggy and Derek yelp in surprise and Caroline gasps.

"It's the Forgotten Queen!" I hear Jeremy cry. "She's watching us from the mirrors!"

That mirror is a screen playing a video, that's all, I try to tell myself. But even solid logic can't keep a chill from creeping down my spine.

Our wagon speeds up, passing the creepy grove of runes and broken mirrors, and then we are back in a regular forest with trees that are bare.

"Okay, that was pretty scary," Derek says, exhaling. "She looked so evil."

George looks thoughtful. "Maybe she's working with the witches. They could be using those runes to pass on messages to each other."

"I thought warlocks used runes," Caroline says, confused. "Or was it mages? What's the difference between all of them anyway?"

"So in the *War of Gods and Men* universe, mages are good guys. Warlocks are mages who went bad. Witches aren't good or bad, and their magic comes from the earth, like trees and water and stuff." Iggy laughs, looking surprised at himself. "Whoa, who am I? Jeremy?"

"Wow, did you get all that from Jer's book? I don't remember any of it." I borrowed the graphic novel on the plane, too, mostly because everyone else was, but I guess I didn't pay enough attention. Sadie's always nagging me about getting bored and skimming when I read, but I don't plan to spend my life with my nose in a book, like her. Still, I can't help feeling the *tiniest* bit worried. "Do you think that stuff will be important to know for the competition?"

George shrugs. "It couldn't hurt. There might be puzzles that test your knowledge."

The twins nod, and my gut clenches. *Playing the* War of Gods and Men *game will be research enough*, I tell myself. *Just because I hate reading doesn't mean I'm not smart.*

Finally, we leave the creepy Witchwood. Our wagon pulls onto a hill overlooking a cozy village full of smoking chimneys and people pushing wheelbarrows. I smell burning wood, damp straw, and the salty scent of the ocean beyond the cliffs. Behind the village sits a beautiful stone castle, turrets sharp against the sky and purple-and-gold banners fluttering in the wind.

"Wow!" Derek chokes out.

"This is amazing!" Caroline says, and Iggy sneaks his phone out to take photos.

I'm speechless. I didn't expect the place to look so ancient, mysterious, and *fantastical.*

"Welcome to the Kingdom of Celadon," the driver says grandly. "That is the Castle of the North Wind, home to King Rothbart and his sister, Princess Errin."

I know the place is actually called Clarebriar Castle, so I guess the producers picked out names from the world of *War of Gods and Men*. Problem is, I don't remember any other names from Jeremy's book, and I have to push away that nagging worry in my gut again.

"You will be staying at Winterhearth House, home of

one of His Majesty's most trusted advisers," the driver continues. "I will take you there now."

We follow the other wagon down into the village, and the townspeople stare at us as we pass by. Everyone is dressed in shapeless, baggy shirts and plain dark pants or skirts. A few of them remove their hats and put their hands over their hearts, while others frown and whisper.

"Some of them don't look very happy to see us," George says.

Iggy shrugs. "If I was just trying to live life, farm potatoes, and move sheep around and I saw ten randos in jeans passing by, I'd think they were pretty sus, too."

"One of us is the child hero, though," Caroline points out. "Shouldn't they be excited?"

The driver overhears us. "Please forgive any rudeness. It is long since we have had hope, what with the threat of the Forgotten Queen looming. We've learned not to trust strangers."

"We'll just have to prove ourselves," I say confidently. By the end of the show, there will be a *lot* of people recognizing that Clip Chu is the cream of the crop. I'll make sure of that.

The wagons pull up to a stone house just outside the gates of the castle. A guy in a suit of armor (minus the helmet) stands in front of it, waiting for us. He has pale skin and brown hair and looks like he's in his late teens. He watches us approach with his arms crossed over his muscular chest and his legs apart in an aggressive stance. A heavy sword hangs at his side.

"Who is *that*?" Caroline breathes. She seems to have forgotten about George.

"Some knight guy?" Derek offers helpfully, as the wagon pulls to a stop.

"Welcome to Pantaera," the knight says, once everyone is standing in front of him. He has an impressively deep voice. I wish I could talk like that, but every time I try, I sound like a frog with a cold. "I am Daniel Redfern, the Captain of the Guard. His Majesty has put me in charge of training you for the next week, and I intend to take that responsibility very seriously."

I stand up a little straighter, even though I know this isn't really a high-ranking knight. He's just some actor who got the part because he's six feet tall, ripped, and has the tousled hair and piercing green eyes of a British boy band member. Caroline's eating up every word he says, though, and even Sadie's face is flushed as his eyes take us in.

Like some of the villagers, though, he doesn't seem happy to see us. He looks tired and worried. "This is all of them?" he asks the drivers, who nod as they unload our luggage from the wagons. He sighs heavily. "Ten tiny children. They look so terribly young."

"He does know one of us is the *child* hero, right?" I hear Lizard mutter to Jeremy.

"Well, if this is what I have to work with, so be it. The drivers will bring your bags into the house, but they will need to take away any, er, *modern* devices," Captain Redfern adds, looking at Iggy.

"Dang, I was hoping he'd forget," Iggy mumbles, handing over his phone.

It takes Jeremy longer than any of us to empty his pockets, since he's also carrying a Kindle, an iPad, a Nintendo Switch, and a pair of noise-canceling headphones. I smirk when the driver automatically puts the headphones around his neck. That's a crack in the "immersive" experience, because how would someone who'd never even heard of Bose know to do that?

The captain sees my expression. "Is something funny?" he asks sharply.

"Uh, not at all . . . sir."

"Good. Because this is a serious matter. You are here to train in the service of King Rothbart." He rubs his face like he's exhausted by the very sight of us. "If I see anyone treating this lightly, they will be dealt with the way I would with any of my *real* warriors. Got that?"

"Yes, sir," everyone says.

"He doesn't think we can do this," Derek whispers to me, and I nod. The captain will be another person I have to prove myself to, and I'm going to show him I'm a cut above the rest.

"Follow me," Captain Redfern says, beckoning. We expect him to lead us into the house, but he walks around the side of it instead, taking us out back.

"Aren't you going to show us to our rooms?" asks the redhead in the Star Wars shirt.

"Shhh, Kris!" Lizard hisses, as the captain stops and fixes the redhead with a *look*.

"Did I not just say that you are here to train?" he asks, and after a long, tense silence, Kris bites her lip and nods. "We're going to the training field. You can rest later." Without another word, he turns on his heel and continues marching toward the back of the house.

A plump, kind-faced older lady appears at the door of the house. "Please forgive him. He's the youngest captain in history, serving the youngest king in history, so he's got a lot on his mind. Just do your best and he'll warm up to you. I'm sure he's really very glad that you're all here." She laughs at our doubtful faces. "I'm Kathryne, the housekeeper, by the way. I'll be taking care of you while you're in Pantaera. But go on now, don't keep him waiting."

She's so nice that we relax a bit . . . but it doesn't last long.

We find Captain Redfern in a large field, talking to other knights. Weapons are scattered everywhere: rusty swords and spears on a table, buckets of bows and arrows, and all kinds of leather and metal doodads littering the ground. Ten horses are tied to a fence nearby.

"Well, here they are," Captain Redfern says, sounding about as excited as someone getting a cavity filled. "Listen up. Tomorrow, you will face your first set of challenges. But before you do, I want to see what your current skill levels are."

I feel a twinge of anxiety. I've been playing soccer for years, so being on a field with a guy barking orders at me should feel familiar. But I know how to play soccer. I'm great at it. Using a sword or a spear, though? I've never even *seen* those outside of a game or a movie.

The captain, however, isn't pointing at the swords or the spears.

He's pointing at the horses.

"Get on," he says.

CHAPTER SIX
CLIP

"SOOOOO . . . THIS IS KIND OF A DISASTER," IGGY says.

Almost everyone has been struggling to get on their horses for the past ten minutes. There was a mad rush for the smallest, nicest-looking ones, and Iggy claimed a little fuzzy brown guy while I picked a cute cinnamon-colored pony with a stylish tuft of hair between his eyes.

Too bad they both turned out to be as unhappy about us as Captain Redfern.

Mine does a jerky tap dance like he's trying to shake me off on purpose. I tighten my grip on his mane, trying not to look scared. There are cameras recording this somewhere, and I don't want the world to know Clip Chu gets nervous on horseback. 'Cause he doesn't . . . much.

"Pet him and talk to him gently. He's just getting used

to you," says Sir Errick, one of the knights. He rubs my pony's neck. "Aren't you, Teddy Bear? You big softie, you."

The big softie bounces me in the saddle. Teddy Bear is a stupid name for a horse who clearly doesn't want to be cuddled or ridden. I glance over at Iggy. "How's it going with Pecan?"

"You mean Pe-*can't*," Iggy says, and his horse gives a threatening snort. "I hope these helmets are legit. I want to keep my neck in one piece before the show even starts." The knights made us all put on elbow pads, knee pads, and riding helmets that buckle under our chins.

"At least our horses aren't the only ones who hate us," I point out.

Kris, the redhead, had bragged nonstop as we were

getting our gear on. "I'm descended from a Russian empress, so our family is, like, totally cool with horses." It turns out her horse wasn't cool with *her*, though, because it pulled away right as she swung her leg over the saddle. She took a light tumble on the grass, but only her ego got bruised.

Lizard, Derek, Caroline, and Molly—the girl who bleached the ends of her hair—needed a couple of tries to get on their horses, too. But Sadie, Jeremy, and George had no problem at all.

"I'm glad you got me into horseback-riding lessons this year," Jeremy tells Sadie happily.

She beams. "I knew they'd help with your confidence."

Captain Redfern tells us to line our horses up in front of him. I hear Jeremy telling the twins, "Dig your heels in gently to make them go," so I do that, and to my surprise, Teddy Bear listens. The only trouble is, he keeps going . . . right past the captain. I have to turn him back around in this awkward circle. Molly and Lizard giggle and Kris smirks, probably glad she's not the only one who embarrassed herself. But I shrug it off, like I meant for it to happen.

Sir Raquelle, another knight, laughs ruefully and shakes her head. "Why do they have to be little children, for goodness' sake?" she asks Captain Redfern, in a voice we can all hear.

"Because the Keeper of Fortunes foresaw a child hero in the Pantaereon," he says.

"I wish you or I could undergo the challenges, sir. We would do better than these babies."

I work hard to keep my face neutral, so the camera doesn't catch me giving her the stink eye. Okay, so maybe a twelve-year-old has never saved the world. That doesn't mean it can't happen! My fingers flex on the reins, itching to show her that she's wrong about me.

The other kids don't bother to hide their annoyance. Lizard rolls her eyes and the twins mutter to each other. Captain Redfern seems to realize we feel insulted and says, "His Majesty commanded me to train these ten youngsters. I will respect his wishes, and so will you."

"Yes, sir," the knight says, bowing her head.

The captain turns to face us. "My soldiers will now hand out your weapons. One by one, you will go through an obstacle course and show me what you can do with these tools. The skills you are about to demonstrate are ones that may be important in the challenges ahead. Don't embarrass me and don't dawdle, because this trial will be *timed*."

"Oh no," Derek groans. Games and challenges with a time limit always stress him out.

The captain picks up an hourglass. "Who wants to go first?"

I see George's mouth open, but before he can say anything, I quickly yell, "Me!"

Two knights come forward to equip me. In under a minute, I've got a (not-very-sharp) sword hanging near my hip, a bow and arrows strapped to my back, and a spear that doesn't weigh a ton, but is long and tricky to hold while riding. I grip it tight, trying not to drop it.

The captain waves me forward, and that's when I see something glinting over his shoulder. One of the knights is holding what looks like logs, but I see a shiny object hidden inside. *Some of the knights are the camera crew*, I realize, so I flash a smile in that direction. Might as well dazzle the audience with my pearly whites before I dive into the challenge.

"Can we stop preening and focus, please?" Captain Redfern asks, sounding exhausted. I don't know what *preening* means, but it can't be good because some of the other kids are laughing. "You have one minute, total, for these tasks. First, fire three arrows at that target. Next, use your spear to knock helmets off a fence while riding past. No slowing down or stopping. Finally, cut down as many scarves as possible with your sword while riding through that archway. Got it?"

"Got it, sir!" I roar.

He flips the hourglass. "Go!"

I dig my heels into Teddy Bear's sides and we trot toward a giant wooden target. Knights stand nearby, but not too close, probably to avoid getting smacked in the face with an arrow. It won't be from me, though, 'cause I'm pretty boss at archery—we did a unit on it in gym class. I pull Teddy Bear to a stop and hand my spear to a knight. Holding the curved side of the bow with my left hand, I line up an arrow with my right and pull it back along with the string. Elbow up, wrist straight. *Pretend it's a video game*, I think, smirking. This is going to be child's play.

I squint one eye, aiming for the middle of the target, and let go. The arrow hits six inches above center . . . and then bounces right off onto the grass.

My face burns. "Shoot!" I whisper. I can't believe I fumbled the first shot.

I try again, this time pulling the arrow back harder. It hits the board and stays there, but I've missed the center by about a foot. I groan, annoyed with myself. This is *not* the strong start I need. How am I going to get Captain Redfern to respect me if I can't even hit a target? More importantly . . . how am I going to *win* the whole show?

"Hurry up!" the captain shouts. "Remember, you only have one minute!"

I fire my third arrow, which also sticks and is at least a *little* closer to the center. I take my spear back from the knight and hurry Teddy Bear down the path, which is bordered on one side by a high wooden fence. Five metal helmets sit on top of it, evenly spaced out.

"Make that horse go faster!" the captain bellows.

I'm annoyed, but I don't want to look like I have an attitude on national TV, so I smile big, like the captain just told me I have beautiful hair. I dig my heels harder into Teddy Bear's sides and he breaks into a bouncy run. I struggle to keep my balance in the saddle.

"Come on, slow down!" I beg, but the horse is *not* having it. He's moving so fast that I miss two helmets and just manage to knock down the others by swinging my spear like a bat.

Suddenly, Teddy Bear is full-on sprinting toward the metal archway. Dozens of scarves are dangling from it, attached to the beam with tiny magnets sewn onto their edges. I swing my sword wildly, hoping to bring a few of them down.

A knight rides up alongside me and grabs Teddy Bear's reins, pulling him to a stop. "You okay?" she asks, and I nod, trying to catch my breath. She leads us back to where everybody is waiting, and Teddy Bear starts calmly chewing grass like he didn't just try to kill me back there.

Captain Redfern has a look on his face like Teddy

Bear just pooped on his boots. "Well, I'll say this: You did it all in under a minute. But with only two arrows on the target, three helmets knocked down, and three scarves cut down, you have a lot of room for improvement."

I can't look anyone in the eye. It was a pathetic start, and no one knows that more than me. "I'll try harder next time," I force myself to say. "Thank you, sir."

A knight helps me dismount and I sink onto the grass. The others call, "Good job, Clip!" and even Sadie says, "Way to go, bro!" But I know it's out of pity. I'd been bragging so much about how this competition would be a cinch . . . and then failed the first task. I feel like a fake.

I take a deep breath and try to focus on watching everyone else go.

They all turn out to be better at one skill than they are at the others. Kris and Caroline get all three arrows on the target. Iggy suddenly turns into a Marvel super-villain and gives this evil roar as he knocks every helmet off the fence. Molly and Sadie tie on every task, while Derek is kind of middle-of-the-road, not horrible but not amazing. I pay special attention to George, who ends up doing about the same as me, except he cuts down more scarves, and I feel a little better. By the time Derek and Iggy join me on the grass, I'm in a much lighter mood.

"Man, *everyone* is on the struggle bus today!" Derek says.

"Most of us haven't even ridden a horse before," Iggy points out. "The captain can't just expect us to know how to use a sword or a bow. Like, if we gave these knights a toaster and told them whoever made the best Pop-Tart would win, do you think they could?"

We laugh, and then I yawn loudly. "Well, at least we can go back to the house and relax now," I say, brushing grass off my pants. "Maybe tomorrow will be better."

"There's still two people who need to go," Derek reminds me.

I shrug. It's just Jeremy and that tiny eleven-year-old, Lizard. Jer's a nice kid, but he's not hero material and neither is she. I'm pretty sure they won't be a threat to me.

But then Captain Redfern flips the hourglass, and a blur rips down the path. It's Lizard on the back of the biggest horse on the field, straight-up *galloping* toward the target. My jaw drops as she pulls the white horse to a stop and expertly nocks an arrow on her bow.

Boom! Two inches above center, and she didn't even look like she was *trying*.

Her second arrow lands a hair above the first. She preps the final arrow and lets it fly, and it hits the target above the others, forming an almost perfect straight line.

"What the . . . ?" Iggy sputters.

"Get it, girl!" Caroline screams.

Everyone is cheering, but even at this distance, I can tell Lizard is laser focused. She points her horse toward the fence, and I watch in numb disbelief as she smashes every single one of the five helmets. *Bam! Bam! Bam! Bam! Bam!*

She tosses her spear to a knight, then hurtles toward the dangling scarves. Several savage swings of her sword, and over a dozen flutter to the ground before she races back to us.

I'm shocked to see that Captain Redfern is smiling. Actually *smiling*, with teeth and everything. "Fifteen seconds to spare! A superb job!" he says. "What is your name?"

"Elizabeth. But everyone calls me Lizard."

He gives her his hand and helps her off the horse, saying, "Lizard, that was the best performance we've seen today. *That* is the kind of speed and agility I am looking for."

Everyone high-fives Lizard, and I force a smile and say, "Great job!" But my stomach feels like it's in knots, because what I never expected this tiny kid to be was a *beast*. She barely even comes up to my shoulder, yet she destroyed that challenge. Who would have thought a shrimp like her could outperform us all? It should have been *me* who did that well and got the captain's praise, not some puny elementary schooler.

I try to calm down as Jeremy prepares his horse and Captain Redfern flips the hourglass over again. *We'll see how Lizard does under REAL pressure tomorrow*, I tell myself.

Suddenly, Sadie starts jumping up and down. "Yeeeeeeaaaaah, Jer!"

"Way to go, Jeremy!" Derek hollers.

My attention snaps back to the field. Jeremy's first arrow has hit the center of the target. *Dead* center. My mouth goes dry as he lets his second arrow fly and it almost does that thing in cartoons where it splits the first one in half. Since our arrows aren't sharp, though, it just nudges it. The cheers are distracting Jeremy, because his third arrow is several inches off the mark, but still— it's an amazing performance from a kid who'd be the first to admit he can't aim or throw.

Jeremy looks like a pro in the saddle as he aims his horse toward the fence, knocks down every single helmet, and then cuts down about ten scarves from the archway before riding back.

"That was very, very good!" Captain Redfern says, and I can't believe that the Gloomy Gus is smiling *again*.

He also helps Jeremy off his horse. "What is *your* name, young man?"

"Jeremy Mithrandir Thomas," Jer says, without skipping a beat, and everyone in our group of friends laughs. Mithrandir is a nickname of Gandalf the Grey, the wizard from the Lord of the Rings, and Jer always uses it as his code name when we play laser tag.

"I'm impressed by your accuracy and timing," the captain says, and Jeremy bows, beaming. "Well, I've seen enough for today. You have all done your best and I am pleased with three people in particular, all of whom will get a head start on tomorrow's challenge."

Everyone stands up straighter, looking hopeful. I tuck a hand into my pocket and cross my fingers, where the cameras can't see. I know it's childish, but I need all the luck I can get.

"Congratulations to Lizard, Jeremy, and *you*. What's your name?"

Caroline goes tomato red when Captain Redfern points at her. It takes her a second to remember her own name. "Caroline," she finally says, and Derek gives her a proud high five.

I watch everyone congratulate Lizard, Jeremy, and Caroline with a bad taste in my mouth, like I swallowed sour milk. Clip Chu, soccer MVP, wasn't even top three.

I see Sadie watching me and I say, "Awesome job, you guys!" so she can't sass me about being a sore loser.

"I hope the rest of you will work harder. The winner of this competition will be someone who shows the world what it means to be a hero, and it didn't look too promising out there." The captain's green eyes sweep over us, and we duck our heads in shame. I know *my* gaze is fixed on my sneakers. "However, I think there's potential here, and I hope you will prove me right."

"Yes, sir," everyone says.

"Go now and rest. I'll come get you for dinner later," the captain says, striding away in the direction of the castle, while the knights pack up and lead our horses away.

George laughs. "That was a disaster. Did you see me almost fire an arrow backward?"

"At least you didn't get your spear stuck in the fence, like me," Derek says, shaking his head. "Maybe I should have done that King Kong roar like Iggy. Right, Ig?"

But Iggy isn't listening. He's staring at something across the field.

Derek pokes him. "You okay?"

"It's Tuba," Iggy says in disbelief. "Come here, Tuba!"

A big black cat is walking toward us. It starts running when it hears Iggy's voice. Iggy bends down and the cat leaps into his arms, purring happily and rubbing its head under his chin.

"Oh, Tuba, you found me!" Iggy says, his eyes wet. "You followed me from the hotel!"

Kris and Molly look puzzled, so Sadie explains, "It's a cat we met at the airport. He jumped on our bus and thinks Iggy is his mom."

"Will they let you keep him on the show?" Caroline asks doubtfully.

"He'll be good," Iggy promises. "He won't make any trouble, will you, Tuba? Come on, let's go." He starts carrying the cat in the direction of the house, and everyone drifts after him.

"Be right there. Gotta tie my shoe," I call. The truth is, I need to be alone for a second after my awful performance on the field or I'm going to scream. I fiddle with the laces on my sneaker, stalling for time, when a shadow suddenly falls over me. I huff with irritation, because Derek always hovers when he knows I'm upset. "I'm fine, D. Go back to the house."

But when I look up, it's not Derek. It's a knight wearing full armor, including a helmet, through which a pair of pale blue eyes twinkle at me. What's weird, though, is that the man's feet are in white socks stuffed into flip-flops that look ready to fall apart.

I stand up, staring at the weird sight. "Can I help you?"

"No," he says brightly. "But you can help *yourself* by not focusing on just one afternoon. I can tell you're disappointed by how you did today."

I frown. "I'm fine, thanks. It's no skin off my back."

"It didn't look that way to me," he says, chuckling.

I am *really* annoyed now. Who is this guy? "Sorry, but you don't know me," I say. "And if you did, you would know I don't give up easy."

"Remember, this is Pantaera. You are in a world you've only known through a screen, and you couldn't have guessed what would happen today. Don't count yourself out early, Clip." With a wrinkled hand, he opens the visor on his helmet to reveal his face. It's old and wise, with a long gray beard, bushy eyebrows, and an expression like he's known me my whole life.

My mouth, which was open to say, *We're not really in Pantaera, you weirdo*, gasps instead. "It's you again!" I exclaim. "The wizard from the hotel! You followed our wagons here, didn't you? How do you know my name?"

He shrugs.

"Oh, I bet Red gave the actors a list of the contestants," I say.

"Actors?" the wizard repeats, looking puzzled.

I laugh. Everyone on this show is so *into* their roles.

"Hey, thanks for the tip. I *was* feeling kind of . . . well, you know. Kind of down about myself."

"Don't feel that way. Remember, anything can happen." The old man winks a pale blue eye at me and then marches away down the field, his sandals flapping against his feet. None of the other knights even look at him as he passes by them.

What he said makes sense, but I can't help feeling a little ashamed that *I'm* the one he chose to say it to. I mean, yeah, this actor caught me alone, but he could have given his pep talk to another kid. Instead, he chose *me*, like I was the worst performer or something.

I need to let it go, though, because I've got all week to prove myself. I might not have won today's task, but there are a bunch more challenges coming.

Clip Chu doesn't lose.

CHAPTER SEVEN
JEREMY

LATER THAT AFTERNOON, SADIE POKES HER HEAD into the doorway of the boys' room. "Hey, are you guys decent?"

"You're supposed to ask that *before* you look in! What if we were in our underpants or something?" Clip growls from the twin bed by the window, where he's sprawled across a woolen blanket (fully clothed, like the rest of us).

Clip's been in a bad mood since the preliminary challenge, even though everyone else is having fun relaxing and eating the tarts, cookies, and fruit pies that Kathryne, the housekeeper, baked for us. I'm not sure how accurate they are to medieval cuisine, but they're delicious.

Derek, whose bed is next to Clip's, plucks at the baggy tan pants and oversized tunic that everyone got as

Pantaera loungewear. "Even if we *were* in underpants, it would be fine 'cause they're just, like, extra-large shorts," he points out.

"The girls got the same clothes." Sadie plops down at the foot of my bed in her own roomy clothes. "For both lounging and for the challenges. What do you think about them, Jer?"

"They feel comfy!" I say. Along with the baggy loungewear, everybody got a competition outfit, too: a tunic and pants in thick forest-green fabric, with a brown leather vest full of pockets to go on top. "I can't believe we're in Pantaera and we get to have our first challenge tomorrow. And soon, Captain Redfern's taking us out to dinner!"

"You make it sound like he's treating us to a restaurant or something," says George, laughing. He and Iggy each snagged a twin bed along the same wall as mine, and Tuba is curled up, fast asleep, on Iggy's pillow. The cat hasn't left his side since we came into the house. "I hope we're having a barbecue in the village. I could go for a nice roast chicken."

"Me too. I hope the food's as good as Red promised," Iggy adds, rubbing his stomach. "All of that horseback riding gave me an appetite. What do you think they'll feed us?"

"Mutton, like in the game?" George suggests.

"Maybe bread and cheese," I say.

Iggy makes a face. "I hope we're getting better stuff than *that*."

"Says the dude who's been eating rabbit food all summer," Clip says in a cranky voice.

"Yeah, but it was worth it!" Iggy says, flexing. "I'm lean, mean, and full of vitamin A."

"Should we go wait for the captain?" Sadie asks. "He'll probably be here soon."

We all get up and follow her into the hallway. On the upper level, Winterhearth House has two big bedrooms (one with five twin beds for the boys, and one with five twin beds for the girls) and two bathrooms, each with a toilet, sink, and shower. Kathryne warned us to keep our showers short, since there isn't a ton of hot water, which everyone else complained about when she was out of earshot. But I'm so excited to be here, I would bathe in the river if I had to. I mean, this is Pantaera! And I, Jeremy Thomas, might have a shot at *not* getting eliminated first!

"How do you feel about tomorrow, champ?" Sadie asks me, once everyone's settled downstairs. The common room is comfortable, with a fire blazing in the hearth, big windows, and soft armchairs. The place also smells good because the kitchen is right next to it.

"Nervous," I admit. "I'm glad I'm getting a head start, 'cause I'll need it."

Derek shakes his head. "Stop being so humble, Jeremy! You rocked it today."

"I wonder what the first challenge will be," Kris says, playing with her long red braid. She was already in the common room with Molly, Lizard, and Caroline when we came down. "I hope it's got something to do with books or riddles. I know a ton about the world of Pantaera."

"Bet you don't know as much as Jeremy," Sadie says loyally.

Kris looks me over. "Have you read the graphic novels?"

I nod. "Yeah, I own all seven of them."

"What about the reference book?"

"I got it autographed by Rowan Ali and Sera Chang when my dad and I went to New York Comic Con," I say proudly. "Along with Red, they're the original creators of the whole *War of Gods and Men* universe, and—"

"I *know* who they are," Kris snaps. "I bet you don't have the *Guidebook to the Mages of Pantaera*, though. It's a rare limited edition, but my mom works in publishing, so I—"

"I have two copies," I say. "I waited outside our bookstore for the midnight release."

Everyone else's heads move between us like they're watching a tennis game.

Kris looks surprised and annoyed. "Okay, well, what about the *Vampire Queen Compendium*? It tells about how the first vampires came to Pantaera—"

"And started their colony in the Dark Wood of Thornbriar. I got two copies of that, too."

Sadie and Clip don't look alike, but right now, anyone could tell they're siblings by their identical smirks. "Pretty sure you're not gonna win this one," Clip tells Kris smugly, forgetting his bad mood. "I bet Jeremy knows more about Pantaera than the actors on this show."

"Nah, that can't be true!" I protest, my face hot.

"Well, *my* money's on Kris," Molly says, and Kris smiles at her. It looks like they've formed an alliance. I studied up on reality TV before we came, and I read that contestants tend to buddy up to survive better. Molly's been acting competitive toward Sadie and now Kris is starting on me, so I guess they think we're threats. I don't mind, though. It's kind of flattering.

"Well, don't underestimate Jeremy," Sadie warns. "He's a puzzle master."

"So am I," Molly snaps. "Stop acting like your group of friends is better than everyone."

Sadie scowls. "We do *not* act like that!"

"Come on, guys, no need to get worked up," Lizard interrupts.

"Agreed. Everyone brings something different to the table," George says reasonably, from where he's sitting next to Lizard. They look funny together, like a big grizzly bear hanging out with a tiny hamster. "I think it'll be fun to see what challenges we're each good at."

"Right," Clip adds. "Don't count yourself out too early, guys. Anything can happen!"

Sadie raises an eyebrow. "Wow, look who's ready to write an inspirational guidebook."

"I didn't come up with that," her brother says. "The wizard did."

"The wizard?!" Lizard and Caroline echo.

"I forgot to tell you guys I saw him again when I was in the field, tying my shoe. He was so weird. He was in a suit of armor, but he still had flip-flops and socks on."

"What did he say?" Derek asks eagerly. "Did he give you hints about the challenges? Maybe he's feeding us clues about the show or something."

"Or maybe he's here to get Tuba back," Iggy says worriedly, looking down at the cat, who followed him downstairs.

"Wait, so that's *twice* now that you've seen the wizard," Sadie tells Clip, frowning. "He showed up in the hotel, too. How come he isn't appearing and giving advice to *all* of the kids?"

"Don't be mad 'cause you were in the bathroom, sis," her brother says airily.

Molly snickers. "Who cares? It's just some actor with a fake beard," she says, rolling her eyes at Sadie. "Don't tell me you believe in wizards now."

"I *don't* believe in them," Sadie says hotly. "But it's a competition, and if some kids are getting an advantage, that doesn't seem very fair, is all."

"He didn't give me any tips," Clip reassures her. "He just gave me a quick pep talk."

"And he told *me* I have to believe in myself," I say. "Also, back in the hotel lobby, he was nice and encouraging. But he hasn't shared any important information or anything."

Lizard taps her chin. "So the bus driver lied to us. She said the wizard wasn't involved in the show, but he definitely is somehow. Maybe he'll appear to you later, Sadie."

"Let's keep an eye out for any more wizard appearances," Caroline adds, and we all nod.

Captain Redfern comes into the room, looking as grumpy as ever. "Good, you're ready. Supper's in half an hour, at a tavern called the Thatch. We will go into the village early so you can explore and get people used to your presence." He raises an eyebrow at the sight of Tuba curled up beside Iggy. "You're not taking that, er, new friend to dinner, are you?"

"Nah, he can stay here," Iggy says sheepishly, leaving the cat snoring by the fire.

The village is a five-minute walk away and looks more fantastical than ever, with the sun setting over it in a blaze of warm light. The air is cooler and crisper than before and smells like hay and roasting meat. I'm impressed to see that the villagers are as diverse as the people in New York City. That definitely isn't true of most of the fantasy books and movies I've read or seen.

"I noticed that, too," Sadie says, smiling, when I mention it to her. "I think it's cool. I bet it's because Red wanted Pantaera to feel more realistic."

The villagers watch us the whole way. I see a mom wrangling six kids and a bunch of pigs, a baker selling hot pastries, an old couple weaving baskets, and farmers pushing wagons and leading oxen. It all feels so real, what with the thatched-roof cottages and rolling fields.

"Hey, Sadie, they brought Lady Gà Gà as an extra," Clip jokes, pointing at a fat brown chicken crossing our path. The other kids look puzzled, so he adds, "Our grandma has a pet chicken named Lady Gà Gà, and that one looks like it. Gà is the Vietnamese word for chicken."

Sadie groans, pretending not to like their grandma's bad pun, and everyone laughs.

I turn to stare at the Castle of the North Wind towering over the village. It looks so epic, silhouetted against the fiery sunset. "This place is ridiculous in the best way!" I exclaim.

"Doesn't it remind you of Disney World?" Caroline asks. "When you first come into the park and there are candy stores and souvenir shops? Except, uh, without the stores and shops."

I can see what she's saying. It feels real, but there's also a *newness* to the place. The sheds seem to be trying too hard to appear old, and some of the flower beds look freshly planted.

"Let's meet at the Thatch in twenty minutes," Captain Redfern says, pointing to a low-roofed building. "Don't wander too far or go to the castle just yet. Understood?"

"Understood," everyone choruses.

At first, we stick together in a big, nervous clump, but then people start splitting up.

I watch Iggy, Derek, and Clip whispering and smirking. After a minute, Clip walks up to a random old man and asks, "Excuse me, where's the nearest Starbucks?" And then all three of them *lose* it, holding their stomachs and laughing as the poor man shakes his head in confusion.

"What about McDonald's?" Derek asks, as Iggy giggles so hard he can barely breathe.

"I don't know what you mean," the old man says.

Clip points to the man's wide leather apron and hammer. "Are you really a blacksmith? Can we watch you make a sword? Do you even know how?"

"Guys! Stop bothering people!" Sadie says, stomping over to yank her brother away. "Just wait 'til Captain Redfern hears about your stupid bet to get an actor to break character."

"And may I remind you clowns, yet *again*, that there are cameras rolling all the time?" Caroline asks, seizing her own brother. "Everything you say is getting filmed!"

"We were just having some fun," Derek protests. "Ever heard of comic relief?"

"Caroline's right, though. We should be acting more like heroes!" I declare. "I mean, look at Sir Parrick of Littlevale. He was a peasant and didn't win Queen Inglebeth's respect right away, but he worked on being noble and courageous so people would look at him differently."

Everyone stares at me like I've started speaking Greek.

"Um, Jeremy? What are you talking about?" Lizard asks.

"You know, chapter sixteen of the graphic novel." I look around the group. "The epic history of Queen Inglebeth and her knights? Didn't any of you read that part?"

"Sir Parrick wasn't a *foreigner* to Pantaera like us," Kris says, shrill and bossy. I hope I don't sound like that when I'm explaining stuff to my friends. "It's not a good comparison."

"It's a great comparison!" Sadie says at once.

"The *best* comparison," Clip agrees fiercely, even though I'm sure he has no clue what I'm talking about. "Let's all be more like Sir Porridge."

"Parrick," Iggy whispers to him.

Kris rolls her eyes. "Don't any of you know that he ends up dying in a dragon pit?"

I hate arguing, but I *have* to speak up when someone's wrong about Pantaera. "Actually, the queen only *thinks* he's dead, but he made a shield out of scales shed by a dragon. He was hiding and safe the whole time the dragon tried to burn him to a crisp."

"Wow!" George says. "That's smooth, using the dragon's own scales against it."

"Right?" I say excitedly. "It's one of my favorite stories in the graphic novel. I can lend it to you if you want. Just give me your address before we go home, and I'll mail it to you."

George gives me a high five. "Thanks, Jeremy, I appreciate it!"

Kris's face is as red as her hair and she opens her mouth to argue more, but right then, we hear shouts and screams ring through the air. Four knights approach the village square, dragging a body that is kicking and fighting them tooth and nail. Captain Redfern runs toward them.

"Come on, guys, we should get over there, too!" I urge my friends.

Up close, we see that the prisoner has mottled gray skin that looks like melted wax, bright yellow eyes with thin black pupils, and a mouth full of crooked, broken teeth.

Sadie clutches my arm. "Um, Jer? What is that?"

A thrill creeps down my spine. I can't take my eyes off the creature. Its ripe stench floats toward us, smelling like someone mixed sweat, dirty socks, and old banana peels in a blender. I almost want to reach for my keyboard or mouse, but then I remember this isn't a game. It's real life. "That," I tell Sadie in a low voice, "is an orc."

"Captain Redfern, we caught him in the Witchwood with *this*." One of the knights holds up a baseball-sized object that's shaped like a teardrop. It glows different shades of purple, reminding me of an amethyst I bought at the science museum, and I cover my mouth in horror.

"Oh no! It's a Crystal of Crestfall, a powerful destructive orb!" I shout. Everyone stares blankly at me. "Captain Redfern, those are dangerous! They can turn a kingdom into rubble in mere seconds. That puppy could level a whole city if it hit the ground!"

"Wh-what?" Sadie chokes out.

"So, like, that's a grenade?!" Caroline screams, scooting backward.

"Oh, heck no," Iggy says, shocked. "How do we know it won't go off by itself?"

"It has to be dropped. It can be deactivated if you recite a spell and twist the bottom three times clockwise, slowly, so as not to release its dark magic into the atmosphere." I know I sound like a walking video game manual, but I don't care. "It's in that encyclopedia I mentioned."

The orc glares at me. "How do you know so much about the orb? Are you a spy?"

"Jeremy's more than a spy!" Derek declares, before I

can respond. "He launched *two* campaigns against your army over summer vacation alone!"

"Right after he leveled up to being a Desert Wizard," Iggy adds. "Be very, *very* afraid."

The orc just stares at them, confused.

The captain gives me an approving nod. "Your knowledge will be of great use this week, Jeremy." Gingerly, he takes the glowing purple crystal and runs his fingers over it.

"It's just a plastic ball," I hear Sadie mumble to herself, her face pale. "It isn't real."

"I've expected this since we caught that band of orcs this spring," Captain Redfern says grimly. "I made sure to study their dark magic and I know the deactivation spell." He speaks the words as he turns the bottom of the crystal, which moves separately like it's on a hinge.

Let darkness seep from these crystal pores
Like ocean waves upon unknown shores

I mouth the words along with the captain as chills run up and down my spine.

Let hate and wrath wash into the deep
Let this evil breathe its last and sleep!

"I render thee useless, Crystal of Crestfall!" Captain Redfern roars. With the final turn, the crystal turns pure white, and for one fleeting moment, a woman's face appears inside of it. She has long black hair, a jagged crown, and a bright red mouth twisted in laughter . . . or fury.

"The Forgotten Queen!" Clip and I yell.

And then she's gone. The crystal becomes dull and gray, and when the captain drops it, it bounces like a harmless rock. A bunch of us still jump backward and scream, though.

The orc looks at the dead crystal with so much anger, it makes me shiver.

"What were you doing with a Crystal of Crestfall on King Rothbart's lands?" Captain Redfern asks sternly. "Tell us the truth and I may let you live."

The orc forces a laugh. "Why should I care what you do with me?"

"I ask again: What were you doing with this weapon on His Majesty's lands?" Captain Redfern's low voice feels like tiptoeing on a minefield, but the orc only gives him a mocking smile. Quick as lightning, the captain swoops down and seizes the orc by the collar, lifting him easily even though he must weigh two hundred pounds. Sadie and Caroline grab each other, looking breathless. "Tell me, or I'll have my knights pull out every one of your slimy teeth."

"I don't know anything," the orc says, looking scared at last. "I'm only a messenger!"

"Rickfeld," the captain says calmly to one of his knights, "take him to the dungeons."

"Wait!" the orc cries. "It's the truth! I don't know much, but I *do* know my leader plans to make more of those. He wants to take over Pantaera in the name of the Forgotten Queen."

"I knew it! He's working for her!" I whisper.

The captain goes pale. "Your leader's making more Crystals of Crestfall? How many?"

"I don't know. But he keeps the ingredients in Frostthorn Castle, the ruins just outside the Witchwood. Our army's using it as a base. To make a crystal, you need three rare items: devil dust, dragon's blood, and the petals of the white mountain rose. We've hidden nine of these around the castle, but only my leader knows where they all are. He doesn't trust us, either."

"If he doesn't trust you, why did he give you such a valuable crystal to bring here?"

The orc turns his hateful glare on us. "To test it out on these *heroes*. Yes, we know of the prophecy and the child who will keep Pantaera from the Forgotten Queen—its *rightful* ruler!"

Captain Redfern shoves the orc at the knights. "Keep this foul creature under constant watch in the dungeons," he tells them, then looks at us. "Frostthorn Castle is half a mile away. If they set a crystal off at that short distance—" He trails off as he looks around at the villagers, who are watching and listening with scared faces. "Come, we must find a private place to discuss what to do. It is time to summon the Keeper of Fortunes."

CHAPTER EIGHT

SADIE

"WOW, SADIE, LOOK AT THIS PLACE!" JEREMY SAYS to me, his voice hushed with awe.

The Castle of the North Wind is both gorgeous and creepy. Captain Redfern leads us into a hall made out of cold gray stone. The ceilings soar above us, held up by massive pillars, and our footsteps echo in the large space. It reminds me of the ancient castles Clip and I toured with our parents when we went on vacation in Scotland a couple of years ago.

We pass faded tapestries showing scenes of war (a lot of men and horses and spears). The windows are high and narrow, and the only light comes from torches. Knights stand everywhere, and there are also . . . cameras. Lots and lots of cameras tucked in corners and dangling from the ceiling, all pointed at us along with other equipment like long metal poles with microphones.

"Whoa, they sure didn't go for subtlety in here," George mutters to Iggy.

I turn to Jeremy as we follow the captain. "Why do you think the orc was giving us so much information? We're the enemy, aren't we? And here he is, being weirdly helpful and telling us all about where his leader's camping out and how to make Crystals of Crestfall."

"I think he was afraid Captain Redfern would torture him," Jeremy replies.

I hear a snort and turn to see Molly behind me. Since we left Winterhearth House, she's pulled her long hair into a high ponytail just like mine and rolled up the sleeves of her baggy shirt the same way I did. "Oh, *please*," she says. "You guys know as well as I do that the orc was just an actor in makeup, giving us backstory so we know what our first challenge will be."

My stomach clenches and I open my mouth to snap at her, but Jeremy tells her calmly, "You can think whatever you want to, and we'll think whatever *we* want to."

Molly shakes her head. "Geeks," she hisses, before walking faster to get in front of us.

"Ugh! She's so horrible," I say, my face burning.

"Just ignore her," Jeremy advises.

I glare at Molly's long swinging ponytail from where she's walking near Iggy and George. "She's always calling us geeks! She's on this show, too, isn't she?"

"I like being a geek," Jeremy says cheerfully. "It means you care a lot about something. I think people who look down on geeks just wish they were geeks, too, 'cause we're the ones who get to have all the fun while *they* have to be boring."

I'm still annoyed with Molly, but I can't help smiling. My best friend is one cool kid.

Captain Redfern leads the group into an enormous dark cathedral. The ceilings rise hundreds of feet above us, and everywhere we look are glowing white candles, which gives an otherworldly feel to the huge empty space. Our shadows flicker over the stone walls as we walk.

A woman waits at the altar, and I practically stop breathing as she gazes down at us.

The Keeper of Fortunes is old, *very* old, with dark brown skin and long white braids worn loose. She is small, but she has the face of an ancient queen, with high cheekbones, lips painted blue violet, and eyes that study us without missing a detail. She wears a strange crown: Half of it is made of white peonies, while the other half is made of autumn leaves. Her robe is also split down the middle: One side is cascading white silk embroidered with snowflakes, while the other is spring green with satin birds sewn all over it. She wears gold rings, gold bracelets, and a heavy gold chain around her neck from which dangles an hourglass charm.

A light shines behind her, outlining her in warm gold so that she's the brightest thing in the cathedral, and a gentle breeze moves her braids and the folds of her dress.

Just good lighting and a fan, I tell myself, because it's terrifying how powerful she looks.

Captain Redfern bows low, and we hurry to do the same.

"We are all servants of time," the Keeper of Fortunes says, in a rich, low voice like melting chocolate. "For what purpose have you summoned me tonight?"

"My lady, I've brought the children you foresaw in your prophecy," the captain says.

The old woman's eyes widen. She comes down the stairs to stand before Captain Redfern. She's so tiny that the top of her head doesn't reach his chest, but she has such a magnificent presence that she seems much taller. "Are you telling me, young man," she says, looking up at him, "that somewhere among these youths stands the child hero?"

The captain bows his head. "Yes, my lady. And we are in need of your advice."

The Keeper of Fortunes studies us. Everybody stands up straight, because no one wants to be caught slouching by this immortal lady who can see through all of time. "Children, do you know what a hero is?" she asks. "A hero is a person who is brave, noble, and determined in the face of adversity. Do you believe that describes you?"

No one looks like they know whether to answer her or not. And then, of course (because my big brother *never* misses a chance to stand out), I hear Clip say, "Yes! It does describe me!"

A few nervous giggles ring out, but they die away at once when the Keeper speaks again.

"A hero must demonstrate five qualities above all: the courage to carry them through fear; the determination to keep going against all odds; the humility to listen to others and admit mistakes; the intelligence to find answers; and the strength to serve the people they protect. You will be tested for these virtues, and we will discover who among you shall join the Pantaereon, the trio of legendary heroes destined to unite this land once more."

Jeremy and I look at each other in silent awe.

The lady, the cathedral, and the glowing candles are all so impressive that I almost forget we're on a TV show. Then I catch Molly's eye and see her smirking at me. I frown and turn away, a little embarrassed that I've already started blending fantasy with reality. But all of the other kids seem thrilled and excited, and none of them look ashamed about it.

"The shadow of doom hangs over Pantaera. Soon,

the Forgotten Queen will gather an army and seize this land for her own." The Keeper waves a hand, and everyone (even Captain Redfern) gasps as a curtain behind her glows and starts projecting faint images. We see a crowned man and two little kids. He puts his hand on the blond boy's shoulder and turns his back on the dark-haired girl, who scowls. She gets into a carriage and drives away, looking out of the window with a fierce expression. She has pale skin and deep blue eyes that are narrowed in anger. Suddenly, her gaze shifts right to us, like she can *see* us watching her.

Derek jumps. "Whoa!"

"That's creepy," Clip says in a low voice.

"She looks like any other kid. Like she could be one of us," I hear Lizard say to George.

The light shifts and the image on the curtain changes. In place of the little girl, we see a tall, slender young woman wearing a crown of daggers and a dark veil that shows only her blood-red lips. I gulp, knowing that she's the girl all grown up and back for revenge.

"She turned evil," Kris murmurs, as the woman's mouth stretches into a cruel smile.

"This is the perfect moment for her to strike," the Keeper of Fortunes says. "Pantaera is weak, and if the magical beings who call it home do not stop bickering and grappling for power, they cannot stand against her. Some are even joining her, lured by her empty promises. Yet there is still hope."

The image on the curtain shows three people in hooded cloaks, standing on a cliff that overlooks the sea. Each person holds an object that sparkles with jewels.

"The gods of Pantaera knew this dark day would come," the Keeper of Fortunes goes on. "Long ago, they crafted three weapons: a sword, a shield, and a plate of armor, each studded with gems that they scattered throughout the land to prevent so much power from sitting with any one group of magical beings. When reunited, the jewels will cast a powerful spell of defense against enemies and protect Pantaera from invasion."

The curtain goes dark.

In the silence, I don't hear anything except for the other kids breathing around me.

And then, suddenly, the cathedral blazes with light from hundreds of chandeliers. We all gasp, blinking at the sudden brightness, and then Jeremy cries, "Look! There they are!"

The curtain has lifted to reveal a golden sword, a gleaming plate of armor, and a brass shield. The sword and the armor are each studded with ten giant, dazzling gems: two red rubies, two bright green emeralds, two deep blue sapphires, two milky white pearls, and two sparkling diamonds. Only the shield is bare, with just ten empty indentations on its surface.

"They're beautiful!" Lizard utters.

Captain Redfern drops to one knee. "I never thought I would see these legendary objects in my lifetime," he says, his voice choked with emotion.

The Keeper of Fortunes puts her wrinkled hand on the sword. "Ten adults were tested in the Kingdom of Verdigris, earning gems to replace on this sword as they completed the tasks." She moves to the plate of armor. "In the Kingdom of Malachite, ten teenagers earned these gems as they competed for the title of hero and put them back onto this armor."

The cathedral is dead silent as she turns to look at us.

"As you can see, the shield is still bare. Who among you will help reclaim its jewels? And which of you will be the third and final hero of the Pantaereon?"

A cold wind sweeps through the cathedral, blowing out most of the candles. I press close to Jeremy and Caroline, trembling as the Keeper of Fortunes' stern gaze sweeps over us.

"This week, you will face the Tests of Courage, Determination, Humility, Intelligence, and Strength, and each challenge will yield two gems of power. Tomorrow will be your chance to find the first two. I know what awaits you," the old woman adds. "I have seen it in the sands of time. Many of the orcs want to join the Forgotten Queen."

"What else do you know, all-seeing Keeper?" the captain asks urgently.

"Some of the sirens will form an alliance with her, too."

Everyone in our friend group gasps. We all borrowed Jer's book on the plane and the first chapter was about sirens: vicious mermaids who sing people to their deaths.

"If enough orcs and sirens join the Forgotten Queen, her army will be that much stronger," the Keeper says grimly. "You *must* stop this, young warriors. Prove yourselves. Send a clear message that you are everything I saw in my prophecy: strong, powerful, and good. Show the orcs and sirens that they should be joining *your* side, not the queen's."

"But how?" George bursts out.

The Keeper of Fortunes gazes at him. "By undergoing the Test of Courage. Invade Frostthorn Castle and find the ingredients for the Crystals of Crestfall so they can be destroyed."

"Oh no," Kris whispers. "We have to go *inside* the orcs' castle?"

"The orcs have hidden devil dust, dragon's blood, and the petals of the white mountain rose in their castle," the Keeper goes on. "But there are only nine such ingredients . . . and there are ten of you. The nine children who find an item will continue the journey."

We exchange glances of dismay. One of us will be eliminated from the show tomorrow.

"But the Test of Courage does not end there," the Keeper says. "The nine remaining children must make a dark and treacherous journey across Glimmervale Marsh, lair of the sirens, which will test the boundaries of your bravery . . . and after that, only eight of you will go on."

"Eight?" Clip whisper-screams.

Iggy gasps. "*Two* people are getting eliminated tomorrow?"

"As I said," the Keeper continues, "two gems of power will be awarded after the Test of Courage: one to the first child to leave the orc castle with an ingredient, and the other to the first child to escape the sirens' marsh. They will have the honor of placing the jewels on the shield."

It hits me right then that I want to stay in the competition. Yes, it might be an ultra-nerdy show. Yes, my classmates might make fun of me for running from orcs, bowing to kings, and listening to an old lady in a costume, and half believing in all of it. And the longer I stay, the more obvious it will be that the story I cooked up to tell at school—that I only did this show because 1) TV is cool, and 2) my friends begged me to do it—will fall apart.

But the truth is: I *want* to be here, now that I've been to the Castle of the North Wind, witnessed an orc get captured, and seen the Forgotten Queen. My friends' excitement is contagious, especially Jer's, and I want to know what happens next. I want to be a part of it all.

"Here's the plan," Captain Redfern says. "My knights and I will clear out the orc castle tomorrow morning, as best we can. You kids will go in and seize those ingredients." Fear and doubt are written all over his face. Clearly, he's wondering if we've got it in us to survive.

Honestly, it's what I'm wondering, too.

But there's only one way to find out.

CHAPTER NINE
CLIP

"COME ON, GET UP! TIME TO GO!" SOMEONE HOL-lers, clanging pots and pans downstairs.

"Ururrghfgghhgfhfhh," I growl, stuffing my head under my pillow. That's what I do whenever Dad tries to get Sadie and me to go on a 5:00 a.m. run with him, or when Mom yells that I'll be late for the bus and that I said "Five more minutes!" fifteen minutes ago. For some reason, though, my pillow is too flat today and doesn't block out the noise. Also, my bed is kind of hard and smells like straw, and my room is *really* cold.

"Clip! Get up!" Iggy shouts in my ear. That's weird. I don't remember him sleeping over.

Somebody yanks my blanket away.

"Hey!" I yelp, lifting my head, and then I realize I'm not at home. I'm in Pantaera, and everyone else is getting dressed. Jeremy is almost done; he's already tugging on his shoes.

"Come on, man, first challenge day," Derek says, yanking on his brown leather vest.

I don't need to be told twice. I crashed and burned in the obstacle course yesterday, and I have to make sure I do better today. Quick as a flash, I jump out of the clothes I slept in and into my competition outfit. George comes back into the room with a toothbrush. "Sink's all yours," he tells me. The other boys look like they're wearing Robin Hood costumes from the clearance aisle at Target, but George actually looks like a hero in his outfit, mature and confident.

I take my turn in the bathroom as the person downstairs, who I now recognize as Captain Redfern, goes on banging pots and yelling for us to hurry up.

In the common room, we find cinnamon rolls, crispy bacon, fried ham, scrambled eggs, and roasted mushrooms and tomatoes, which I've never had for breakfast before. But hey, I'm not turning down food. I'm a pro at eating fast, since I'm used to wolfing down snacks on the bus before playing away games at other schools, so I'm done before everybody else.

"I hope you're all ready." Captain Redfern's hair looks freshly washed and gelled, and he seems a *tiny* bit less grumpy. "My knights cleared out Frostthorn Castle this morning. They did their best, but there may still be orc guards, so be careful and avoid capture at all costs. Jeremy, Lizard, and Caroline, you were our leaders in yesterday's task. When you get to the castle, you three will have a one-minute head start, and then the others will follow. Understood?"

"Understood!" everyone says.

My heart thunders with excitement. I've stormed a castle before, but only in the video game. This scavenger hunt is going to be *so* much more fun in real life, and I'm gonna rock this because I'm Clip Chu and I am a champ, and no one will doubt that after this.

Captain Redfern leads us outside and we see the horses we rode yesterday. I spy Teddy Bear and make like a cheetah in the opposite direction, trying to pick another ride. But then the captain calls out, "Everyone, please mount the steeds you had before."

"Aw, man," Iggy mumbles, slouching toward Pecan.

Teddy Bear *literally* gives me side-eye. This horse has so much sass, I'm telling you. At least he stands still as I climb into the saddle. "See how easy that was? Work with me today, okay?" I ask, and he snorts like he's saying, *Don't push your luck, man.*

Iggy gets into the saddle fine, too, but he looks

worried. "I wish I knew where Tuba's gone," he says. "Why would he just leave in the middle of the night without saying goodbye?"

"How should I know? He's not my cat, and he's *barely* yours." But because Iggy looks so sad, I add, "Maybe he'll be in the house when we get back. I mean, he did follow you from the hotel."

Iggy brightens. "That's true."

"All right, people, let's go!" Captain Redfern says.

"We ride at dawn!" Jeremy screams, raising his clenched fist with a fierce expression. It's dorky, but there's so much excitement and energy in the air that the other kids echo his cry and I find myself grinning and lifting my fist, too.

Captain Redfern leads us through the village, back up the hill, and into the Witchwood, where he motions for us to be silent. My hands tighten on the reins, remembering how we saw the Forgotten Queen and someone in a cloak sneaking through the dead trees. The last thing I want is to fall off my horse and have to deal with a witch. No, thanks.

In a minute, we turn down a new path and suddenly burst out onto sprawling green hills with the wild Irish sea roaring in the background. The producers couldn't have timed it better, because at that moment, the sun rises, sending a mystical rose-gold glow over the ruins of an ancient castle. Half of the building looks like it got blown apart by cannons and it's eerie and silent, but also beautiful, with cracked towers and ivy-covered walls.

The captain leads us to the back of the castle, signaling for us to dismount and huddle around him. He's probably only eighteen or so, but his serious expression makes him seem older. "Today, you have an important duty," he says quietly. "Find the ingredients for the Crystals of Crestfall in this castle and bring them out to be destroyed. You will save many lives. Here are some examples of what you're looking for: devil dust, dragon's blood, and a white rose petal."

We crowd closer as he shows us three glass vials. One contains what looks like pepper, another has a thick red liquid that reminds me of tomato soup, and the third holds a flower petal.

"Nine of these vials are scattered throughout the castle," the captain explains. "Each of you must find *one* and then escape through the main doors. Since there are ten of you, one person will be left behind and will no longer be considered for the Pantaereon. Got it?"

Everyone gulps and nods.

"The first person to find an ingredient and escape the orcs' castle will win a gem of power," Captain Redfern reminds us. "So will the first person to get through the sirens' marsh."

Every nerve in my body is on fire. I'm ready to rock. It's that feeling I get before every soccer game, when I'm about to sprint onto the field and kick butt.

Captain Redfern points at Caroline, Jeremy, and Lizard. "You three, come with me."

They disappear inside, and the rest of us look nervously at each other.

"How are you guys feeling?" I ask.

"I'm worried about the orc guards," Sadie admits.

Molly snorts. "They can't hurt you. It's a TV show, remember?" she says, and even though I wanted to say the same thing, I don't like her being sassy with my sister. That's *my* job.

"You're fast. You'll be okay," I tell Sadie. "What about you, Derek? Iggy?"

Iggy punches his open palm. "I want to see the orc who tries to stop me."

"Doesn't look like it's a timed challenge," Derek adds. "It's just whoever the first nine kids are to find an ingredient and get out. So I'm good!"

"Where are we supposed to be looking?" Kris asks.

George shrugs. "Everywhere you can think of, I guess. Shelves, corners, furniture—"

Captain Redfern jogs back out. "Okay, everybody, it's your turn now. Be careful and work fast. I'll see you on the other side of Glimmervale Marsh. Go! Make me proud!"

It's like buffalo storming the plains as we race inside. I hear a weird noise that sounds like someone cheering, and then it's muffled, like they remembered they're not supposed to make any noise. "Our families," I realize aloud, grinning. They're watching the action somewhere, hidden away, and I'm ready to crush it even more for my parents and grandparents.

Turns out I was right to worry about George, because he and I are the strongest runners in the pack. We plunge through the door, neck and neck, and enter a hallway of doors. Iggy and Derek are right on our heels, so I make sure to run farther down. I tear into a random room and find a moth-eaten canopy bed and a rickety old dresser. You better believe I am all over that place: ripping away blankets and sheets, punching pillows, checking under the bed, and yanking open the dresser drawers, but no glass vials turn up.

I run back outside and almost collide with George.

He eyes my empty hands. "Nothing in there?"

I look at *his* hands, too. "Nope. Nothing for you, either?"

He shakes his head and we run for the next door, but I get there first.

"All yours," George says, hurtling into another room.

My heart pounds like crazy as I hear the other kids' frantic searching. "Ten kids, nine ingredients," I mumble, to motivate myself. "Come on, there's gotta be something—"

I hear Derek scream. I rush back out to see him holding a vial full of black pepper. "Devil dust!" he says, beaming, and I flash him two thumbs-up as he charges away down the hall. I might not have been the first to find an ingredient in our group (minus Caroline, Jeremy, and Lizard), but hey, at least my best friend was.

Back in the room, I find five chairs around a cold fireplace. I grab a metal poker and search through the ashes, and I even shake the chairs in case a vial's hidden in the legs. Nothing.

Out in the hall, everyone is still running around like headless chickens. It's too crowded and the vials are supposed to be all over the castle, so I decide to bust this Popsicle stand. I jog to the end of the corridor, go up a flight of stairs, and find another hall snaking along the opposite side of the castle. George is already here, running so fast he looks like a blur. I frown, annoyed that he had the same idea.

"Clip, be careful! I think I heard voices in there!" George calls.

But I'm on autopilot as I plunge toward a closed door. When my brain and body are in action mode, nothing can stop me. I skid inside the room . . . and immediately come face-to-face with two orcs sitting at a table, drinking from heavy brass goblets. "Aw, crap!" I say.

They're just as ugly as the one from yesterday, with lumpy skin and puke-yellow eyes, but I don't waste time admiring them because the table snags my attention. There's a tray full of half-eaten food, and next to it is a vial with a single white rose petal.

"Intruder!" one of the orcs shrieks.

The guards lunge at me and my life flashes before my eyes . . . until a giant feather pillow comes out of nowhere, smacking an orc right in the face. It's George, who must have raided a nearby bedroom. "Hang on, Clip!" he shouts, slamming another pillow into the other orc's face.

A million thoughts race through my mind, like: *He just rescued me, which is nice*, and *Oh, shoot, I owe him now*. But the most urgent thought is: *I can't let him take that vial!*

I nose-dive for the table, snatch it, and shove it into my pocket. I spot a second exit across the room and consider barreling through it and leaving George to deal with the orcs alone. But he *did* just save me, and he also tried to warn me about this room. If I had listened to him, neither of us would be in danger of getting captured. "Ugh!" I growl in frustration. I grab the goblets that the orcs were drinking from and toss the contents into their faces before they can grab George.

"Auuuuughhhhhhh!" they scream, even though it was definitely just water.

George nods a thank-you at me, and I nod back. It's all we have time to do before we're running in opposite directions: him back out into the hall, and me toward the second exit. I fly down some stairs and find myself in a big empty kitchen—a good sign, since the main entrance can't be far if I'm on the ground level. I jog through the door and down a hall full of mirrors.

I can't help checking myself out in one of them. I gotta say, my hair looks pretty good, and this ridiculous Robin Hood getup doesn't look too bad on me, either. I look like an epic fantasy hero! The only thing I don't like about my reflection is that creepy lady behind me.

Wait a second.

"Auuuuuugh!" I squawk, whirling just in time to see the image of a tall, veiled woman in one of the mirrors behind me. My heart practically jumps out of my chest as I realize that 1) it's the Forgotten Queen, with her creepy crown of daggers, and 2) I'm completely alone in the hall. She's only in that mirror. I can't see her eyes through her dark veil, but I feel sure she's watching me because of the way she smiles. She holds up a long white finger with a sharp red nail and wags it at me, like she's saying I'm in trouble. And then she vanishes.

All I see in the mirror now is me, looking way less than an epic fantasy hero and more like a panicked kid, with round scared eyes and a gaping mouth. What the heck just happened? I stand there, frozen, my heart still thundering as I stare at my reflection.

The sound of running footsteps snaps me out of it. I bet another kid found their vial and is searching for the entrance now, too. I sprint through the hall of mirrors, careful not to look into any of them in case the evil queen chick appears again, and pump my fists in triumph.

"Yes!" I whisper, relieved.

Two doors stand open, leading onto a stone terrace outside, with no guards in sight. I rush toward them and almost have a heart attack when I see movement from the corner of my eye.

Someone is slipping down the other end of the hall, and for a terrifying second, I think the Forgotten Queen has somehow stepped out of her mirror . . . but no, it's a person in a long, periwinkle-blue robe who doesn't seem interested in stopping me. I hear a flapping noise, like flip-flops hitting their feet, as they run in the opposite direction and into a room.

"The wizard!" I think back to what he told me yesterday on the field. Man, was he right about not counting myself out too early! I chuckle and hurry onto the terrace, which is roped off except for a section that curves around the side of the castle. It leads to a newly built, warehouse-like structure. The door is open, and it is pitch-black inside. I can't see anything, but I can hear lapping water and someone singing a low, haunting melody.

The Keeper of Fortunes told us that the second half of the Test of Courage would involve vicious killer mermaids . . . and I guess that's one of them singing now. There's no time to think, though, because the other kids (especially George) might be on my tail.

I check to make sure that my vial is safe in my pocket, take a deep breath, and rush into the building, where I'm swallowed up by the darkness.

CHAPTER TEN
JEREMY

CAPTAIN REDFERN TAKES CAROLINE, LIZARD, AND
me inside the castle and points us down a roped-off hallway. My stomach always hurts when I'm nervous, and
right now it feels like I ate too much candy. I gulp, knowing I'm about to throw a wrench into the orcs' evil plans.

"This is a shortcut right into the heart of the castle,"
the captain tells us. "You will need to go in one at a time.
Who wants to go first?"

"Me," Caroline says at once. She jogs down the hall,
her sandy-blond braid swinging.

The second she disappears, Lizard blows past me like
a tiny impatient tornado.

And then it's my turn. I hurry after the girls, shaking so hard that I accidentally run into the wall. *Calm
down, Jer*, I tell myself. *You are here to save the world.* A

true hero never gets nervous before battle. Did Aragorn tremble before facing the evil armies of Mordor? Did Luke Skywalker panic before confronting Darth Vader? No way.

Caroline and Lizard are nowhere in sight, but I can hear them searching through drawers and dragging chairs across the floor. It sounds like they're tearing the place apart.

I take a couple of deep breaths. Dad always tells me to face any challenge with intention, meaning that I need to work with focus and care. So I start by trying to be thoughtful. What do I know about orcs?

1. They are super sneaky.
2. They like to hoard and hide treasure.
3. They're not very smart.
4. They love to go underground.

I decide that the hiding places of the vials won't be too tricky. They might not be in plain sight, but they shouldn't be too ridiculously hard to find.

A tapestry catches my eye, showing a peaceful forest scene with deer, birds, and fish. It might be a good place to conceal a glass vial. Sadie and I love this book series called the Ninety-Nine Kingdoms of Windermere, and the characters always seem to find secrets hidden around tapestries. I run my hands over the heavy fabric, and then lift it to peek underneath.

"Jackpot!" I whisper, as it reveals a secret doorway.

It leads to a tiny chapel with stone benches and four stained-glass windows. As I look at the pretty glass, I get that feeling Mom likes to call my *intuition*. It's like a sixth sense that tells you there's more than meets the eye, and right now, it's telling me that a stained-glass window would also be a perfect place to camouflage a vial. Not in plain sight, but not too difficult.

I climb onto a bench in front of an old-fashioned, gold-framed mirror and run my hands over the first two windows. I'm starting to wonder if this was a totally bananas idea when my fingers suddenly brush against an object that's been attached to the glass with something sticky. When I pluck it off, I see a vial full of thick, orange-red liquid.

"Dragon's blood!" I gasp, holding it up to the sunlight.

My heart feels too big for my chest. I almost want to cry because I've found something so magical. See, it's almost *impossible* to collect dragon's blood because they only give it as a reward for courageous deeds. Dragons bleed different colors depending on which region of Pantaera they come from, and each color has a unique magical ability. Orange-red blood like this holds the gift of seeing the future. I bet the dragon whose blood this belongs to could tell me who is going to win the competition.

I'm so awed and inspired that it takes a second to remember I'm still in a dangerous orc castle. I tuck the vial in my pocket and decide to make sure the coast is clear first. I don't know if the girls went somewhere else, but it doesn't matter. I need to focus on getting *me* out of here.

I'm about to clamber down from the bench when I catch sight of my reflection in the mirror . . . and see the Forgotten Queen standing right next to me. I let out a choked scream and fall backward onto my butt, my mouth dry with terror. But the next second, I realize I'm still alone in the chapel. The queen is only in the mirror, her face turned toward me. She laughs silently, shaking her head at me like she's saying, *You fool! How can* you *defeat me?*

"Just wait and see," I say fiercely, even though I'm shaking like a leaf on the floor. "I won't let evil win! You'll never take over Pantaera. Not on my watch!"

I must sound way braver than I feel, because her image vanishes like it was never even there. Letting out a long breath, I get up and hurry back out into the hall.

I don't see any enemies around, thank goodness, 'cause I'm pretty sure I used up my last crumbs of courage just now.

Since I'm a slow runner, my best bet is to not let any orcs see me in the first place.

I move sideways, keeping my back against the wall, my knees still trembling from my encounter with the Forgotten Queen. I try to pretend that I'm playing laser tag with Sadie and our friends—having fun, keeping quiet, and sneaking past enemy territory.

"You got this," I whisper to myself, as I scuttle along like a scared crab. "You're a hero, Jeremy Thomas. You're not gonna get caught by the orcs!" Mom always tells me to talk to myself the way I would to my best friend, and that's what I would tell Sadie if she were here.

The pep talk gets me to the end of the hall. My intuition tells me to turn left, so I do that, admiring the place as I go. I know that Frostthorn Castle once belonged to the Goldhew lords, but they fell into ruin when the last Goldhew made a not-so-smart alliance with an evil warlock.

I follow my intuition around several corners and find a set of doors leading onto a terrace. "Oh, thank Gandalf!" I say, relieved. I scurry outside, jog around the side of the castle, and discover a gigantic wooden building in the back. The doors are open and it's pitch-dark inside. I hesitate, wondering if this is the right place, and then I hear a woman singing in a low voice.

"'The Dirge of Deadwater,'" I gasp, recognizing the music from the video game. "The melody that plays at the beginning of the siren puzzle!"

Last year, for my birthday, Dad took me to the *War of Gods and Men* panel at New York Comic Con. We waited three hours to get in, but it was so worth it. One of the things the writers talked about was the music and how it helped them build the world of Pantaera and revealed more about whoever sang it. The lyrics of the dirge are in the sirens' language, but when translated into English, it's about how these deadly mermaids want to feast on the flesh of mankind.

And right now, I am listening to the song *in person*.

"This is the coolest thing that's ever happened to me!" I declare, and then suddenly I remember that *I* have the flesh of mankind and there's, like, a 98 percent chance the sirens will want to eat *me*. But this is part of our Test of Courage, and there's no way out but through.

By now, *all* of the kids are in the orc castle, and they could catch up to me any second, especially the fast soccer guys like Clip or Derek. I need to get my butt in gear.

"Fake it 'til you make it!" I say. "Come on, Jeremy. You are brave and powerful, and those sirens aren't gonna know what hit 'em!"

Suddenly, I hear a weird noise that sounds like someone yelling, "Yeah! That's right!" and then another person goes, "Shhh!" and a dog barks. It sounds a *lot* like Chickpea.

But I don't have time to think about it. I hustle through the door and let my eyes adjust to the darkness. I am standing on the banks of a vast marsh that looks like a maze of stale-smelling water and mossy plants. Dim torches are scattered here and there, shining a pale light on the mist that blankets everything. The place smells earthy and damp, like a humid greenhouse. Floating in front of me is a line of small rowboats, each tethered to a pole with rope.

I count them. Nine kids will make it out of the castle, and there are still nine boats . . . which means I'm the first one here!

And then . . .

"Hey, Jer!" Caroline says, breathing hard as she runs in after me. "Are you okay? Did you find your vial? Am I in the wrong place? Is Lizard here yet?"

"Yes. Yes. This is the right place. Not yet," I say, answering her questions in order.

Caroline touches a cattail bending into the water. "Wow, the producers are *really* not cheaping out on this set. These rocks and plants are all real."

We both jump when a woman's head and shoulders suddenly pop out of the water. She has pale, green-tinged skin and long golden hair that floats around her like dead weeds. A plant is wrapped around her upper body like a tank top, leaving her neck and shoulders bare, and I see creepy flaps of skin waving just beneath her jaw on either side.

"She's got gills!" Caroline whispers to me.

The siren smiles at us with sharp white teeth, then starts singing in English.

You think you're heroes of a tale
But let me tell you true
No heroes live to cross our marsh
So why should it be you?

Caroline and I look at each other. Are we supposed to answer the question?

"B-because we're brave," I stammer, my heart thundering. I am talking to an *actual* siren. "And because we have the courage to make it to the other side."

The siren sings in response:

Then off you go, into a boat
Proceed with utter care
Sirens may or may not help you
Only listen if you dare

And then she slips underwater and doesn't come back up. If she's swimming, she's doing it without a single sound, and if she's still there, she can hold her breath better than an Olympic swimmer. There's no noise except for the gentle lapping of water and other sirens singing quietly somewhere deeper inside the marsh.

Caroline shrugs. "On we go, I guess." She unhooks a boat from its pole, hops into it, and picks up the oars. "You gonna be okay, Jer? Want to stick with me?"

I want to say yes, but that's not what a hero would do—not when he's trying to prove his courage. "No, thanks!" I say, stepping gingerly into another boat. "Good luck. And be careful! It sounds like the sirens might give us clues, but they might also trick us."

"Good luck to you, too!" she says, then rows off into the maze.

I grab the oars, copy her arm movements, and manage to inch forward a bit—until I feel a sharp yank on the back of my boat. I'm about to panic when I realize it's still tethered to the pole. Sheepishly, I slip off the rope and this time, I have no problem moving down the waterway.

Rowing my boat might be fun . . . if the marsh wasn't *terrifying*.

The torchlight is so faint, I can see only about three feet in front of me and can't make anything out except for the outlines of boulders and trees bending into the water. I gulp and look around nervously, wondering if someone is watching and waiting to ambush me. I'm pretty sure I will pee my pants if I see the Forgotten Queen again.

It feels like a horror movie: a kid paddling a boat alone in pitch darkness with no sound but splashing water and women singing in eerie voices.

Suddenly, the waterway splits into three paths. I hesitate, not sure which one to pick.

In the distance, I hear the same siren singing her song to somebody else:

You think you're heroes of a tale
But let me tell you true . . .

Uh-oh! That means another competitor has entered the marsh, and I'd better get a move on. I make a snap decision to pick the path all the way to the right.

Something splashes nearby and I scream and nearly

drop my oars. A siren with dark brown skin and wide, long-lashed eyes bursts out of the water and starts to sing:

Do you feel certain that you know
That third path is the way to go?

"No, I don't feel certain," I say weakly, clutching my heart. I regret my answer at once, because she might try to use this information against me. Sirens are devious and love getting humans into trouble. I mean, they were responsible for starting the Great Sea War a century ago.

But she vanishes under the water without another word.

"Oooookay." I'm not sure if that's a good or a bad sign. I'm jittery and sweaty, and I think I hear Clip and George shouting somewhere behind me, so I row my boat down the third path. Right away, I'm worried that I chose wrong because it starts spiraling weirdly in on itself.

But at the center, I find another waterway going straight through some low-hanging trees. My tired arms already feel like Jell-O. "Don't give up," I whisper, trying to ignore the ache.

I hear a rustling sound in the trees to my immediate right and whirl around in alarm. "Who's there?" I demand, but nobody answers. A small creature slinks through the undergrowth. It has a long, skinny tail that curves into the air and two pointed ears. It disappears into the thick shadows before I can see exactly what it is, and then I hear voices on the other side of the trees.

"I'll try going this way!" I hear Lizard say clearly. "Maybe it won't be a death trap."

"Or maybe it will," Iggy replies, sounding doubtful.

This means at least five other kids are in the marsh with me right now, so I row faster. I had a one-minute head start on this challenge, and I need to make sure it counts.

The waterway splits again into two forks. The left one goes alongside a cliff, while the other plunges deep into the trees. Two sirens sit on a boulder between the two paths, illuminated by the torches blazing on either side. They have wet black hair, sly smiles, and silver tails that begin at their waists and end in two sharp fins. One of them is wearing a tank top of thick yellow leaves wrapped around her torso, while the other wears red leaves.

They start singing in perfect harmony:

You see two paths before you
And only one is right
The other one will trap you
And you will need to fight

"Fight what?" I squeak.

They ignore me and continuing singing in eerily beautiful voices:

One question you are allowed
But listen with great care:
One of us will always lie
While one has truth to share

And then I do something I never thought I would do in a marsh full of killer mermaids.

I laugh. "This is the riddle from *Labyrinth*, that movie Aunt Elaine loves!"

Labyrinth is an old film Sadie and I watched with my aunt last Thanksgiving break. A girl named Sarah has to rescue her brother from the Goblin King, and on her quest, she runs into all kinds of obstacles. One of them is a riddle given to her by two guardians blocking two doors.

"So there are two paths," I say, thinking out loud. "And two sirens: one who always lies, and one who always tells the truth. I get to ask *one* question to figure out which path to take." I pause for a second, replaying the movie in my head. "Okay, here's the solution. I ask one of you which path the *other* siren would tell me to take. It doesn't matter which one I ask."

The sirens don't respond.

I point to the one in the yellow tank top. "Let's say you're the one who always lies, and I ask you which path the other mermaid would tell me to take. Whatever you tell me is going to be a lie, so I should do the opposite of what you say."

A girl's piercing scream echoes in the distance, followed by an enormous splash of water, and I tense up. I hope that wasn't Sadie, and I hope everyone else is okay.

"But let's say you're the one who always tells the truth," I go on. "That would make the other mermaid the liar. So again, I would just do the opposite of whatever you tell me."

Both of the sirens smile. I got it right!

"Okay, here's my official question for you," I say to the same siren in yellow. "Which path would the other mermaid tell me to take?"

In response, she sings:

Your reasoning is sound
And what you ask is fair
She would tell you to go left
So listen, if you dare

"I'm turning right, then! Thanks!" Quickly, I paddle down the right fork, which leads me to a straight-shot waterway with an open door leading outside. "Yes! Freedom!"

I'm sweating buckets and I know I'll be sore tomorrow, but I couldn't care less. I laugh and cheer all the way out. I, Jeremy Thomas, have survived both the castle *and* the marsh!

On the shore outside, I'm greeted by a beaming Captain Redfern, half a dozen knights, the Keeper of Fortunes, and Caroline, who is jumping up and down with joy. Lizard and Iggy are scrambling out of their own rowboats in front of me. A few knights wade into the water to help me, and I almost collapse when I step out because my legs are shaking so hard. But I manage to hand my vial of dragon's blood to Captain Redfern.

"Excellent work, Jeremy!" he says warmly.

"Very well done," the Keeper of Fortunes agrees, somehow managing to look just as epic and mysterious in broad daylight as she did in the dark cathedral.

"Thanks!" I say, right as my knees finally give out and I collapse onto the grass.

"Are you okay, Jer?" Caroline asks.

Iggy runs over to help. "Hold on, buddy, I got you. You feeling all right?"

My face hurts from smiling so big. "I feel *more* than all right. I feel like a hero!"

CHAPTER ELEVEN
SADIE

"YEAH, SADIE! GO, GO, GO!" EVERYONE YELLS AS I row my boat into the sunlight. I'm shivering and my wet clothes are plastered against my skin. I feel like I want to cry, because going through that marsh was the scariest thing I've ever done.

Captain Redfern and his knights help pull my boat to shore as Caroline, Iggy, Lizard, and Jeremy all cheer. I immediately fall onto the grass because my knees feel like jelly.

Jeremy hugs me even though I'm soaking wet, because that's the kind of amazing friend he is. "Are you okay, Sadie?" he asks, looking worried.

I give him a weak smile. "I'm fine. I just fell out of my boat near the whirlpool. And also, I saw the Forgotten Queen again."

"Whirlpool?!" Jeremy and Caroline repeat.

"What? I didn't see a whirlpool!" Lizard says, sounding jealous.

Iggy shudders. "I saw the queen, too. In a mirror inside the castle."

My throat feels tight and my eyes burn, and I try my hardest not to cry. "Well, she was in the marsh, too. Remember where the waterway splits into three paths? I wanted to take the middle one, but a siren messed with my head, so I ended up going left. It brought me to a mini-waterfall and I screamed all the way down and fell into a whirlpool at the bottom."

Jeremy gasps. "That was you screaming?"

I shiver. It hadn't been *that* far to fall, but it's horrible when you can't see anything in the pitch darkness. "The water wasn't deep, so I just got back in my boat and kept going. I ran into a big mirror in a dead end and . . . and *she* was in it. The queen. I panicked." I gulp back tears as Jeremy, Caroline, and Lizard all hug me. Iggy kneels in front of us and gives the toe of my sneaker a sympathetic squeeze. "Anyway, I backtracked and somehow found that three-way split again, and this time I took the path all the way to the right."

"With the *Labyrinth* door riddle," Jeremy says, beaming.

"Yeah! I'm sending your aunt Elaine a thank-you card for making us watch that movie."

"You should be glad you didn't take the middle path," Iggy tells me. "Lizard and I got stuck in some weird multi-level maze. We found about a zillion dead ends."

Lizard nods. "I thought we'd never escape!"

Captain Redfern takes my glass vial of devil dust and hands me a thick fleece blanket to wrap myself in. "Nice job, Sadie," he says. "You were very courageous today."

"Indeed. I am impressed with all of you," the Keeper of Fortunes tells us, with the hint of an actual smile on her ancient face. "You have shown great bravery."

My friends help me onto my feet and Iggy spreads his arms wide, saying, "All right, top five! Bring it in!" We do a big, happy, jumping group hug.

And in that moment, I forget I'm on a TV show. It just feels like my friends and I have had the kind of adventure you only read about in books. It was so easy in the darkness of the marsh to forget that it was all pretend. I sigh, feeling glad I don't have to go back in there.

"Finish line!" somebody screams.

Everyone whirls to see Clip and George fighting tooth and nail to reach the riverbank first. My brother wins by a hair and throws himself onto land. His clothes are soaking wet, too, and his eyes search the group for me. Instead of looking annoyed that I finished the challenge before he did, he looks concerned. "You okay, Sadie? You fell overboard, too?" he asks.

"Yeah, but I'm fine. You?"

"Same." Clip shakes himself off like a dog, then trades Captain Redfern a vial with a rose petal for a fleece blanket of his own. "George and Derek and I got stuck in a trap for *ages*. I thought we were goners for sure, and there'd be a three-way elimination or something."

Caroline gasps. "You guys saw Derek? Where is he? What happened to him?"

"I don't know. I thought he was right behind us." George lets out a breath. "It was my fault we got lost in that maze in the first place. I was so sure it would lead us to the exit, and I told Clip and Derek to follow me. But I was wrong, and I'm sorry."

My brother's eyes widen. Clip hates admitting mistakes, so I guess his mind is blown that George can just admit that. "It's okay. You helped us get out of that tangled fishing net trap."

I count the kids on the riverbank: Caroline, Lizard, Iggy, Jeremy, George, Clip, and me. "Ten of us started this competition, and seven are here. So there are three people in the marsh?"

"No, just two," Jeremy corrects me. "Somebody got

left behind in the orc castle, remember? Only one more person can stay in the competition with us."

Caroline paces the riverbank. "What's going to happen to the last kid in the marsh?"

"Don't worry, the knights will bring them out here," Captain Redfern reassures her.

Suddenly, we hear splashing as the eighth competitor rows out of the marsh. I cross my fingers, hoping it's Derek . . . until I see the small, dark-haired figure of Molly Wan.

"Oh no, Derek!" Caroline groans, covering her face.

"Wait, so Derek's eliminated?" Iggy asks, upset.

Clip sighs. "I thought he was gonna make it!"

Nobody's happy to see Molly because we all wanted Derek instead. I might have felt bad for her, except she gives a giant smirk when she sees me. "Didn't you have a boat, too, Sadie?" she asks me. "You look like you swam your way across the marsh."

I clench my teeth, but before I can respond, a knight rows out with Kris and Derek. Kris's red hair is a mess and she's covered in dust, and Derek has a fleece blanket wrapped around him.

Clip hurries over to him. "Hey, man, what happened?"

"I'm fine," Derek says, looking sheepish as he and Kris climb onto dry land. "I tried to take a shortcut, got trapped in a wave pool, and fell into the water."

Caroline throws her arms around him, her eyes full of tears. "I can't *believe* you, D!"

"Don't worry," he tells her brightly. "Now I get to go watch the filming with Dad, so you're representing the Marshalls now, okay? Here's my vial, Captain Redfern."

"Wonderful job, Derek," the captain says, patting his shoulder. "I now have nine vials, thanks to all of you, and I will have them destroyed right away." He and the Keeper of Fortunes go off to the side with a couple of knights, talking in low voices.

Derek looks around at the rest of us. "How's everyone doing? Sadie, you fell in, too?"

I blush. "Yeah, but I'm okay."

"I didn't even get to look for a vial in the orc castle," Kris wails. "I was searching the library, and two orcs came in and sat down for *forever*, so I had to hide behind a dusty old bookshelf. It was so unfair!"

Clip frowns. "Why didn't you just run for the door?"

"Because they're orcs!" she cries, and my brother looks away. I can read his expression like a book: This was the Test of Courage, and Kris Kurso definitely did not pass. "The wizard didn't even come in to help me. I saw him walk by the library door."

"I saw him, too!" George and Iggy say together.

"He was in the marsh for me," Caroline says, and Lizard adds, "Yep, for me, too!"

Clip nods. "I saw him in both the castle *and* the marsh."

"Same," Jeremy agrees. He looks at Iggy. "And I think I saw a cat. Maybe it was Tuba!"

I look around at them, feeling left out. "Wait, so all of you saw the wizard? Show of hands, who saw him during this challenge?" I ask, and everybody raises their hands except for me and Molly. "How about the Forgotten Queen? I saw *her*, at least."

This time, all of us raise our hands. As the group starts talking excitedly about when and where they saw the evil queen, I turn to Jeremy. "Why do you think I haven't seen the wizard yet?" I ask, chewing my lip. "Everyone else has run into him by now, and he talked to you guys and gave you advice. Do you think it means something?"

"Don't worry," Jeremy reassures me. "I think you'll see him soon. I have this feeling the wizard appears to anyone who *wants* to see and believe in him."

"Ugh, who *cares*?" Molly breaks in. "It's just some weird actor in a costume. It's not a *real* wizard. Stop acting like a baby and pouting about it, Sadie."

"I didn't ask *you*!" I snap. "And quit calling me names."

I notice Clip watching us and wait for him to jump in

and defend me, but he doesn't say a word. He just turns back to Iggy and Derek and keeps talking to them like nothing happened.

"Come on, Jeremy. We don't have to stay here and be treated like this," I say, seizing my best friend and dragging him away from Molly. "Ugh, she's so mean to me! There's nothing wrong with wanting to see the wizard, too, when everyone else has!"

"You know, I think *she's* upset about not seeing him, too," Jeremy says thoughtfully.

I let out a cough of disbelief. "But she called me a geek for wanting to see him!"

"Kris and I are way bigger Pantaera nerds than you are," he points out. "I mean, pretty much everyone else on this show is, because you don't even play the video game. But notice how Molly doesn't bully any of *us*."

"Why me?" I ask, looking around at the other kids. Everyone's smiling and chatting and laughing. They all look so happy to be in Pantaera. They look confident in a way I don't feel.

"Maybe 'cause she knows she can get under your skin. And 'cause she's jealous."

I raise my eyebrows. "Of me?"

"Of people like us," Jeremy says cheerfully. "She wishes she could love things really, *really* hard, the way we do. Imagine what it's like to be ashamed of loving things hard!"

I get a weird feeling when he says that. Almost like I feel *sorry* for Molly or something.

Captain Redfern and the Keeper of Fortunes come back and shake Kris's and Derek's hands. "Thank you for all you've done for Pantaera," the captain tells them. "My knights will take you back to your own world now. I wish you the best of luck."

"I commend your efforts," the Keeper adds. "Well done."

Derek hugs, high-fives, and says something nice and encouraging to every kid. When it's my turn, he whispers, "You got this, Sadie!" and I practically melt into a puddle.

Kris still looks upset. "Bye," she mumbles, as the knights take her and Derek away.

And then, there we are: the top eight competitors on the show.

The Keeper of Fortunes faces us. "The Test of Courage has revealed that you are all brave enough to continue. You survived a castle and a marsh full of many dangers, and there is no doubt in my mind that the child hero is one of you standing here."

My stomach lurches in terror and excitement. I'm still

in the competition. *Sadie Chu, a hero of the Pantaereon,* I think, trying out the title. It sounds good, but unreal, too.

"Whoa, a siren!" Lizard shouts, pointing at a woman who has just burst out of the water.

"And an orc!" George adds, as a hulking, gray-skinned creature approaches us.

"Stay calm. I summoned them here to host the Test of Courage," the Keeper of Fortunes says. She raises an eyebrow at Captain Redfern, who whipped out his sword at the sight of the orc, and he lowers it sheepishly. "Some orcs and sirens may be tempted to join the Forgotten Queen, but many others hope for peace. Remember what I told you about the objects of power: the sword, armor, and shield? And how, long ago, the gods of Pantaera scattered the gemstones among the magical beings in the land?"

We nod.

She waves a knight forward. He lays the plain brass shield on the grass. "There are ten jewels to be collected for this shield. Today, two will be given to the children who excelled at the Test of Courage." She points at Jeremy, whose eyes grow round with surprise. "You were the first to find a glass vial and escape the orcs' castle. Please step forward."

"Way to go, Jer!" I say, patting him on the back.

Everyone cheers as Jeremy shuffles forward, looking thrilled and embarrassed.

"Kog," the Keeper of Fortunes says to the orc, "you hold the Gem of Courage that was given to the orcs. Will you present it to our young warrior?"

The orc pulls a huge, shining ruby from his pocket and we all gasp. The jewel has been cut into a perfect square and glitters every shade of red in the sunlight.

"All orcs may seem evil and bloodthirsty, but it isn't true," the orc says in a nasal, high-pitched voice. "Some of us believe in the Pantaereon, the child hero, and peace, and we refuse to follow the Forgotten Queen. In that spirit, I present you with this Gem of Courage." He holds out the ruby to Jeremy with both hands. "You have won the honor to place it upon the shield."

My best friend accepts the gem with trembling fingers and sheer joy on his face. He bends, fitting the ruby into one of two square indentations on the shield. It snaps on with a *click!*

The Keeper looks at Caroline. "You were the first competitor to escape the sirens' marsh. Step forward."

Blushing, Caroline approaches the riverbank, where the siren holds out a second ruby.

"Many of my kind also hope for the peace that the

Pantaereon will bring," the mermaid says, her gills flapping creepily against her neck. "Take this Gem of Courage that was given to the sirens long ago. You have earned the honor of placing it upon the shield."

"Th-thank you," Caroline stammers, and snaps her ruby into place beside Jeremy's. The brass shield looks much better now with a little decoration.

Everyone cheers again and Captain Redfern says, "Well done, everyone. We will now go back to the house so you can eat and rest. Your horses await." I hear Clip and Iggy groan quietly. "And make yourselves presentable, because this evening, I will introduce you to His Majesty."

Jeremy gasps. "We get to meet King Rothbart?"

"I think you've earned it," the captain says, smiling. "Don't you agree?"

Jeremy and I are the first ones downstairs after a nap and a shower. We find a yummy predinner snack prepared by Kathryne: freshly baked bread, three kinds of cheese cut into slices, warm molasses cookies, veggies and dip, and ice-cold lemonade.

"Can you check my teeth when I'm done?" Jeremy

asks me. "I don't want to meet King Rothbart with food stuck in them."

"Sure, if you'll check mine." I nibble one of the cookies. It's soft and crumbly and sweet. "Do you think the king will like us, or be unimpressed like Captain Redfern?"

"I hope he'll like us. And the captain's coming around. He's been smiling a lot more lately." Jeremy layers a slice of cheese between two bits of bread, making a tiny sandwich. "I think we made him proud today. Those challenges weren't easy."

I shake my head. "I can't believe I made it through the Test of Courage. I really thought I was gonna fall apart in the marsh when I saw the Forgotten Queen."

"I didn't think I would last a day, either," Jeremy admits.

"I feel like Derek should have made it instead of me," I say. "Or even Kris, since she knows so much more about Pantaera than I do. I don't know if I deserve to be in the top eight."

"But Derek and Kris didn't make it, and *you* did," he points out. "We both got past the orcs and the sirens. So it feels a little more possible that we might survive the next challenge, too, you know? We're still here, and we deserve to be!"

I smile. Jer is the kind of kid who's always cheerful and positive, which makes it hard for me to feel bad about myself for long. "You're right. Nobody else seemed to doubt themselves. Clip was all smug, like he was thinking, *Duh! Of course I'm in the top eight!* And George and Lizard and the rest of them . . . they just seem so confident, you know?"

"You should be, too," Jer says, his mouth full of cheese.

A thought occurs to me. "Maybe that's it. Maybe Molly's picking on me 'cause she senses that I don't feel good about myself. Well, I don't want to be like that anymore. I want to be confident and strong." I sit up straight, like a hero. "I earned my place in the top eight."

"Yeah!" Jer says enthusiastically. "You toughed it out!"

I pound my fist on the table. "I toughed it out!"

"Say, 'I'm amazing'! Come on, say it!"

"I'm amazing," I say sheepishly. It feels silly to say that out loud . . . but it also feels good. "And so are you, Jer! We're gonna rock the next challenge, whatever it is!"

"I'll cheers to that," he says, grinning, and we clunk our mugs of lemonade together.

Soon, everyone joins us for snacks, and before long we are all marching back up to the Castle of the North Wind with Captain Redfern. He is definitely loosening up, like Jeremy said, because he chats with us and points out interesting sights the whole way there.

Clip and George walk together, talking about someone they both follow on Twitch, while Iggy and Lizard discuss *Animal Crossing*, this game they love. I stick with Jeremy, glad to still have my best friend with me. Caroline and Molly seem lonely without Derek and Kris.

In the castle, the captain takes us to a hallway full of oil paintings. A young man waits for us there, gazing up at the artwork. He looks like he might be in his late teens, like Captain Redfern, and he has dark hair, olive skin, and a golden crown on his head.

I gulp, suddenly nervous. "Should we bow?" I whisper to Jeremy.

"Yep!" Jeremy says. "Thank goodness I looked up what type of bow is appropriate."

Behind us, the other kids haven't noticed the king yet.

"So anyway, I tiptoe toward this tarantula, right?" Iggy says to Lizard, still talking about *Animal Crossing*. "And I know it's gonna be worth, like, ten thousand bells. And then I realize I forgot to equip my net! That thing was all over me, and I blacked out and—"

"Psst! Guys!" Clip hisses, and everyone falls silent.

Captain Redfern bows to the king, bending at the waist with his right arm folded across his stomach and the other draped over his back.

"That's the royal court bow of the Kings of Everheart," Jer whispers to me, his eyes shining. "You have to remember to slide the right foot back slightly. That's very important."

We all try to copy the bow, with varying degrees of success.

King Rothbart doesn't seem to mind. He has the kind of friendly face that you would feel comfortable asking for directions. "Hello, Daniel," he says to the captain, and then his brown eyes crinkle as he smiles at us. "Welcome, young warriors. I am so grateful you're here. You left your world to fight for mine, and that means more than I can say. Thank you."

His voice is warm and kind. He looks way too young to be a ruler, and I remember what Kathryne, the housekeeper, told us: that both King Rothbart and Captain Redfern keep having to prove themselves because of how young they are.

"The Keeper of Fortunes tells me one of you will be the child hero, fated to save the realm," the king continues. "But to me, every one of you is already a hero. Tell me your names."

Clip looks flustered when His Majesty approaches him. "Clip Chu, sir," he says, shaking the king's hand and bending clumsily at the knees. Clearly, he's already forgotten the bow.

When everyone has introduced themselves, the king says, "Glad to meet you. I think—"

Six knights burst into the gallery, interrupting him. They look sweaty and panicked, and their leader, a short and stocky woman, bows hastily. "I beg your pardon, Your Majesty, but there's something urgent the captain and his warriors must see at once," she says.

Captain Redfern excuses himself to the king and beckons for us to follow him and the knights outside. The sun has set and it's getting dark, but we can clearly see the Keeper of Fortunes on the drawbridge, gazing down at the moat below. On the other side of the rushing water, there are burning objects stuck into the ground. Plumes of smoke rise in the air, but for some reason, the objects don't crumble into dust. They stand tall and whole and blazing.

"Feathers!" King Rothbart exclaims. He must have followed without any of us noticing.

The Keeper of Fortunes nods. "The phoenixes have paid you a visit, Your Majesty."

"What does it mean?" he asks. "Is it a message of

friendship? They've been quiet, and it's hard to guess whether they will align themselves with me or the Forgotten Queen."

"It is not a message of friendship . . . but it is not the opposite, either. It is a *possibility* that they will join you, depending on how these young warriors perform. Yes," the Keeper of Fortunes adds, as we look at each other in realization. "This will be your next challenge: the first half of the Test of Determination. Tell me, what do any of you know about the phoenixes?"

Every single pair of eyes swivels to Jeremy.

"I know that whenever a phoenix releases a feather, it burns for seven hours, my lady," he says. "Seven is a sacred number to the phoenixes."

A smile creases the Keeper's lips. "Correct. We must let them finish burning. Tomorrow morning, you will gather them and bring them back to this side of the moat. They will unlock a puzzle. This task is not for the fainthearted, and it will test the limits of your determination . . . but I am told by the phoenixes themselves that whoever succeeds will receive a gem."

We all exchange nervous glances. I look down at the roaring water with dread, wondering how we're going to cross it. Some of the other kids don't seem too thrilled, either.

Captain Redfern nods. "Warriors, meet me back here on the drawbridge at first light."

"The fate of Pantaera rests upon your shoulders," King Rothbart adds gravely, looking around at us. "Rest well, and good luck."

CHAPTER TWELVE
CLIP

THE NEXT MORNING, AFTER BREAKFAST, WE HURRY to meet Captain Redfern on the drawbridge.

"Did you sleep at all, Clip?" George asks me.

He and I are leading the pack. He seems like a cool guy. We like the same movies and follow the same gamers on Twitch, so there's always a lot to talk about during our downtime. But when we're on and competing, I have to remind myself that he's my biggest rival.

"A couple of hours," I say, glancing over my shoulder to check on Sadie and Jer. They look as tired as I feel. "I'm not sure anyone got much rest. Besides snore-storm Iggy anyway."

"Hey! I heard that!" Iggy says indignantly.

I snicker. "Yeah, and we all heard *you* rumbling like an earthquake last night."

"Well, excuuuuuuuse me for breathing!"

As we hurry through the village, a few residents actually call out, "Good morning!"

"Why are they so friendly all of a sudden?" Lizard asks, panting. Even with short legs, she's managed to keep up with the three of us big guys. I can't count her out as a rival, either.

"Maybe they're warming up to us, like the captain is," I suggest.

Captain Redfern, the Keeper of Fortunes, and a dozen knights are waiting for us by the edge of the moat. Across the water, the phoenix fire has died out to reveal eight separate bundles of shiny golden feathers, spaced out in the dirt and glowing in the early morning light.

"Wow!" George and Iggy both say.

"Oh no," I hear Sadie grumble to Jeremy. "*That's* how we're getting over there."

Eight wooden rafts toss in the water, spaced six feet apart. Each sits on a track made of two thick ropes stretched across the churning moat. There aren't any oars, which means we'll have to get on our stomachs and paddle with our hands, fighting the current the whole way. No wonder Sadie isn't thrilled, because this is going to be tough for anyone who isn't very strong.

I'm grinning, though. "Hope you're all ready to get a little wet!"

"That rope track should help," Lizard says, when Jeremy and Sadie groan. "At least we won't go sailing down the moat to who-knows-where."

"Welcome to your Test of Determination," the Keeper of Fortunes says. "If you excel and prove yourselves to the phoenixes, they may join King Rothbart against the forces of darkness. They have left behind eight bundles of feathers and eight accompanying puzzles. Sir Grayheart?"

One of the knights walks over to a table, which holds what looks like a stack of small wooden shoeboxes. He picks one up and shows us the eight tiny holes along the top.

"Paddle across the moat, collect a bundle of feathers, and bring it back to this side," the Keeper explains. "Each feather is a different length, and each hole in your puzzle block is a different depth. Figure out how to insert the feathers so that they are the same height, all the way across. That will unlock the message hidden inside. Understood?"

Everyone nods.

My chest tightens a little. It might not be *too* hard for me to paddle across, but the puzzle part will be tricky.

I've never been good at stuff like that, not like Sadie and Jeremy.

"Only seven of you will move on after this challenge," Captain Redfern speaks up. "The last person to collect their feathers and solve their puzzle box will be eliminated."

I hear George gulp, which makes me hopeful that his nerves will trip him up.

"And the *first* person to solve the puzzle box will receive a Gem of Determination," the Keeper of Fortunes adds. "The phoenixes only appear to human eyes at twilight, so they will not be here to present it to the victor. But they have assured me that the jewel will appear to the worthiest and most determined competitor."

A jolt of excitement runs through me. I just know that jewel is gonna be mine!

"Everyone, on your rafts," the captain says, and we all scramble to claim one. I plop onto my stomach, feeling the water rushing beneath me. George and Iggy take the rafts on either side of me, which is handy because I can keep an eye on them. "On your marks, get set . . . go!"

I start whirling my arms fast like a windmill, but my raft only moves a tiny bit forward. The current is so powerful that for every foot I gain, I get held back a few inches. I clench my teeth when I see George's massive football player shoulders trying to pull ahead of me with fire and fury. He keeps getting pushed back by the current, too.

Breathing hard, I turn my head to check on everyone else. Lizard and Caroline are right on Iggy's tail, and Sadie, Jeremy, and Molly are working hard at the very back. Jeremy's face is scrunched in concentration, and as I watch, I'm surprised to see him catching up to Lizard. He's not the strongest or fastest kid, but he's *determined*. And that's what I need to be, too.

I keep paddling, ignoring the burn in my shoulders. I'm already soaked, but the water is surprisingly warm. *Focus and get the feathers*, I tell myself. *Don't give up.* When I watch the show later, I want to see myself looking like a winner. I want to be the one who's crowned the child hero and gets to hang out with Red on the movie set in LA. He's going to be so impressed when he hears my video game ideas, and maybe Sadie and my parents won't think I'm such a failure then. *Clip, let's write a game together*, I imagine him saying, and picture the awed looks on my family's faces. I grin and paddle even more furiously.

The opposite shore gets closer . . . and closer . . .

"Huuuuuurk!" George grunts as his raft hits land. He

pulls himself onto his feet and grabs a bundle of feathers, and then he's on his stomach again, paddling back.

I hit the shore a few seconds later and do this half roll, half stumble because my tired limbs are shaking so hard. I grab my feathers (which are made out of a very light metal), throw them on my raft, lie on top, and start making my way back to the other side.

I gasp for air as I flail my arms even harder, fighting the water, and my neck and shoulder muscles scream at me. My determination pays off, though, because I catch up to George.

Captain Redfern hands each of us a wooden puzzle block once we're both on dry land.

I shake mine and hear something rattle inside. I throw myself onto the grass and start sticking my feathers into random holes on the block. I don't have a strategy, aside from hoping I'll get lucky and find the right combination. There's no time, because I *have* to beat George. I want to win a gem and get to stick it on the shield, like Caroline and Jeremy did yesterday. *It's not over 'til it's over*, I think, frantically arranging my feathers.

George seems to have the same "stick 'em in randomly and hope for the best" technique.

"Remember, the feathers are different lengths, and the holes are different depths," the captain says. "Find the right order so that they're the same height, all the way across."

A third raft arrives. I glance up and I'm *shocked* to see Jeremy, which just further proves that this challenge is more about determination than athletic ability. He must have kicked serious butt on his raft to catch up to me and George. I start panicking, because I was counting on my head start over our puzzle experts Jer and Sadie. My feathers are a mess, sticking out at half a dozen different heights. *Don't freak out*, I try to tell myself. *Go slow.*

Plunging headfirst into a challenge without a plan hasn't helped me on this show so far. In the orc castle, I barged into that room and almost got myself captured, and in the marsh, I kept rushing down the wrong path because I never stopped to think. I need to take it easy, like Jeremy, who's studying his feathers carefully. I pull mine back out and lay them on the ground. "Okay, here we go. These are the same length," I whisper, picking up three of them. I stick them into random holes until they're all the same height. My heart leaps . . . until I try to fit the other feathers in and none of them line up. "Aw, *man!*"

By now, Lizard, Iggy, and Caroline are back, too, and working on their puzzles. Molly and Sadie arrive last, within seconds of each other. My sister plops down nearby and Molly, who seems as eager to keep an eye on the competition as I am, sets up shop right next to her.

"You okay?" I ask.

"Fine, thanks!" Sadie says, and gets cracking on her puzzle.

There's complete silence as everyone focuses, and then . . .

"Done!" George holds up his block. Every golden feather is the same height, making a perfect line across. A little door has popped open, revealing a scroll and a silver key.

Captain Redfern reads the scroll out loud. "*The were-wolf village.*"

We all pause and look around at each other, confused.

"Don't just sit there! Keep going!" the captain yells, and I jump and turn my attention back to my puzzle. "This is only one piece of an entire message, and I need the rest! Quick!"

Jeremy is the next one to hand in his scroll.

"*Find the antidote,*" Captain Redfern reads aloud.

At this point, we're even more desperate to finish. Werewolf village? Antidote? I'm dying to know what the whole thing says. Groaning, I pull out my feathers *again* and lay them out on the grass . . . which is probably what I should have done right off the bat. I arrange them by length, then insert the longest and the shortest into the block until they line up perfectly.

"Done!" Sadie shouts.

Captain Redfern takes her scroll. "*These keys will.*"

"Here's mine!" Caroline says.

"*And save a life,*" the captain reads.

Sweat drips from my brow. I'm on the right track, because *finally* the last feather goes in and they're all the same height. I hear a click as a compartment in my block pops open.

"Done!" I cry, practically throwing my scroll at Captain Redfern.

"*To ingredients in,*" he reads out loud.

I wipe my sweaty face, shaking at how close I came to losing. For all my big talk, I've been on the struggle bus the *whole* show. At least I've been able to pull myself together and try to think things through, but . . . this is not the way I was hoping to show my heroic awesomeness.

Iggy, Molly, and Lizard are still working. The Keeper of Fortunes is nearby, watching them, which seems to make Iggy even more nervous. He's doing what I did at first: sticking the feathers into random holes and hoping they magically line up. They don't, of course, and he groans and yanks them all back out. *Come on, Iggy*, I think, chewing on my nails.

Lizard is the next to finish. She jumps up and down impatiently as Captain Redfern unfolds her scroll and reads aloud: "*Open seven doors.*"

Sadie and Jeremy lay the scrolls on the grass, trying to piece the whole message together.

Now, it's a tense battle between Iggy and Molly to see who stays in the competition. I can tell Iggy's getting frustrated. I've seen it happen on the soccer field, when things don't go his way and he gets stuck in his own head. His face is bright red as he works.

And then Molly grins with triumph. "Done!" she says, the bleached tips of her ponytail nearly smacking the captain's face as she hands in her scroll.

"*And the phoenixes will,*" Captain Redfern reads out loud.

Iggy sits back on his heels and gives an exhausted laugh. "Well, guess I'm out."

My stomach sinks, and I cover my eyes with my hands. I've already lost Derek in this competition, and now I have to lose my other best friend, too.

"Don't give up yet, Iggy. We need your piece of the message, too!" Captain Redfern urges him. "Sadie! Clip! You're closest to him. Help him out, will you?"

My sister and I hurry over. "Pull the feathers out and put 'em on the ground," I say.

"Arrange them by size first," Sadie advises.

Within minutes, we've got Iggy's puzzle block finished, too.

"Phew! Team Chu to the rescue," Iggy says, smiling. He might get frustrated sometimes, but he's not a sore loser. "Sorry I couldn't do it faster, Captain Redfern."

The captain pats his shoulder. "Your scroll says: *Join your cause.*"

"Perfect! The message is complete!" Jeremy says, taking Iggy's scroll from the captain.

"Go on. Do the honors and read it for us," Captain Redfern tells him.

Beaming, Jeremy stands up tall and breaks out in an epic, fake English accent. "*These keys will open seven doors to ingredients in the werewolf village,*" he reads aloud. "*Find the antidote and save a life, and the phoenixes will join your cause.*"

"Whoa!" Caroline exclaims. "That's as good as a promise, right?"

"Sounds like it," George agrees.

"They're joining us!" Lizard and Sadie grab each other and do a little dance.

Captain Redfern wears an expression that reminds me of my coach: proud, but about to tell us there's more work to be done. "There's more work to be done," he says, right on cue. He turns to the Keeper of Fortunes.

"The werewolf village is Hollybottom, isn't it, my lady?"

The old woman nods. "They are allies of the phoenixes, and I hear their elder is deathly ill. If you save him, you will prove to both the werewolves and phoenixes that our cause is worth joining. This could turn the tides of war." She lifts her eyebrows and looks around at all of us. "Well? Are you ready for the next part of your Test of Determination?"

"Yeah!" everyone shouts.

"Iggy, we are proud of everything you have accomplished, but your road ends here," Captain Redfern says gravely. "Please hand me your key and say your goodbyes."

Iggy hands over the key that was inside his puzzle block, then heads for me first. We give each other a tight one-armed hug. "Win this for me and Derek, okay?" he says, and I nod.

He hugs everyone else, too, but before the knights can escort him away, there's a loud and happy meow and a big, fluffy black cat launches itself at him. "Tuba, you're back!" Iggy cries. The cat rubs its head against Iggy's chin lovingly, its amber eyes bright. "Aw, you're still proud of me even though I failed, aren't you?"

"You didn't fail," Captain Redfern and I say together.

For someone who got eliminated, Iggy seems pretty

happy now that the cat who adopted him is back. "Bye, everyone, and good luck!" he says, as he and Tuba walk off with the knights.

Captain Redfern hands Iggy's key to George. "As the winner of the phoenix challenge, you will have the advantage of *two* keys in the next task. Well done."

My gut clenches, but I clap with the others as the captain pats George's shoulder. *I'm still here, and it's not over until it's over*, I remind myself.

A large wagon pulls up. Captain Redfern helps the Keeper up, then hops in next to her. "Let's go, warriors. The werewolf elder is dying, and there's no time to lose," he says, and the last seven kids in the game climb up in back. "To Hollybottom, the village of the werewolves!"

CHAPTER THIRTEEN
JEREMY

HOLLYBOTTOM IS ABOUT A TEN-MINUTE RIDE AWAY.
Our wagon has to climb a steep hill to reach it, and at the
top, we get a stunning view of the sea sparkling in the
sunshine. It looks like a glittery turquoise ribbon stretching behind the village of thatched-roof houses.

"Isn't Pantaera pretty, Jer?" Sadie asks with a happy
sigh.

"Yeah, it is," I say, my heart soaring at the view.

Molly rolls her eyes. "You mean *Ireland*. Or have you
forgotten this is all pretend?"

"Maybe *you're* pretending," I say lightly, as Sadie
tenses up. "But I'm immersed, like we're supposed to be.
It's more fun playing the game in the spirit it was meant
to be played."

"Yeah! What he said!" Sadie says fiercely.

Molly flips her bleached hair. "Only dorks actually *believe* that this is real," she says flatly. She turns her back, like she doesn't even want to be associated with us, and jumps into Lizard, Caroline, and George's discussion about their favorite superhero movies.

Sadie catches sight of Clip, who's sitting on my other side. "Why don't you ever stick up for me?" she demands. "You never help me out, like Jer does. Some big brother you are!"

"I can't always be there to fight your battles," he says calmly.

She crosses her arms. "Whatever. You don't know what it's like to be bullied."

"Actually, I do."

Sadie and I exchange glances. "Yeah, right," she says, shaking her head. "Clip Chu, the most popular kid in school? Soccer MVP? Who would bully *you*?"

"I wasn't always popular," Clip points out. "When I was in third grade, this fifth grader named Ben Anderson found out I wasn't doing great in math. He and his friends tortured me about it. They kept laughing and saying they didn't know Asians could be bad at math."

"What?!" I say indignantly. "That's racist."

Sadie's eyes widen. "Wasn't Ben the captain of your soccer team last year?"

"Yeah," her brother says. "As soon as I got on the team, he was a lot nicer to me and pretended he had never bullied me. But he would still say dumb stuff, so I made sure to fight back whenever he did. I wanted him to know I was tough and wasn't gonna take it anymore."

"Did you tell Mom and Dad about it?" Sadie asks quietly. "Or a teacher?"

Clip shakes his head. "I should have. But I talked to Derek and Iggy and that helped. See, it's a power thing," he adds, his face serious. "Bullies don't feel good about themselves, so they try to make *you* feel bad about yourself, too. And you shouldn't let them."

"It makes sense, Sadie," I chime in. "I mean, you haven't been feeling confident in Pantaera. I bet Molly doesn't, either, and she's making fun of you to hide how bad she feels."

"See? Jeremy gets it," Clip says smugly, jabbing a thumb at me.

We glance at Molly, who's still listening to the other kids discuss the Avengers movies.

"I want to have fun in Pantaera like all the rest of you," Sadie admits. "I *am* having fun. So maybe I should stop letting her make me feel bad about it."

Clip nods. "There you go!"

"That's right!" I say. "Repeat after me: I'm Sadie Chu and I'm here to have fun!"

"I'm Sadie Chu and I'm here to have fun," she says, her cheeks pink.

"We can't hear you," Clip says, cupping a hand around his ear.

"I'm Sadie Chu and I'm here to have fun!" she says, more loudly.

Molly turns around and gives her a *look*, but the other kids whistle and clap and Caroline hollers, "Woooo! That's right, girl!"

Sadie leans back, looking proud and embarrassed, as the horses pull the wagon up in front of a gate surrounding a group of small houses. We've reached the village of Hollybottom, and I crane my neck eagerly to see the werewolf inhabitants coming out to greet us.

"Wait, these are werewolves?" Lizard asks. "Why do they look like regular people?"

"Werewolves only transform under the full moon once a month," I explain.

George looks at me. "I think I remember Hollybottom from the game. It's a safe haven for werewolves, right? They can live in peace, since there's so much prejudice against them."

"Right!" I say brightly.

Captain Redfern helps the Keeper of Fortunes off the wagon, and she motions for us to gather around them. "The elder is a respected werewolf," she informs us. "His people are peaceful and have stayed out of the great war so far. But it seems they may be changing their minds and preparing to fight alongside their friends, the phoenixes."

A woman walks toward us. She looks to be in her thirties and she's beautiful, with light brown skin, wavy black hair, and dark eyes. She stands in a challenging kind of way in her simple dress and muddy boots, with her hands on her hips. "You are the Keeper of Fortunes?" she asks. "You told me you would bring heroes to save our elder's life. These are mere babies."

Clip and George frown, and Lizard makes a loud "tuh!" under her breath.

"Watch your tongue, madam," Captain Redfern snaps at the woman, before the Keeper of Fortunes can respond. "King Rothbart, the Keeper, and I all trust in these courageous young warriors, and you had better do the same."

Sadie and I look at each other, amused. The captain has *definitely* changed his tune since we began this competition and it feels good to hear him defending us.

"These *babies* are your elder's only chance to escape

his poisoned deathbed, Elspeth Thurhold." The Keeper might be tiny and ancient, but the young woman backs away at her tone.

"Elspeth Thurhold?" I exclaim, and everyone looks at me. "You're the only non-werewolf living in Hollybottom. You're a witch who was found outside the village as a little girl. The blacksmith adopted you out of pity, even though none of the other werewolves trusted you."

Elspeth's jaw drops. "How do you know all of this?"

"Ummm, your story is in appendix B of the *War of Gods and Men* encyclopedia," I say sheepishly, as she scowls at me in confusion. I decide to keep going anyway. Might as well, since I've already started. "Your special skill is healing, but when the werewolves get sick or injured, you kind of, uh, hold back your knowledge. 'Cause you're annoyed with them—and with the elder— for being mean and prejudiced against you when they should know better."

The other kids are grinning, and Captain Redfern folds his lips tightly, crosses his arms, and looks down at his boots. If I didn't know better, I'd think he was trying to hide a smile.

"Oh!" George yelps, turning to me in excitement. "Elspeth is in love with the elder's son, isn't she, Jer? And he won't let them get married. I remember that from the game, too!"

Clip gasps. "Oh yeah, that potions puzzle from level sixty-two, right?"

"Yep! You're both right," I say proudly.

The Keeper of Fortunes arches an eyebrow at Elspeth. "Well, is this enough proof for you that these young people can help?" she asks dryly. "If you truly love the elder's son, you will want to see his father saved. There is no time to waste. Lead us to the antidote."

"Follow me," Elspeth says with a grudging sigh, taking us to one side of the village. We see a thick plywood wall that stands about six feet high. Set into the wall is a row of seven doors, each with a silver lock that matches the keys we got from our phoenix puzzle boxes.

"This is it," Clip whispers, rubbing his hands together eagerly. "This is the challenge!"

"The elder was poisoned by an orc blade," Elspeth says. "The orc was trying to force him to join the Forgotten Queen, and he refused. It's the only thing I respect about him, aside from being my dear Phillip's father. I can make the antidote he needs, but let's just say I haven't felt like gathering the ingredients. That will be *your* task. Bring them to me and I will save his life."

The Keeper of Fortunes nods. "Warriors, this is the second half of your Test of Determination. You each have a unique silver key. Find the door that it will open. There are three additional layers of doors you'll need to pass through in different ways, to collect three ingredients for the antidote. Be quick, because the first person to finish will receive a Gem of Determination from the werewolves . . . and the person who is farthest behind will be eliminated from the competition."

Captain Redfern points at George. "As the winner of the phoenix challenge, you have a one-minute head start and an extra key. If you're ready to begin, then go!"

"Yes, sir!" George jumps into action, wielding a key in each hand, and tests them both on each door. On his fourth try, we hear a click as the lock disengages. He whoops, calls out, "Good luck!" to the rest of us, and then barrels through to the other side. I catch a glimpse of low tables with sacks on them before the door swings shut again.

"Those must be the ingredients," Sadie whispers to me, and I nod in agreement.

"Okay, the rest of you, go, go, go!" Captain Redfern cries.

It's like Black Friday shoppers running to grab the very last PlayStation as the remaining six kids run full throttle toward the wall.

"Hold on, everyone!" I grab a fallen tree branch and throw it in front of George's closed door. "I'm marking this one. That way, we won't waste time trying to open it."

"Oh, good idea, Jer!" Lizard says approvingly.

There is no talking, just the jiggling of doorknobs and the rattling of keys as everyone runs around testing the doors. Suddenly, Lizard gives a shout of triumph and flies through her door. Clip plunges through his door next, and then Molly, leaving just Sadie, Caroline, and me.

And then, bam! My key clicks in the lock and I'm through, too! I don't have time to celebrate, though, because my shoe catches on the doorframe and I fall flat on my face.

"You okay?" Sadie asks anxiously.

I scramble to my feet, my face hot. "I'm great!" I declare, hurrying through the door into a wide-open space with six low tables. Four of them are empty. The others have grabbed their ingredients and are now climbing a second plywood wall. Wait a second . . . *climbing*?!

A squeak escapes me as I watch Lizard struggle with a rope dangling from the wall.

A door pops open behind me. "Come on, Jer!" Sadie says, and we grab the last two sacks.

Part of me is thinking: *Yes! I'm not the last to finish!* And another part is thinking: *Oh no, Caroline!* She's been left behind, and now she won't be able to continue on with us.

"That's both the Marshall twins gone," Sadie says sadly.

The second plywood wall has no doors. Instead, it has six thick ropes secured to the top. Each rope has huge knots all along the length, to make it easier to grab on to.

"Oh no. I can't do this," I say in a small voice.

"You can! I know you can," Sadie tells me encouragingly.

But the gym class flashback hits me full force: Mr. Bechtel making us climb a rope dangling down from the ceiling. "You have to *try*, Jeremy," he had said, and I had grabbed the rope miserably. "Your feet need to leave the ground, son," Mr. Bechtel had added, and everyone (except Sadie) had laughed at me. I had reached for the next knot up, missed, lost my balance, and landed hard on my butt on the padded mats as the other kids laughed even harder.

Now, Sadie looks at me sympathetically. "Listen, maybe we don't *have* to do this. If Caroline's out, that means we're still in the running. Top six. Should we even keep going?"

That brings me back to my senses.

I might have given up in gym class. But I didn't give up in the castle, the marsh, or the moat. Not once. I kept going every single time, and now I'm here, one of the top six competitors.

"Of course we have to keep going!" I declare, as a sudden burst of courage fills me. "For the good of Pantaera, we *must* go on! Come on, Sadie! No way out but up and over."

I shove away the bad memory and grab a rope. The big knots are helpful and the wall also has grooves in it for our toes. The climb is only six feet high, but it's hard and I'm shaking within seconds. Somehow, though, Sadie and I make it halfway up, struggling the whole time.

Sadie gasps for air. "We can do this!"

I nod, already exhausted.

And then, against all odds, we've gotten high enough to see over the wall.

There's another wide-open space below us. George and Clip are already at the next wall, Lizard is grabbing her second ingredient, and Molly . . . is crumpled in a heap at the bottom of the wall we're on, cradling her right foot in her hands.

"Oh, geez, is she hurt?" Sadie mutters. "Let's get down there and check."

I swing my leg over the wall and gulp. I'm looking forward to coming down even *less* than I looked forward to climbing up. "Here goes nothing," I say weakly, and let go. My knees bang into the wall on the way down and I land on my butt, but I'm not hurt. And I did it!

Sadie and I hurry over to Molly. "Are you okay?" we ask.

Molly winces. "I landed weird on my ankle, but I don't think it's broken," she says, moving her foot gingerly. "I'm fine. Just go."

"You don't *look* fine," Sadie says doubtfully.

"Just go, okay?" Molly snaps. "Go play your little game of pretend and leave me alone."

I watch Sadie's face turn red. But then she takes a breath, and I can tell she's thinking about our conversation with Clip. "Yeah, I *will* play the game," she says. "I want to be a warrior and see the wizard and help Pantaera. And I want to have fun, too. So if you want to call me a geek or a dork or whatever, fine. Being mean is boring, and I don't care what you think!"

Molly stares at her, stunned.

I look between them, beaming because I'm *so* proud of Sadie.

"I *know* I'm cool and I know I'm nice, too. Which is why I'm not leaving without making sure you're okay first." Sadie holds her hand out to help the other girl stand up.

A moment passes, and then Molly takes Sadie's hand. She grits her teeth as she gets onto her injured foot. "I rolled it coming down, but I think I can hop back to Captain Redfern."

"We could help you keep going, though," I offer. "You can put an arm over us, and—"

"The next door has to be opened with a treadmill and I can't run when my ankle's like this," Molly interrupts me. "Besides, it's probably against the rules if you help me."

"A treadmill?" Sadie and I echo.

The third plywood wall has a row of doors in it, just like the first one. Clip and George are gone, but Lizard's still working. She looks like she's at a medieval gym, jogging on a wooden treadmill connected to ropes and gears that slowly lift the door up in front of her.

Molly looks down at her shoes. "At least I'm still in the competition. So you guys go ahead . . . and, um, thanks for checking on me. You didn't have to."

"Sure we did," Sadie says. "You're a fellow competitor, aren't you?"

Molly blinks at her, and then turns and hops away without another word.

"Nice job!" I whisper to Sadie. "You handled that like a champ!"

"Thanks to you," she says, smiling. "And I hate to admit it, but thanks to Clip, too."

We grab our ingredients and each take a treadmill on either side of Lizard, whose door is now high enough for her to slip under. She gives us two thumbs-up and runs through.

I hate running even more than I hate climbing. I've never seen a point to running unless you're being chased by zombies. But this treadmill is *fun*, probably because I'm on it for a reason: to open a door. "We gotta tell Mr. Bechtel to buy these for the gym at school," I say, breathing hard. "Maybe then I'll actually *want* to finish a mile."

"Right?" Sadie gasps.

After several minutes of huffing and puffing, our doors lift and we scurry through.

Several feet in front of us is the fourth and final wall, which has no doors or ropes. Lizard is lying flat on her stomach in front of it, pawing at the dirt underneath it with both hands. It reminds me of my dog, Chickpea, digging in the backyard. Clip and George are nowhere to be seen, but I spy two big kid-shaped holes under the wall beside Lizard.

"We've got to dig *under* the wall?" Sadie screeches.

I stare around the grassy space, which has three low tables. All of them are empty, and I sigh with relief. "I don't think *we* have to. Lizard's taken the last ingredient, so she's going to get third place. I guess we're done!"

Sadie sinks onto the grass, relieved. "Phew! I wonder if Clip beat George? If he did, we'll only have to hear him brag about it for, like, the next three years."

I sit down next to her, stretching my aching arms. "We did it!" I say cheerfully. "We got through the Test of Courage *and* the Test of Determination. Only three more to go!"

"I bet our parents are so proud," Sadie declares.

"My dad's probably shocked I made it this far. He didn't think I would."

"That's not true, Jer!" she argues. "He just didn't want you to get hurt, that's all. My parents and grandparents are the same way. It's not that they don't believe in us."

I pluck a blade of grass and twirl it in my fingers. "Are you sure? 'Cause it sure feels that way sometimes with my dad."

Sadie pokes me in the shoulder. "Hey. Remember the big lesson in pretty much every fantasy story: It's not about the size of the hero, it's about the size of the hero's *heart*. And you've got a heart the size of North America, Jeremy Thomas."

I beam. "You do, too, Sadie Chu."

She holds out her knuckles. I tap them with mine, glad that my best friend and I are still here doing our jellyfish fist bump, even in the middle of saving the world.

"Come back, everybody!" we hear Captain Redfern call, so Sadie and I scramble to our feet. Elspeth, the Keeper, and the other kids (including Caroline) are waiting for us back where we started, along with two newcomers. Both men have dark brown skin and close-cropped tight curls, but one is young and strong and is helping the other, who is elderly and frail, onto a wide tree stump.

"Sit here, Father," he says. "My dear Elspeth will have the antidote ready for you soon."

The old man gives a weak cough. "Can I trust her, Phillip?"

"I can *hear* you, Elder, and trusting me is your only choice," Elspeth says, annoyed, stirring a cauldron that's bubbling over a low fire. She holds out her hand to Clip, who gives her his three sacks, and she empties them into the cauldron. There's a glittering powder, something that looks like sea salt, and a vial of bright blue liquid. As she mixes the potion, a cloud of bright blue smoke suddenly billows up, making everyone gasp.

"I hope this works," George mutters.

"It will," I say confidently. "Elspeth is one of the best healers in the history of Pantaera."

"As the winner of the werewolves' challenge," Elspeth tells Clip, "you have the honor of administering the potion. Please pour a spoonful over the elder's injured leg."

Phillip gently rolls up his father's pant leg to reveal

an awful greenish-yellow wound. The other kids look grossed out, but I'm excited. "Oh yeah, that's definitely an orc blade wound!" I cry. "You can tell by the color. That's how their poison reacts with blood."

Phillip looks at me in surprise. "You're very knowledgeable."

"He knows everything there is to know about Pantaera," Sadie informs him.

Clip holds a spoonful of the potion over the elder's leg. "Um, it's still kind of hot," he says nervously, but Elspeth gives him a nod to continue, so he dribbles a bit onto the wound. It doesn't seem to hurt the old man, so Clip dumps the whole spoonful. A minute later, all we can see is smooth, dark brown skin on the elder's leg. The injury has completely disappeared!

Everyone bursts into cheers and applause.

"You've done it! I can't believe it!" The elder's face is brighter and more full of life as he gazes at Elspeth in shock. "I owe you an apology. You saved my life, and I thank you."

Elspeth gives him a cool nod. "I didn't do this alone, Elder."

The old man looks at Clip, who's still holding the empty spoon. "You were the quickest to collect the ingredients for my antidote," he says, then turns to Captain

Redfern and the Keeper of Fortunes. "I must confess: I thought little of the prophecy. I didn't believe a child could save my life, let alone all of Pantaera, but today I have been proved wrong." He reaches into the pocket of his tunic and pulls out a round, bright green emerald.

"Wow!" Sadie murmurs. "It's beautiful."

"This Gem of Determination was given to the werewolves long ago," the elder says to Clip. "You were the first child to find all three ingredients for the potion, so I give the jewel to you as a mark of my confidence in the prophecy. Do not fail Pantaera."

Clip takes the gem and stares at it in awe. "I won't."

Suddenly, we hear a loud *crack* and whirl to see another tree stump splitting in half by itself. We all gasp again, because rising from the center is a second sparkling emerald. "It is as the phoenixes promised," the Keeper says, picking it up. "Their Gem of Determination has appeared because they have deemed one of the children to be worthy. This young warrior crossed the castle moat, collected the phoenix feathers, and solved the puzzle before any other. George, please step forward."

George accepts the gem from her with a proud smile.

Captain Redfern holds out the brass shield, which glitters with Jeremy's and Caroline's rubies from yesterday.

The boys snap their emeralds into place, grinning as everyone applauds.

"And now, we must say goodbye to Caroline." The captain gives her a kind smile. "Thank you for all you've done. The Keeper and I are proud of how far you've come."

Caroline blushes. "I'm glad to help out," she says, and gives each of us a hug before a knight takes her away to rejoin her dad and Derek in the real world.

"That's four kids gone," Sadie whispers to me, sounding both sad and amazed.

"I know. We made it to the top six!" I whisper back.

The captain's eyes twinkle. "Congratulations to all of you still standing here. I think you have more than earned the reward I planned for you tonight . . . a celebration feast!"

CHAPTER FOURTEEN
SADIE

"COME ON, SADIE, HURRY UP!" CLIP HOLLERS UP THE
stairs. "I don't want to be late for the feast. Captain
Redfern says we're the guests of honor!"

"You guys go," I call back. "I have to dry my hair."

"I can wait for you," Jeremy offers.

"Nah, it's okay. I'll meet you there!"

It's later that evening, and everyone has been relaxing at Winterhearth House since we got back from
Hollybottom. Molly claimed the shower first, and then
Lizard, so I lay down on my bed to wait my turn and
ended up napping for two hours. Now I'm scrambling to
get ready for dinner. I rub my head with a towel, wishing
I had an electric hair dryer, and finally just give up and
comb and braid my wet hair before hurrying downstairs.

The house is empty. The other kids have all gone into

the village, where Captain Redfern promised us a bonfire party with *tons* of food to celebrate us passing the Test of Determination. I'm about to head there when I spot someone sitting in the common room, facing the fireplace. Outside, the sun has set and the space is dark and cozy, lit only by the dancing flames.

"Hello?" I ask, frowning.

"Oh, hello," says a voice I don't recognize.

Slowly, I approach and see an elderly white man with a lined face and pale blue eyes that crinkle in a smile. He's wearing a periwinkle-blue robe and flip-flops, and he has a big black cat snoozing on his lap. He has a long gray beard and a big nose, and on the table beside him is a pointed periwinkle-blue hat. "Good evening, Sadie," he says kindly. "It's nice to meet you."

"It's you! The wizard!" I gasp, my heart leaping. *Finally*, I get to see him like everyone else! He looks just as weird and cool as the other kids said. Remembering my manners, I add, "It's nice to meet you, too. And hi, Tuba. I thought you were with Iggy."

The cat opens an amber eye and meows in greeting.

"Won't you have a seat?" the wizard asks, pointing to the chair next to his.

I was starving a second ago, but all thoughts of dinner have flown right out of my head. I sit down, trying not to stare at him because it's rude. But it's hard *not* to because he looks so strange. "I thought I wasn't going to get to see you," I say. "All of the other kids spotted you in the hotel and the castle and the marsh, and I didn't."

The wizard's eyes twinkle. "Just because you didn't see me doesn't mean *I* didn't see *you*. I've been watching over all of you kids, and I'm very proud of you, Sadie."

"Thanks," I say shyly. "I still can't believe I made it into the top six."

He shakes his head. "That's not quite what I meant. I'm proud of you for standing up for yourself yesterday. With Molly."

"You heard that?" I ask, and he nods. I wonder where he had been standing so that he could listen in on us and not be seen. "My best friend, Jeremy, thought I might get to see you if I *really* wanted to. Is that why you're here? Because I told Molly I wanted to see you?"

The old man just smiles mysteriously. "I'm glad you're not letting her call you names like *geek* anymore. I know you really didn't like that word."

"It's not that. I mean, it's just a word, and there's nothing wrong with being a geek. Jeremy calls himself one. What I didn't like was the mean way Molly was saying it to me."

The wizard gives me a sympathetic nod. He seems

so nice and understanding that I feel like I could share anything and he would only listen and not judge.

"Jer and Clip think she doesn't feel good about herself, and that's why she's been picking on me," I say. "She can tell I haven't been feeling good about myself, either. But it doesn't matter what she thinks, or anyone else. 'Cause if *I* don't feel good, then I gotta fix that, right?"

"That's right," the wizard agrees.

I fiddle with the end of my damp braid. "I didn't want the kids at school making fun of me for being on this show and pretending, but no one else seems worried about that. Everyone's having fun, like Jer and George and Lizard. Clip, too. And Caroline and Derek and Iggy . . . even the kids who got eliminated were just enjoying it. I want to, too. I want to feel confident."

"Here's what I've seen," the old man says. "You're the kind of kid who cheers on your friends, is kind to everyone, and helps a person in need, even if that person hasn't been very nice to you. That's a lot of things to be confident about, don't you think?"

I look down, embarrassed. "I guess so."

"You *guess* so?"

"Umm . . . okay, I *know* so," I correct myself sheepishly.

The wizard gives me an approving nod. "That's the

ticket. Now, this was a lovely chat, young Sadie, but I think you ought to get going or the others will worry."

I get to my feet reluctantly. "Thanks! I hope we meet again sometime," I say, and the old man gives me a cheerful wave. I head for the door, and then turn back around. "Are you going to chat with Molly, too? I think she wants to meet you."

But both the wizard and his cat have disappeared. The chair in front of the dying fire is empty, like all the other chairs in this room. I am totally alone.

"What?!" I gasp, looking around. There's only one exit from this room, and I'm standing right in front of it. No way could the wizard have left without me seeing him, unless there's a trap door or secret passageway I don't know about. Yeah, that must be it.

I shrug and start walking toward the village, my heart light. I even pick a bright yellow daisy and stick it over my right ear. The wizard thinks I should be proud and confident, too! No matter what anyone else says. I reach the center of town and see a huge bonfire illuminating several banquet tables that groan under the weight of a gigantic feast. There are roast turkeys, glazed hams, a pot of piping hot vegetable stew, loaves of freshly baked bread and butter, and a stack of fruit pies that fill the air with the smell of butter and caramel.

"Sadie!" Jeremy calls. "What took you so long?"

I hurry over to the kids' table. "I saw the wizard! He was so cool!" I fill them in on the encounter but leave out the part where he and I talked about Molly. She listens to me as she twirls her ponytail around her fingers, eyes on the ground. "He vanished into thin air, though."

"Yeah, he does that," Jeremy says, laughing.

"That's his thing," Lizard agrees. "I guess it wouldn't be as magical if he, like, walked out the door and got into a Jeep and drove away."

George cracks up. "A Jeep?! I guess that's more wizard-y than a Toyota."

"Why aren't you guys eating?" I ask, my stomach growling at the smell of the food. "I feel like I could put away an entire roast turkey by myself."

Clip snickers. "No way, sis. You're the size of a cricket."

"Oh yeah? Watch me!" I say.

"Okay, fine. If you eat a whole roast turkey, I will *let* you win tomorrow's challenge," he says smugly. "I'll wait at the finish line and let you through when you show up an hour later."

I put my hands on my hips. "Let's hope it isn't the Test of Humility, 'cause humble is something you're not, Clip Chu!" The Chu siblings are a good team, sometimes . . . that is, when my big brother's not being a jerk, like he has been all day after winning at Hollybottom.

"We're waiting for the go-ahead from Captain Redfern

before we start," George says, answering my question. "I guess the villagers don't think we have enough food yet."

We watch as several people come out of their houses, carrying trays and plates piled with food, and add them to the already crowded banquet tables. Kathryne comes over to pour us some ice-cold apple cider (which Jeremy explained isn't accurate to the time period, but he's letting it slide since we're not old enough to drink ale and the cider is *really* good).

Finally, Captain Redfern waves us over. "Go ahead and eat, warriors! Don't be shy! You've done a wonderful job on your first two challenges and you deserve this feast."

"Okay, if you insist, sir," Clip jokes.

I get in line with Jeremy, and Molly comes up behind us. I notice she's taken down her ponytail and changed it to a braid, like mine, and even plucked a daisy to put over her ear, too. *If she really thought I was uncool*, I realize, *she wouldn't copy me*. I can't help feeling a little sorry for her, even though she's been so mean to me.

"My ankle's feeling better," she says. "Thanks again for checking on me today."

"No problem, I'm glad you're okay."

She smirks. "So you got your wish of seeing the

wizard, huh? Did he cast a magic spell or make anything disappear?"

I choose to ignore her sarcastic tone. "Nope. He just gave me a lot of encouragement."

Molly can't seem to think of a response, so I start piling food on my plate and head back to the table with Jeremy. And for ten solid minutes, everyone—including the villagers, Captain Redfern, and the knights, who all joined us for dinner—are completely silent because the food is *that* good. People start getting up for seconds and thirds.

When the meal is over, the captain lifts his mug of apple cider high in the air. "I would like to propose a toast. Congratulations to our six remaining competitors, who have excelled at both the Tests of Courage and Determination. To our young warriors!"

"To our young warriors!" the villagers and knights repeat.

"Do any of our heroes want to say a few words?" the captain asks, smiling.

Clip taps Jeremy on the shoulder. "That's all you, bro!"

"Jer! Jer! Jer!" we all chant.

Jeremy grins, but before he can speak, some of the villagers start screaming. They scramble away from the feast, looking panicked as they dart into the shadows.

"What's going on?" Molly asks, her eyes round with fear.

"Someone's coming!" Lizard hisses.

A tall, slender figure emerges from the darkness. Captain Redfern and his knights whip out their swords and form a protective circle around our table.

"I can't see anything!" Clip complains, hopping onto the bench. We copy him, and when we see the newcomer in the light of the bonfire, we understand why everyone was so terrified.

The woman is six feet tall, thin as a rail, and dressed in black, with a scarf wrapped tightly around her neck. Her skin is white as bone, and I'm not talking pale like "she hasn't left her house in six months 'cause she's been marathoning Netflix" pale. I'm talking pale like "I hate garlic, I can turn into a bat, and I can't see my reflection" pale. Her hair and eyes are dark, but her lips are red, with two sharp fangs emerging between them.

"Oh, man, that's a vampire," Jeremy says weakly.

George gasps. "Is she going to bite us?"

"Oh, heck no!" Clip yells, holding his soup spoon like a dagger.

"In the name of the king, stay where you are!" Captain Redfern shouts, and the vampire stops and holds out her thin hands, so we can see that she's not carrying any weapons. In the shadows, she looks mysterious and beautiful and very scary. "Who are you? Why are you here?"

"I am Lady Scarlet of the House of Blackbirds, and I'm on your side," the vampire says in a soft, musical voice. "I'm a traitor to my clan. Many vampires plan to join the Forgotten Queen and wage war on Pantaera, but I only want peace for my people."

Captain Redfern frowns. "The House of Blackbirds is the most powerful vampire clan in existence. No one who wished to survive would even *think* of betraying them."

"What makes you think I wish to survive? I don't care about myself," Lady Scarlet says. "Yes, Captain, some vampires actually want to prevent bloodshed. I'll do what it takes to make sure no one else comes to harm because of the Forgotten Queen."

"I don't believe you," the captain says flatly.

The vampire sighs. "The Keeper of Fortunes visited me in a dream. She told me of a group of young knights from another world, one of whom is the child hero we've all been waiting for."

"She saw the Keeper of Fortunes?" George whispers, looking around at the rest of us. "She can't be all bad, then, can she?"

"No, she can't," Jeremy agrees in a low voice.

"I lead a group of vampires who want to prevent war in Pantaera. I have proof that the Keeper summoned me to help find the child hero." Lady Scarlet pulls out a long gold chain from under her scarf. A huge white pearl dangles from it, along with a shiny black pendant. "This pearl is a Gem of Humility, given to the vampires long ago by the gods of Pantaera."

"And *that's* a Sun Pendant!" Jeremy bursts out.

Lady Scarlet looks surprised. "That's right, young man. How do you know?"

"The encyclopedia, probably," Lizard whispers.

"The appendix?" George guesses.

"Nope. The *Vampire Queen Compendium*," Jeremy says cheerfully. "There's a whole chapter on the Sun Pendants. Only six of them exist, and the gods of Pantaera gave them to the most noble vampires, to help them walk in full sunlight. You're telling the truth, Lady Scarlet."

She smiles at him. "Thank you for believing me. Yes, the Sun Pendants were given to me and my lieutenants. And the Keeper has asked me to host the first part of the Test of Humility."

Captain Redfern lowers his sword. "Then you stand with King Rothbart?"

"I do," Lady Scarlet vows. "My vampires and I want

a better world. We want to complete the Pantaereon . . . that is, if these young people can prove themselves to us. Because a true hero does not just plunge into danger, banners flying. They must also be willing to admit mistakes, be truthful, and listen to others, no matter how hard that may be. In a word, they must be *humble*."

I smirk at Clip, and he sticks his tongue out at me.

"When and where will the Test of Humility be?" Captain Redfern asks.

"Tomorrow at sunrise. Come to Shadowheart Manor and I will explain everything. For now, take these." She places some keys on a table, and then melts back into the darkness.

For a moment, there is silence.

And then everyone starts talking at once.

"Our next challenge is in a *vampire castle*?" Lizard exclaims.

"What do you think we'll have to do?" Molly asks, looking worried.

"Stake one of 'em through the heart?" Clip suggests.

"First of all, that is *way* too violent," I point out. "And second of all, why would we do that? Lady Scarlet said that they're peaceful vampires who want to join our cause."

"Maybe we have to go through the kitchens and throw out all the garlic," George jokes.

Everyone laughs and the mood lightens, but my stomach is still clenched. "I don't know how to feel about this," I tell Jeremy. "I know Lady Scarlet's on our side, but she looked scary."

"I know, but at least we'll be together," he reassures me.

We sit back down, but I've lost my appetite. This show is starting to feel more and more *real*. I came in knowing that cameras were on us, and I wanted to keep my distance and remember that we were just pretending. But now I shiver, remembering how the firelight made Lady Scarlet's pale skin glow. And I think of how the wizard just disappeared without a trace.

Well, the producers *did* promise us an immersive experience.

Tomorrow's challenge might test our humility . . . but I have a feeling it's going to test my courage again, too.

"WHAT DO YOU THINK'S TAKING SO LONG?" I ASK, trying to peer through a window.

It's early the next morning, and we barely had time for breakfast before Captain Redfern dragged us onto the wagon again. The ride to Shadowheart Manor took about half an hour ("They must be running out of castles in a five-mile radius," Clip suggested) before we got to a large old house. The captain told us to wait, then disappeared inside. He's probably been gone only five minutes, but knowing that he's walked into a vampire lair makes it seem way longer.

"I don't see anything. I can't tell if it's because it's dark inside or if they have curtains up." George's face is pressed to the window next to mine, his hands cupped around his eyes. "Do you see anything through that one, Jeremy?"

I shake my head. "Nope."

"Maybe the captain got kidnapped," Clip says thoughtfully. "Maybe our task is to go in there and rescue him. I'm game! I could march in there and take 'em down and—"

"What does that have to do with humility, though?" Sadie argues. "That's the *opposite* of showing how humble you are! I think we should stay here like he told us to."

"Don't forget, Lady Scarlet is helping us," I remind everyone. "I agree with Sadie. We should hang tight. Captain Redfern might get mad if we don't follow his instructions."

"But what if he doesn't come back?" Molly asks anxiously. "What if he has no choice?"

Luckily, Captain Redfern comes out right at that moment, accompanied by Lady Scarlet.

"We're ready for you now," Lady Scarlet announces. "The first part of the Test of Humility is simple: Escape Shadowheart Manor with your lives."

Everyone gasps.

"Just kidding, ha ha!" she says, smiling. "Don't worry. My vampires and I gave our word to the Keeper of Fortunes that you will all leave safe and sound, no matter what, and you will not be touched or harmed in any way. That's a promise. Okay?"

We nod, but none of us looks convinced.

Lady Scarlet hands us each a leather belt to loop around our waists. Each belt has a silver key tied onto it with a red cloth flag, which dangles down along our legs. "Your task is to search for the Reflection Room, a chamber full of mirrors, which will be your exit. Your keys will open the door. To make this more challenging, my vampires and I will be hiding throughout the house, and we will try to steal your flags. As I just said," she adds, "you yourselves will not be touched or harmed. And we will only *walk*, not run after you."

Sadie and I exchange glances, and Lizard lets out a nervous, high-pitched giggle.

"Here's the catch: If your flag gets stolen, you *must* return to the beginning and start over," Lady Scarlet says. "Humility is about accepting your weaknesses and trying again when you encounter defeat. The first person to reach the Reflection Room will receive a Gem of Humility, but the last person to find the exit will be eliminated from the competition. Is everyone clear on that? Are there any questions?"

Clip raises his hand. "Are we allowed to fight the vampires who try to steal our key?"

An odd look crosses Lady Scarlet's face. Her mouth trembles, almost like she's trying not to laugh. After a moment, she says, "You may not fight. There is no violence allowed. Those flags are designed to flutter as you move, so we can grab them without touching you."

"Please don't punch anyone," Sadie begs Clip. "It would be *so* embarrassing!"

"Sheesh! I was just *asking*! I wasn't planning on actually doing it," her brother retorts.

"Clip," the captain says, "as the winner of the werewolf challenge, you will have a one-minute head start. On your mark." Clip does this low, dramatic lunge. "Get set . . . GO!"

Clip bursts through the door, followed by Lady Scarlet.

"Wanna stick together, Jer?" Sadie asks me. "She never said that was against the rules."

"Yeah!" I say gratefully. I know the vampires are nice and they're just testing us, but the thought of them jumping out of hiding to snatch my flag is kind of scary.

"All right, everybody in!" Captain Redfern calls.

George and Lizard barrel through the entrance, with Molly, Sadie, and me trailing close behind. At once, we are confronted in the main hall by a vampire with curly red hair and a cape. He raises his eyebrows as we all freeze and stare at him, unsure what to do.

"You know," he says in a calm, thoughtful voice, like he's about to tell us the weather forecast or something.

"There's an ancient proverb that says: *Courage is often caused by fear.*" And then, without warning, one of his long arms swoops out toward the flag on Lizard's belt.

"No way, pops!" Lizard screams, diving around his other side.

"I know an ancient proverb, too. It goes: Check yourself before you wreck yourself!" George bellows, as the vampire lunges for his flag next. But George manages to do this graceful spin and slips past him on the other side, escaping down a hallway.

"Go, go, go, while the vampire's distracted!" Sadie shrieks at Molly and me.

I run for my life, skirting along a staircase and diving into an empty room. I squeeze myself behind some bookshelves, panting as I wait for Sadie and Molly to join me . . . but they never show up. They must have run to the other side of the hall, and now everyone is split up—which must have been the point of stationing that guy at the entrance like that.

I am all alone in a vampire castle.

I let out a shaky breath and stay still, listening. There's no sound, so I creep out from my hiding place. That's when I see a huge mirror with a fancy gold frame, leaning against the wall. What's truly weird and scary is that I can't see my reflection in it, almost like I'm a vampire, too. But then I realize it's a *doorway* disguised as a mirror, and my fear melts into excitement.

"That's right!" I say under my breath. "Lady Scarlet is a Blackbird. A glass-walker!"

In the *Vampire Queen Compendium*, I learned that the House of Blackbirds is famous for using mirrors in a way that most of their kind don't. Vampires in this game world tend to fear and hate reflective surfaces, but not the Blackbird family. They turn mirrors into doors they can walk through. It's kind of like saying, *Oh, what? You think I'm scared of these? I'll show you!*

Suddenly, I hear voices in the hall. Panicking, I slip through the mirror doorway and into an old-fashioned bedroom. Unfortunately, the voices are growing louder every second, and this chamber is a dead end. I look around in desperation and see a big wooden wardrobe.

When I pull open the doors, I almost cry out with relief. This bedroom isn't a dead end after all. There's a *second* empty mirror frame inside the wardrobe! I hop inside and shut the door—and just in time, too, because through the crack, I can see a blond vampire woman enter the room. Quickly, I step through the second mirror . . . and bump into a warm body. I'm about to let out an earsplitting scream when a hand claps over my mouth.

"Shhh, it's just me, Jeremy!" Clip whispers.

"Phew! I thought I was a goner!" I whisper back. "Where are we?"

"Some kind of portrait gallery, I think."

The wardrobe opens onto a long hallway lined with suits of armor, one of which Clip and I are currently standing behind. The windows are covered with heavy dark fabric, and a couple of dim, flickering chandeliers show dozens of paintings of all shapes and sizes on the walls.

"So much for my head start," Clip mutters. "This place is a maze, 'cause I've been here before. I ran upstairs, got trapped in a room with two vampires, and lost my flag."

My jaw drops. "You had to start over?"

"Yep. And now I'm back here again." He clenches his teeth. "What a waste of time! I could be at the Reflection Room by now. I try to tell myself to just stop and *think* on this show instead of running in headfirst, but I keep getting into trouble."

"It's hard to remember in the heat of the moment," I say sympathetically.

"I think I heard Lizard scream a second ago, so I'm laying low for a minute." Clip jerks a thumb at the empty mirror frame behind me. "Where does that go?"

"A bedroom. Listen." Quickly, I explain about the House of Blackbirds. "I have a theory. You said the house is like a maze, right? I think that if we find more of these empty mirrors, they could be a direct path to the Reflection Room. Like they're leading us straight to it."

Clip nods eagerly. "You're a genius, Jer! But how will the other kids know? Was there anything about the Blackbirds or glass-walkers in your graphic novel?"

"No, it was in a different book. And I'm just guessing here. I'm sure you *can* get to the Reflection Room without knowing the backstory, but maybe it would take longer. The others will figure it out." I scan the length of the gallery. "Maybe one of the paintings is a doorway."

"Let's look," Clip says, stepping around the suit of armor. "But we have to be careful. Whatever happened to Lizard sounded like it was close by."

I wipe my sweaty palms on my pants. "I hope Sadie's okay. She's scared of vampires and we were supposed to stick together, but we got split up."

Her brother waves a careless hand. "She'll be fine. It's good for her to face her fears."

I'm not sure Sadie would agree, but I nod, and we start studying the paintings.

A minute later, I spot an empty gold frame three feet above the floor. "Look!" I say, but before we can climb in, a dark-haired vampire in a purple velvet suit appears.

Clip swears, grabs me, and yanks me down the hall. "I can't shake that dude today!"

Lady Scarlet said the vampires would only walk after us, but it's still scary to be pursued no matter how slowly they're going. Clip and I hurtle into a high-ceilinged library, slam the door shut, and block it with a chair. A minute passes, and then the knob turns as the vampire tries to get in. We find a metal staircase in the corner and run up to the second floor. My heart is beating so fast, I feel like it might come right out of my mouth.

Suddenly, a vampire with long brown hair pops out at us from behind a bookshelf.

"Come *on*, lady, give me a break!" Clip shouts at her. "Jeremy, run! Save yourself!"

"No, I'm not leaving you!" I grab a heavy book off the shelf, whisper an apology to it, and fling it at the vampire's feet to distract her. It works, because she looks down at it in surprise, giving Clip and me time to run into another room and flip the lock into place.

"Thanks for helping me back there," Clip says, panting.

I lean against a wall, trying to catch my breath. "No problem. I think we need to go back down to the gallery and climb into that empty mirror. Are you coming with me?"

"Yeah, is that okay?"

"Sure! You just seem to like being a lone wolf, that's all."

"Well, if there's one thing I've learned from laser tag, it's that teaming up can be necessary sometimes," Clip says, grinning. "Look, there's a second exit over there. Let's see if it takes us to the stairs."

"Lead the way," I say weakly.

CHAPTER SIXTEEN
SADIE

"ARE YOU SURE WE SHOULD GO THAT WAY?" MOLLY
asks.

I rub my itchy nose. "No, of course I'm not sure. But it's my best guess."

"But *why*?"

"Because there are three doors in this room," I say, trying to be as patient as I can with her. "The one we came in goes back to the entrance, and I tried *that* door over there and it's locked. So our only option is the third one."

"Let's just start over. Clearly, we're not even close to the Reflection Room."

I sigh and scratch my nose again, trying not to sneeze. I'm hiding under a dusty desk with none other than Molly, who has attached herself to me like a staticky sock and complained about every decision I've made in the fifteen minutes we've been wandering through this maze.

"Listen. If you want to start over, be my guest." I make sure to sound braver than I feel, because as annoying as Molly is, I *really* don't want to go through this castle alone.

"Are you bananas? I can't start over by myself. What if I run into that vampire again?"

I've *had* it with this girl. "You're the one who keeps saying that we're just pretending," I point out. "You've been calling me a geek for the past three days because Pantaera feels real to me, and now you're afraid, too?"

She clenches her fists. "I'm not afraid! I'm just *tense* because of you."

"Oh, so now it's my fault?!"

"Yeah, it is!" Molly says loudly. "It's because you think everything is real, including the vampires, and you're worried and it's stressing me out. Of course I know it's all pretend. Duh!"

I grit my teeth. "There's nothing wrong with feeling like Pantaera is real. It's more fun that way. And if you want to pick on me for that, go ahead! At least I'm not boring like you, 'cause that's what bullies are! B-O-R-I-N-G, boring!" I climb out from under the desk and leave her. Standing up for myself is *hard*, but I'm proud that I did it.

"I'm not a bully!" Molly shouts, following me. "Take that back!"

"You've been calling me names and being mean and making fun of me this whole time," I say, putting my hands on my hips. "What do you think that makes you, then? Maybe if you weren't so afraid of having fun, you would see the wizard, too!"

She doesn't say anything. She just stands in front of me, red-faced.

I take a deep breath. "I think you're worried about what other people think of you. I worry about that, too. But you shouldn't pick on someone to make yourself feel better."

Molly stares at her shoes, her lips trembling.

"I love epic fantasy, okay? I like watching Clip and Jer play video games. I like being on this show and pretending to be a hero in a magical world. I'm proud of that, and it doesn't matter what anyone else thinks. So *there*!" I turn and go into the other room.

"Wait! Don't walk so fast!" Molly cries, hurrying after me. This room looks like an armory full of helmets, spears, and shields, and there's no light inside except for a few candles. All of the windows are covered with thick black fabric. "I told you, it's just a creepy dead end!"

I ignore her. Something weird hangs on the wall: an

antique gold frame that looks out of place. There's no painting inside, and when I walk over, I discover that it's actually the opening to a crawl space. "Whoa! I wonder where this goes?" I mutter. "A shortcut, maybe?"

Molly crosses her arms. "I am *not* going in there."

I wish Jeremy was here, 'cause he would know what to do. He would have a random but useful fact that would help. I make a snap decision. "I'm going in. The only other choice is to go back to the beginning, and I don't want to do that. *You* can if you want."

"But what if it's trying to trick us? Sadie. *Sadie!*"

I ignore her and climb into the crawl space, which is wide enough to fit a grown man.

Molly follows, still whining and complaining.

I move forward on my hands and knees, knowing I will never hear the end of it if we *do* get trapped. As I crawl, my head hits something soft and heavy, like a curtain.

"Shhh!" I hiss, hearing footsteps through it. After a moment, I peer around the edge of the curtain and see a long corridor. "No one's here. Let's go."

"Great, another stupid hallway," Molly moans. "We're gonna get lost again."

"No, I don't think so," I say excitedly, making the short drop to the floor. Old-fashioned portraits of people in giant wigs and poofy dresses line the wall, but I'm not looking at them. I'm looking at an oak door across the way, which has a dozen tiny mirrors in gold, silver, and bronze frames hanging around it. My reflection flashes in them as I approach. "I think we might be on the right track! I haven't seen mirrors anywhere else."

Suddenly, Molly grabs my arm and lets out a squeak. I see it at the same time: the reflection of the Forgotten Queen in one of the bigger mirrors. Her face is turned to the side, covered by the heavy, dark veil, and her crown gleams as she turns her head to look right at us.

"Hey!" someone calls. We both yelp in surprise and turn to see a tall vampire standing at the end of the hallway. He stares at us from under a black top hat.

Molly takes off through the oak door, not even bothering to wait for me. I run after her down a set of stone stairs, which end at a locked door, also with mirrors hanging around it.

"Quick, try your key!" I urge Molly.

"No, *you* try yours!"

"But why? You're right there!" I feel like I'm about to pee my pants because I can hear the vampire's slow footsteps on the stairs behind me. "Hurry *up*, Molly!"

Tears stream down her round face. "No! I can't do it!" she wails.

I swear, I'm about to shake this girl. "Why the heck not?!"

We scream as the vampire in the top hat comes into view. He stops on the landing above us, though, and doesn't come any closer. "She can't open the door because she lost her key," he says calmly, in a crisp British accent. "Didn't you, young lady?"

My jaw drops. "What? Is this true?"

Molly hangs her head and sniffles. "Yeah. I lost my key at the entrance. That vampire grabbed my flag when we were running past him."

Horrified, I look down at her belt. In all of the excitement, I hadn't even noticed that it was missing a flag. "Are you *kidding* me? Why didn't you say something?"

Molly is crying so hard that she can't speak.

The vampire crosses his arms. His expression is a mixture of stern and amused, and he looks so much like a disapproving dad that Molly and I both calm down a little.

"I would have had to start over from the beginning," Molly blubbers. "So I decided to stick with you and get to the Reflection Room. I don't want to finish last!"

"So you were using me this whole time?" I screech.

Molly starts crying again.

"Come along, dear," the vampire says kindly to Molly. "Let's go back to the entrance together. You can get another key and try again, all right?" He looks at me. "Your key will open the Reflection Room. Solve the puzzle and you'll be set. Do you need anything else?"

I blink up at him. "Um, no, thanks."

Whimpering, Molly follows the nice vampire upstairs. She looks so ashamed that I can't help feeling bad for her. But Lady Scarlet *did* say that humility is about learning to start over.

Sighing, I unlock the door and step into a brightly lit chamber. The light of dozens of candles bounces off thirty different mirrors set up all around the room.

"Hey, Sadie!" George says, looking relieved. He's standing in the middle of the room with a scroll of old parchment, his forehead damp with sweat. "How are you doing?"

"Fine, you?"

He shakes his head. "Not great. Here, take a scroll." He points to a table that holds two rolled-up pieces of parchment. "I think there were five to begin with. Clip and Jeremy are done, and you and I are here, so that only leaves one for Lizard or Molly. Have you seen them?"

I fill him in on what happened to Molly.

George lets out a low whistle. "Sheesh! It's just like in the zombie movies! She's that person who gets bitten but doesn't tell anyone until it's too late."

I open my scroll to find a couple of handwritten lines. At first, I think the old-fashioned script is what makes it so hard to read. And then I realize: "Whoa, it's backward!"

"Yeah. We have to figure it out to get the exit to open." George nods toward the far wall, which has a big wooden door with no knob. "It must operate on some kind of mechanism that won't swing open until we figure out what these scrolls say."

"Okay," I say, looking around. Mirrors cover the walls and even part of the floor. Some stand around the room or lean against tables. "If the writing is backward, we just have to hold it up to any mirror, right?" I test a tall mirror on my left. To my shock, the script is *still* backward. I walk around, trying different ones, but none of them will reverse the message.

George lets out a tired laugh. "See what I've been dealing with?"

"Okay, there has to be a logical explanation. When you look into a normal mirror, it flips the image. So if I raise my right hand, it looks like my reflection is raising the *left* hand."

"Exactly. And if you have a shirt with writing on it, it would look backward in a regular mirror. But check this out." George reaches under his tunic and pulls out a small necklace with three letters dangling from it. "This is a good luck charm from my dad. We have the same name and initials: George Carter Quinn. GCQ, right? You see that?"

"I see that," I confirm.

"Get a load of this." He holds the necklace in front of a big oval mirror. The reflection still reads GCQ. The letters aren't backward at all, and a chill goes down my spine. "Creepy, right? These are like funhouse mirrors at the fair. I look kind of weird in them, too. Different."

I snap my fingers. "That's it, George! These are special

mirrors," I say, my excitement rising. I stand in front of a full-length rectangular mirror. My reflection *definitely* looks odd . . . and I realize it's because it's not flipped. It's not a mirror image of me, like I'm used to. The freckle on my left cheek is also on my reflection's left cheek. When I lift my right hand, my reflection also lifts its right hand. "These mirrors show us what other people see when they look at us. The image isn't reversed. They're *true* mirrors!"

"True mirrors?"

"Jeremy and I learned about these in science class. A true mirror is two normal mirrors attached at a right angle. Ninety degrees. The light bounces off differently, so the image doesn't get reversed." I turn in a circle. "This room is full of true mirrors. They won't help us figure out what the scrolls say because the script stays backward. But I bet that somewhere in here—"

A smile forms on George's face. "There's one *regular* mirror? Brilliant, Sadie! Let's split up. I can take this wall, and you take that one?"

"You got it!" I try every mirror on my wall, but none of them are normal. "No luck here."

"Me, neither," George says. "Let's check the ones on the floor."

Minutes later, we still haven't found anything. I turn

my attention to the standing mirrors. "It's gotta be one of these, then," I say, approaching three full-length ones that look like they're straight out of a fairy tale. One has a silver frame etched with roses, while the other two are decorated with sparkly purple gems. I hold up my scroll to each one. "George! Over here!"

He runs over to where I'm standing in front of the silver rose mirror. "Awesome! Let's see what these say," he says, and we hold our scrolls up to the glass.

The message is the same on both pieces of parchment, and we read it aloud together:

> *Humility means seeing yourself as you truly are*
> *And having the courage to love all of it.*
> *Congratulations!*

The door swings open and sunlight floods the room. George and I hurry outside to find Captain Redfern, Lady Scarlet, Clip, and Jeremy waiting for us. The Keeper of Fortunes is there, too, and her stern expression is as close to a smile as I've ever seen it.

Jer hugs me. "You did it! You guys figured it out!"

"It was all Sadie. I'd still be stuck if it weren't for her," George says, and Clip blinks at him, looking shocked that he could just admit something like that.

"You would have figured it out eventually," I tell George.

"Jeremy helped me out, too," Clip says sheepishly. "I didn't know what the heck was going on. I thought something had happened to my eyes!"

Lady Scarlet beams. "What did you think about the task? Did any of you lose a flag?"

"I did, almost right away," Clip confesses, and I gasp. "I'm still mad at myself about it. I was going too fast and not taking the time to think, and a dude with a top hat was like, 'Cowabunga!' And hopped out from a corner of the room."

"He did *not* say 'Cowabunga!'" I protest.

My brother grins. "Maybe not. But he did grab my flag, and then he was nice enough to say sorry and walk me back to the entrance so I could start over."

"That's the same guy who made Molly go back." I tell everyone what happened to her.

"That's so shady," Clip says, shaking his head in disapproval. "She's like that one person in a zombie movie who pretends they didn't get bitten."

"That's what *I* said!" George yells, and they high-five, laughing.

"Well, hopefully Molly has learned her lesson," Captain Redfern says.

The door opens again, but it's not Molly who comes out. It's Lizard.

"Yo, that was *so* fast!" George says, amazed. "Sadie and I haven't been out here five full minutes, and we didn't see you come into the room!"

"My aunt and uncle run the state fair in my town," Lizard says with a grin. "I know a lot about trick mirrors. And I got lucky and found the normal one pretty fast."

"The Test of Humility is almost complete," the Keeper of Fortunes says, smiling at us. "And here stand our top five competitors. Congratulations!"

Right as she's done talking, we hear a strange sound like people cheering from an open window on an upper level of the manor. "Woo-hoo! YEAH! That's what I'm talking about!" We also hear a dog bark twice, before all of the noise dies away into silence.

Quickly, Captain Redfern cries, "Yes, indeed, congratulations to all of you!" at the same time that Lady Scarlet says in a loud voice, "Wonderful work, everyone!"

They look so proud that we forget about the mysterious cheers and barks.

"Woo! Top five!" George crows.

Jeremy looks dazed. "I can't believe it. There were *ten* kids at the beginning, so this is half of what we started with. And one of us will be the child hero."

Clip crosses his arms smugly. "The cream's rising to the top."

"Will another person be eliminated today?" Lizard asks.

The Keeper shakes her head. "No. You are our top five, and whoever wins the second half will have a head start on tomorrow's challenge," she says, and we all whoop with joy. "Shall we go and say goodbye to Molly, who will now return to her own world?"

Lady Scarlet leads us around the side of the house to the front entrance, where Molly and the vampire in the top hat are waiting. Molly shakes hands awkwardly with everyone, looking so upset that we all make sure to say something nice. Even Clip tells her, "Good job!"

When it's my turn, she and I look at each other for a moment. "Um, Sadie?" she asks timidly. "Can I talk to you in private?"

"Yeah, sure," I say, surprised. "If that's okay with Captain Redfern."

The captain looks a little confused, but nods.

I follow Molly back into the castle and we stand in the empty front hall.

She takes a deep breath and says, in a small voice, "I'm sorry. For using you and not being nice. I guess I was jealous, because you're so popular."

"Me?" I ask, stunned. "Popular?"

"Yeah. You have so many friends here, and your brother, too." She looks down at her shoes. "Everyone likes you, and I guess I wanted to be the one person who *didn't* like you. I ended up wanting to be your friend anyway, but it was too late. You already hated me."

"I don't hate you!" I exclaim. "And it's not too late to be friends. I've wanted to be friends since the beginning, but, like . . . you kind of made it hard."

We look at each other and a giggle escapes Molly, and I laugh, too.

"I had fun on this show, too," she admits. "And you were right. Sometimes I felt like it was real, not pretend. I just wish I could have seen the wizard, too. He sounded so nice, and—" She breaks off abruptly and lets out a shriek, pointing behind me.

I whirl, my heart thundering, but it's just the wizard. He walks toward us, smiling, his flip-flops flapping against his feet. "Oh my god, please do *not* scream like that in a vampire castle," I tell Molly weakly, clutching my chest.

But she's not listening. She's staring with wide, teary eyes at the wizard, who beams down at her. "Hello there, Molly," he says warmly. "I've been watching over you, even if you haven't seen me. And I'm proud of everything you have accomplished here."

"Y-you are?" she squeaks. "Even though I . . . I lied today?"

The old man raises his bushy gray eyebrows. "Did you learn a lesson?"

Molly nods.

"And did you just apologize to Sadie and admit your mistakes?"

"Yeah," she says softly.

The wizard shrugs, his eyes twinkling. "Like I said, I'm proud."

"Girls!" Captain Redfern calls from outside. "Are you done talking yet? We need to get Molly back to the real world safely, so we can start the next part of the challenge."

"Just a sec!" I call back, and then I reach out and hug Molly. After a second, I feel her hugging me back. "Apology accepted. You really kept me on my toes!"

She laughs.

"And we're totally friends now," I say. "Have a nice trip back!"

"Thanks, Sadie. And good luck," she says, pulling away. She turns back to where the wizard is standing . . . but once again, he's completely disappeared. He must have tiptoed away so quietly that we didn't even hear him. Molly stares at me with wide eyes.

I grin. "Yeah. He does that."

The nice vampire leads Molly away, and the rest of us follow Lady Scarlet, the Keeper, and the captain back through Shadowheart Manor. All of us are quiet and deep in thought. I know *I* don't feel like talking. I feel happy about making up with Molly, and also a weird mix of relief, excitement, and anxiety that there are only four other kids left on the show besides me.

Jeremy pokes me. "Hey! Did everything go okay with Molly?"

I fill him in on our chat. "She did kind of help me, you know," I say thoughtfully. "She got me to admit that I *am* having fun and it's okay to be immersed. I'm glad about that."

"Me too."

I sling an arm over my best friend's shoulders. "But most of all, I'm glad we're still in this together!" I say.

"You know it." He holds out his fist, and we do our happiest jellyfish yet.

CHAPTER SEVENTEEN
CLIP

SO THIS IS THE TOP FIVE, I THINK. I STAY NEAR THE back of the group, sizing up the remaining competition as the grown-ups lead us through the manor.

Lizard walks in front with as much confidence as if she owned the place. I'd never have guessed she'd still be here, but it turns out she's as tough as she is tiny and she's doing a great job keeping up with us older kids. Behind her are Sadie and Jeremy, discussing the history of Shadowheart Manor. Now, those two, I *really* didn't think would last . . . but then again, I did underestimate them in laser tag and I can't make that mistake again here. Jeremy knows Pantaera better than anyone, he's got serious brains, and he throws himself into every challenge like it's real. As for my sister, she's a lot braver and more determined than I gave her credit for.

Then there's George, who's swinging his arms and whistling *Super Mario* music as we walk. Now, *he's* the one I could see going all the way to the final. He's tough like Lizard, smart like Jeremy, determined like Sadie, and strong and fast like me. He's the real deal, the whole hero package. And he's got something else, too, that I can't put my finger on.

George catches my eye. "We've got an awesome group left, huh, Clip?"

"Yup," I say. "I think the kids who made it this far deserve to be here."

"Well, *you* do, and so do Lizard and Sadie and Jeremy. You guys are all winners to me." He looks thoughtful. "But I've mostly been lucky. I found a vial pretty fast in the orc castle, you and Derek helped me out in the marsh, and Sadie gave me an assist with that mirror riddle. So it feels like I've been kind of coasting a little, you know?"

I suddenly realize *that's* what I can't put my finger on about George: He's humble. He's a great competitor, yet he's the first to admit whenever he needs help or messes up. Me? I don't like admitting that stuff because it makes me feel weak. For some reason, though, I don't think George is weak when he's being modest. I think he's cool.

Sadie's always telling me off for bragging, and now I see what she's saying (not that I would *ever* tell her). Between someone who runs his mouth all the time, and someone who sees himself clearly and tries to do better . . . well, I think I'd rather be the second one.

"You *do* deserve to be here, though," I say to George. "You've got this humility thing down . . . and I've, uh, been lucky a couple of times, too."

He laughs. "But you're Clip Chu, hero material! Haven't you been saying that all along?"

I flush, feeling a little ashamed. "A hero's gotta have more than just confidence, though. Even with all my big talk, I haven't done as well as I said I would."

"Hey, man, I don't think there's anything wrong with knowing you're good," George says kindly. "And sometimes, if you're unsure, just *saying* out loud that you're gonna kick butt makes you believe you will. Fake it 'til you make it, and all that. You know?"

"I guess." I scuff my shoes. "Honestly, I think everyone who's left has just as much of a chance at winning as I do. Maybe even a *better* chance."

"We'll see what happens," he says. "Right, Sadie?"

I look up, surprised to see that my sister is now walking with us. I wait for her to say something sassy about how my giant ego has finally deflated, but she doesn't.

All she does is put an arm around my shoulders, and she's so much shorter that she really has to *reach* to do it. I guess she heard what I said and thought it was cool. Gratefully, I put my arm around her scrawny little shoulders, too, and we walk like that the rest of the way.

The Keeper of Fortunes stops us in front of a large door. "Welcome to the second half of the Test of Humility. As I said, no one will be eliminated, but the winner will have an advantage in tomorrow's task, so aim high. Inside, you will find the floor covered in scrolls of parchment. Every scroll has one of five different witch runes. Each of you must find and collect all five."

Excitement shoots through me like electricity. This challenge sounds like it's going to require speed, and speed, I've got. I think back to what George just said, about faking it 'til you make it. *I'm gonna kick butt*, I tell myself. *I'm going to prove that I have a reason to brag.*

Jeremy's eyes are shining. "Witch runes?"

"Yes, the witches have agreed to host this challenge, though they are like the phoenixes and do not often choose to appear to humans. Their Gem of Humility will magically present itself if one of you is deemed to be worthy. Some witches may have joined the Forgotten Queen, but many others stand with King Rothbart and support the child hero." Her eyes sweep over us. "This task will test your humility because it's possible to complete alone, but you'll find that teamwork will help. Who knows if the player next to you has the rune you need? Feel free to trade and work together. Humility means asking for help and admitting that you may not have all of the answers."

A week ago, I might have snorted and thought, *Ask for help? Fat chance!* That's not in the Clip Chu Rule Book. But today, I want to show that I can be as humble as George.

Captain Redfern pushes the door open. "You have ten minutes to find five different scrolls. Call out when you're done. The first person to do so will win the witches' Gem of Humility. On your mark, get set . . . GO!"

I try to channel Usain Bolt, the legendary Jamaican sprinter, as I race into an enormous ballroom . . . and almost wipe out on a pile of scrolls. The Keeper wasn't joking when she said the floor would be *covered*. There are hundreds, maybe thousands, of rolled-up pieces of parchment in messy stacks everywhere. It's like a ski slope, except with paper instead of snow.

"Careful!" Sadie says, and I give her a thumbs-up.

I've been rushing through these tasks so far and making silly mistakes, so I decide to slow down and take in the surroundings. The ballroom is about the size of a football field, and the ceiling soars hundreds of feet above us. It's well lit and empty except for the sea of scrolls.

Everyone seems to be staying near the door, so I move farther into the room to attack a mountain of parchment tucked against a pillar. I start opening random scrolls, all of which have the same bright red infinity symbol that looks like the number eight turned sideways. I stick one in my pocket and keep searching, but all I find is the same rune.

"Jer, do you have any green ones?" I hear Lizard call from across the room.

"Yep! Trade you for an orange?" Jeremy asks.

Green? Orange?

"Why are all of these stupid ones red?" I mutter, getting up and moving to another stone pillar. I find more red infinity symbols, and I'm starting to get frustrated when I finally find a blue rune that looks like an O with three lines through it. Two down, three to go! I know this task is about being humble, but if I end up completing it all by myself, I wouldn't *hate* that.

The minutes trickle by, and all I can find are red and blue runes. I know no one's getting eliminated and I'm in the top five no matter what . . . but I still don't want to finish last.

I'm pawing through the scrolls, feeling like I should move somewhere else, when my hand hits something warm. I frown. It feels like a big toe. The big toe is connected to a foot in a white tube sock and a flip-flop, which peeks out from under a periwinkle-blue robe.

I fall backward in shock at the sight of the wizard. "Dude, what the *heck* are you doing?"

He puts a finger to his lips. "Shhh! And sorry, didn't mean to scare you."

"I saw you in the orc castle," I tell him. "And the marsh, too."

His bushy eyebrows go up and down. They look like two gray caterpillars.

"What is the point of you? Like, what's your role on this show?" I know my questions are a little rude, but he only shrugs at me. "Okay, you know what? I don't have time for this."

"Hold on now. I'm here to remind you not to count yourself out," the wizard says, tapping his nose knowingly. "You may brag a lot, young man, but only because you don't want the others to know you're worried about losing. Fake it 'til you make it, right?"

I gawk at him. "You heard George say that in the hall?"

"Beg pardon?"

"Wait. If you were listening to our conversation, how did you get in here so fast?"

The old man lifts his shoulders and spreads his hands, smiling.

"Never mind," I say, shaking my head. "I have three witch runes left to find and I'm running out of time, so I'll see you around."

"Yes, go!" he agrees, making a shooing motion. "Don't forget what I said!"

"Weirdo," I mumble, jogging across the room. He's gone when I glance back, but I don't have time to wonder about him. I dive into a pile of parchment, and out of the corner of my eye, I see George nearby with *three* scrolls in his pocket to my two.

He looks up. "Found any green ones?"

"Nah, just blue and red so far," I say.

"Oh! I need the blue. Wanna trade me for an orange one?"

I hesitate. There were a million blue scrolls where I just was, but if I point him over there, he would be *that* much closer to winning. One more color, and the victory will be his.

George breaks into a smile, like he knows what I'm thinking. "Never mind, it's okay. And the orange scrolls are near that window." He points, then turns away and keeps working.

You don't want the others to know you're worried about losing.

I clench my teeth as the wizard's words echo through my mind. Clip Chu might not be the most humble guy on earth, but he's not a jerk, either. "Hey, George," I say, and he looks up. "There are a million red and blue runes over there."

"Thanks!" he says, and takes off.

I go to the window he pointed out and find the orange runes, just like he said. The symbol looks like the letter V set inside of a diamond. "Only two left to find," I say under my breath.

"Jer! I found two purple ones!" I hear Sadie call.

Purple and green are all I need.

I glance at George, who's pocketing a blue rune. He now has four out of five scrolls, and I have only three. *Focus*, I tell myself sternly. I start tearing through a pile nearby, glad that the parchment is soft like cloth so there's no danger of papercuts. (Even though I would *totally* sacrifice my fingers to win.) Suddenly, I spot a green rune that looks like a drawing of a bird.

Now all I need is purple to win!

"Three minutes left!" Captain Redfern yells from the doorway.

"Three minutes?" Lizard groans.

I am in full-on panic mode, searching for the purple rune, when I see Sadie ten feet away, waving one at me. It has a square with the number seven inside it, inked in . . .

"Purple!" I gasp.

She raises an eyebrow. "You need this one?"

"Yes, please," I say, trying not to sound too desperate. Any second now, George is going to find his fifth and final rune. "What do you want for it?"

"Wow! Clip Chu admitting he doesn't have all the answers and wants to trade?" she asks, but in a nice, jokey kind of way. "I need a green one."

"Perfect! I'm sitting in a whole pile of them."

"That's the last one I need, though," Sadie says. "If you give it to me, we tie for first."

The old Clip Chu would turn her down flat. The old Clip Chu would say, "No way, sis!" and run over, grab the purple scroll, and scream, "I'm done!" to Captain Redfern. But it's weird: I don't know where the old Clip Chu is anymore. I think I left him back out in the hall, when I realized that I want to be less like him and more like George.

So I say, "A tie for first sounds great to me," and I get up and swap scrolls with my sister.

Sadie beams up at me. "On three? One . . . two . . ."

"We're done!" we yell together.

"All right, everybody, stop what you're doing!" Captain Redfern calls.

"Noooooooooo!" Jeremy does his Darth Vader scream. "I only needed one more!"

"Me too," George and Lizard say together.

We head back to the entrance, where we find that the shield has appeared at the Keeper of Fortunes' feet. The light sparkles on the two rubies and two emeralds decorating the surface. "I saw some marvelous examples of teamwork in here," the Keeper says. "Captain Redfern and I are proud of all of you. And now, it is time to present the vampires' Gem of Humility."

Lady Scarlet smiles. "Clip and Jeremy, step forward.

You were the first to find the Reflection Room and solve the riddle. Which of you will place the pearl upon the shield?"

I don't even hesitate. "Jeremy solved the puzzle. He should get the pearl."

"You helped!" Jeremy protests.

"Nope, I'm not taking it," I tell him. "It's yours."

"Very well. Then I believe this is yours, Jeremy." Lady Scarlet takes the pearl off her necklace and hands it to Jeremy, whose smile lights up the entire room. I've never seen a kid so happy to hold what's probably just a piece of plastic, but it was worth letting him have it.

Suddenly, we hear a loud whirring sound, like a motor running underneath the ballroom floor. A few feet away, something starts rising up from the ground, pushing aside a mountain of scrolls on its way up. It's a small marble pedestal, and sitting on top is a round white pearl identical to the one Jeremy is holding.

"Another gem!" Lizard cries.

"The witches have kept their word," the Keeper of Fortunes says, moving over to pluck the pearl from its stand. "Their Gem of Humility has appeared because they deemed one of you to be worthy of it. Clip and Sadie, you were the first to locate five different witch runes. Which of you will place this gem?"

Again, I don't hesitate. I guess I'm on a humility roll here, and I don't hate it. "Sadie should have it. She came up with the idea of swapping with me."

"But you *agreed* to the swap," Sadie points out. "Even though I told you we would tie for first. You weren't ashamed of winning with me."

"Why would I be ashamed of winning with you?" I ask, even though I know what she means. The old me wouldn't have liked sharing a victory with his annoying sister . . . but this is the new me, and *he* likes the way everyone's beaming proudly at him.

"Come on, Team Chu!" Jeremy says heartily. "Let's put the pearls on together!"

I look at the Keeper of Fortunes. "Do you think the witches would mind?"

"I don't see why they would," she says, smiling.

Sadie accepts the pearl and holds it out to me, pinched between her pointer finger and thumb. I pinch the other side in *my* pointer finger and thumb. We kneel next to Jeremy and attach the Gems of Humility into their rightful places. There must be a magnet inside of them, because I hear a loud and satisfying *click!* as they snap onto the brass shield.

Everyone else cheers as Jeremy, Sadie, and I get up, grinning.

I realize that I really don't mind sharing the victory. I made it to the top five on this show, and I get to have this awesome moment with my sister and our friend.

And if that's what humility is all about . . . then I think I like it.

CHAPTER EIGHTEEN
SADIE

THE NEXT MORNING, EVERYONE IS BACK ON THE wagon and huddling under fleece blankets to keep warm. The air is so cold, I can see my breath, and nobody looks fully awake. Next to me, Jeremy's head keeps drooping toward my shoulder, then jerking upright, and then falling again.

"Sorry, Sadie," he says, letting out a huge yawn.

Lizard yawns, too, and then both Clip and George yawn. Everyone watches as I try to fight the urge, but soon enough, an enormous, jaw-cracking yawn wins out.

Clip slaps himself on the cheeks. "We need to wake up, guys! New challenge today."

Jeremy's bloodshot eyes pop open. "Uhhhh?"

"But it's so early, and it's freezing out," Lizard complains.

"And we stayed up a *little* too late last night," George adds.

Yesterday, we came back to a delicious feast at Winterhearth House. Kathryne went all out and made us roast chicken, wild mushroom pie, and a cinnamon sugar cake. We stayed up late eating, swapping stories about the challenges, and laughing until our sides hurt, but we paid for it this morning when the captain yelled for us to get out of bed before the sun was up.

I rub my bleary eyes and look across the sprawling green countryside we're traveling through. "Where did the captain say we're going again?"

"We're meeting the Keeper of Fortunes by the sea," George says.

"I hope it's the Test of Intelligence today and not the Test of Strength." Lizard yawns so widely, we can see all of her teeth. "I can barely keep my head up right now."

"I've been keeping track of the magical beings who've been hosting these tasks," Jeremy says, looking a little more alert. "The only ones left are mages, warlocks, elves, and dragons."

I groan. "Dragons? None of us are in *any* condition to slay a dragon today."

"We're just going to look like a big buffet to it," Lizard

agrees. "What's the difference between mages and warlocks again?"

"Mages use good magic," Jeremy explains. "And when a mage goes bad, that's when they become a warlock. This is just in the *War of Gods and Men* universe."

"I thought they were all wizards," I say, confused.

Jeremy nods. "They are. *Wizard* is an umbrella term for magical people."

"Oh, that reminds me!" Clip says. "Remember *the* wizard? With the flip-flops? I saw him yesterday when we were looking for the witch runes. He was hiding in a corner, being weird as usual. I asked him what he was doing there, and what the point of him even is—"

"Clip! That's so rude!" I interrupt, horrified.

My brother shrugs. "It's a good question, though! Every other grown-up in Pantaera has a reason for being here. Like, Captain Redfern is our boss, right? Our *coach*."

"And the Keeper of Fortunes tells us about the different tasks," George chimes in. "And Lady Scarlet and other people give us backstory. They all play a role."

Clip points at him. "Exactly. But the wizard is just *there*. He was trying to be nice, 'cause I was worried about not finding my runes. Maybe he pops up to stop us from panicking?"

I snort. "I could've really used his help in the sirens' marsh, then."

"You did fine on your own," Clip says, and I beam. He's been a lot nicer to me lately, and less arrogant, too. I think it's because he looks up to George and is trying to be more humble and friendly like he is. I sure hope the change is permanent.

"Did the wizard have Tuba with him?" Lizard asks.

"Nah, I don't think Tuba's his cat anymore," Clip says. "He's one hundred percent Iggy's now, whether Iggy's dad likes it or not."

Suddenly, everyone gasps as an incredible view appears: dramatic cliffs plunging into the sea, like a waterfall made out of rock. The ocean is so blue that it almost hurts to look at it. Perched on top of the cliffs is a building of pure white stone, with a clock tower wrapped in green vines. Captain Redfern and his knights are leading our wagon toward it on their horses.

"A cliff? Do you think we'll have to scale it?" George jokes.

"The producers wouldn't make us do that, would they?" Jeremy asks worriedly.

"No way," I say. "It must be a thousand feet high!"

Captain Redfern doubles back, pulling his horse alongside our wagon. "We're going to take the cliff path halfway down," he calls. "It's safe, but you can never be too careful, so, everyone, stay in your seats and keep your hands in the wagon at all times. Okay?"

"Okay," everyone says.

He and the knights ride up to the edge, where there's a path about ten feet wide that slopes steeply downward. One by one, they descend, disappearing below the level of the ground. As the wagon follows, I peer over the side and instantly wish I hadn't.

The cliffs drop straight down to white-capped waves crashing violently against the rocks. I close my eyes and gulp, feeling dizzy. No one else seems bothered by the zillion-foot drop, though. Lizard actually stands up so she can see better.

George grabs the back of her tunic, like a mother cat trying to wrangle a hyper kitten. "Liz, will you *please* sit down?" he moans. "I know you heard what Captain Redfern said!"

She ignores him. "Look! Dolphins!"

"Where?" Clip demands, and he and Jeremy stand up a little, too.

George throws his hands into the air, exasperated. "If any of you fall off this wagon and into the ocean, I'm not diving in after you. Just so you know."

"Relax, *Dad*. We just want to see the cute dolphins,

not swim with them." Lizard taps Jeremy's arm. "See, Jer? They're jumping up and down in the waves!"

I stay in my seat, but turn to look, too. The dolphins look like they're a mile off the coast, but we can see them clearly, little bouncing gray shapes breaking the ocean's surface.

The wagon makes a sharp turn, drawing our focus back. We enter a huge, open-air room without a ceiling that's been cut into the side of the cliff. The Keeper of Fortunes stands at the foot of a stone staircase leading right up to the entrance of the building with the clock tower. Next to her is a tall girl in her late teens, with pale skin and long blond hair in a thick braid. Both of them are wearing thick cloaks to protect them from the chilly sea breeze.

"Your Highness," Captain Redfern says to the blond girl, looking both surprised and annoyed as he climbs off his horse to bow. We all get off the wagon and do the same. "Does King Rothbart know you're here?"

The girl rolls her eyes. "My brother might be the king, Daniel, but I don't need his permission to go everywhere. I wanted to meet the young warriors today."

"Princess Errin, it is a dangerous time for you to roam the countryside alone," the captain says disapprovingly. "You didn't even bring any guards to protect you."

The princess ignores him and smiles at us. "It's wonderful to meet all of you. I've been hoping to see you in
action at one of your challenges. You don't mind if I stay,
do you?"

"Of course not, Your Highness," Clip says loudly, and
I snicker. My brother's always been a sucker for a beautiful princess. "You can stay as long as you like!"

Princess Errin beams at him. "It's settled, then."

Captain Redfern still doesn't look happy, but he turns to the Keeper of Fortunes without further argument. "My lady, here are the young warriors, as requested."

"Very good," the old woman says. Sunlight gleams off her high cheekbones and her dark velvet cloak billows as she faces us. "Today, I summon you to the Cliffs of Whitesea to face your greatest challenge yet. Above us, you see the Abbey of the Grey Mages, which has stood upon these cliffs for countless ages of mankind. Once, the mages practiced good and healing magic here . . . but never again. The Great Betrayer made sure of that."

Suddenly, the image of a man's face is projected onto the stone wall behind her. He has white skin, dark brown eyes, and a jagged scar down his nose, mouth, and chin. His smile is cold and cruel, and as we watch, he waves a magic wand that looks like a twisted tree branch. It lets out a bright red light that knocks over a group of people in gray robes. They don't get back up.

"The Great Betrayer was once a mage," the Keeper of Fortunes goes on. "As a penniless orphan, he was taken in by the mages, who taught him all the magic they knew. But when he grew older, he betrayed them. He forced them out of their home and filled it with dark magic."

Shivering, I look up at the tower with its chains of ivy swaying in the wind. It's so easy to picture this evil man glaring down at us, and I *really* hope we don't run into him in there.

"His spell prevents the mages from ever setting foot in the abbey again . . . that is, unless one translates and speaks a magical phrase aloud," the Keeper says. "But it contains seven different words in seven different languages. As part of your Test of Intelligence, you must enter the mages' library and seek the books that will help you decode it."

Jeremy and I are practically dancing with glee. Libraries, languages, and decoding magical phrases are one billion percent up our alley, and everyone knows it. Clip mumbles to himself, George twists his hands together nervously, and Lizard lets out a heavy sigh.

"Pencils and paper will be provided," the Keeper of Fortunes tells us. "Please note that this is *not* a team-based challenge. You must work alone. Multiple books in the library will hold the answers you seek, so you don't need to fight over any of them. Do you understand?"

"We understand," everyone choruses.

"The first person to complete this challenge will receive the mages' Gem of Intelligence, which they have entrusted to me," the Keeper goes on. From a pocket of her billowing robes, she produces a huge sapphire, deep blue in color like the ocean. "They asked me to give it, along with their gratitude, to the one who helps them return to their library."

"Clip and Sadie, step forward," Captain Redfern says. "As the winners of the previous challenge, you will both have a one-minute head start. Wait here while I see if everything is ready." He jogs up the stairs and disappears into the abbey.

Clip gives Princess Errin a cheesy grin. "A head start is nice, but I probably won't need it. I haven't needed extra time on any of the challenges, not even the last one."

I roll my eyes so hard, it's amazing they don't get stuck in my brain. Just as I was starting to feel proud of him, he's back to his old bragging self as soon as a pretty princess is around.

"Oh? Wasn't your last challenge the Test of Humility? You know, about being *humble*?" Princess Errin asks innocently, and everyone laughs.

"Oh, snap!" George shouts. "Someone call the burn unit!"

Clip laughs, too, and the princess smiles at him to show she was joking.

"Okay, Clip and Sadie!" Captain Redfern calls from the top of the stairs. "Come on up!"

CHAPTER NINETEEN
SADIE

THE MAGES' LIBRARY IS A BIG ROUND ROOM THAT soars several stories high, with light filtering in through the windows and a giant brass bell hanging from the ceiling. Aisles upon aisles of bookcases stretch out across the floor, and six metal ladders have been installed on the walls to allow access to shelves that spiral all the way to the top, hundreds of feet above us.

I gulp. I'm definitely not climbing that high if I can help it.

Captain Redfern points to a plaque above the main entrance. "This is the phrase you will need to translate. Remember, each word is in a different language, and everything you need is in this room. When you're done, come see me by this door. Don't shout out the answer. Got it?"

Clip and I nod. "Got it."

"Your task begins now. Go!"

I take a deep breath, shaking with nerves and excitement, and read the words on the plaque:

Urggle Buhcoco Lupinelle Querste Pexomera Incitafo
Sluewess

"What *is* this, a long sneeze? What languages are those? And how are we supposed to know which books can translate them? This place is *huge*." Clip chews on his nails, which he always does when he's panicking. "Well, Sadie? Don't you have any ideas?"

I can't lie: I love it when my ultra-confident brother loses his cool. All of a sudden, we get a challenge that *isn't* athletic, and he's turning to me for help. Which is against the rules.

"Ideas?" I repeat. "Uhhh, how about . . . don't freak out?"

He throws his hands up. "That's it? That's your advice?"

"Yeah, 'cause you're freaking out, and it's freaking *me* out! So stop!"

"Don't tell me not to freak out if you don't want me to freak out," he snaps. "If you tell me not to freak out, I'll freak out more and that'll freak *you* out more, too!"

I put my hand up. "I don't have time for this. And we can't help each other, remember?"

"Fiiiiiiine, whatever!" he says.

I grab a pencil and scribble the phrase on a piece of paper. Clip immediately copies me, but I ignore him and take off through the bookshelves.

There are a million great things about being best friends with Jeremy Thomas, King of the Geeks, and one is that his epic fantasy knowledge has rubbed off on me. I actually *recognize* a couple of words. I might not know their meanings, but at least I've seen them before.

When I borrowed Jeremy's graphic novel on the plane, I had laughed at the word *Pexomera* because it sounded like a high blood pressure medication or something. Even Jer had joked that the witches' language sounded like the prescriptions his dad writes out for patients.

"Okay, if I were a witch dictionary," I mutter, "where would I be?"

Usually, in a library or a bookstore, there would be signs to tell you what section you're in. But it looks like the mages either forgot to make signs or didn't need any.

I decide to pick a random aisle. I scan the spines

for titles, authors' names, or *anything* to help me, but everything is jumbled. Some volumes don't even have words—just drawings or languages made up of shapes or numbers. This is going to be trickier than I thought.

I hear Captain Redfern's voice at the entrance, calling down to Jeremy, Lizard, and George, and a minute later their footsteps scurry into the library.

"Come on, come on," I mutter, scanning the shelves. And then I see a mustard-yellow book with familiar symbols, two of which I remember from yesterday. "Witch runes!"

I take it down, excited, but when I flip through, I discover that the whole thing is written in runes—there's no English at all. That's not going to help me. I put the book back and check out its neighbors: a green book with illustrations of the sun and planets, and a red cookbook. As I scan the witch recipes, a piece of old parchment flutters out. It reads:

Pexomera = Darkness

"Yes!" I exclaim, then clap a hand over my mouth. I jot the word down and replace the book—just in time, because a second later, my annoying brother pokes his head into the aisle.

"Did you find something?" Clip asks eagerly.

"Maybe I did, and maybe I didn't. Mind your own beeswax!"

"Ughhhhhhhh!" he says.

I scoot past Clip, so energized that I decide to try one of the ladders. I can go just *halfway* up the tower wall, which doesn't seem too scary. I see Jeremy jog around the corner with pencil and paper clutched in his hand. "How's it going, Sadie?" he asks cheerfully.

"It's going! Good luck," I say, and he waves and vanishes down an aisle.

I check my paper. I recognize another word: *Buhcoco*. Two weeks ago, Iggy came over to play *War of Gods and Men* with Clip. I watched them do a siren puzzle with *Buhcoco* in it, and Iggy had joked that if his parents let him adopt another cat, he'd name it Buhcoco Loco.

"I need the siren books," I mutter, running my fingers over the spines. You'd think these mages would hire someone to organize their library or cast an alphabetizing spell or something.

I decide to climb just a little higher. From here, I can see the whole library and everyone else. George is sprawled out on the floor with a pile of books. Lizard is on another ladder across the room, so high up that she looks like a fly on the wall. Jeremy is bent over a table, scribbling on his piece of paper, while Clip is pacing and chewing his nails.

I turn back to the shelves in front of me and notice something interesting. There's a green book, a yellow book, and a red book with witch runes on their spines, lined up exactly like the ones I just looked at. Curiously, I open them. "They're the same books!" I whisper, and I open the red cookbook to find another piece of parchment that translates *Pexomera*.

I turn, look out at the library again, and notice pops of green, yellow, and red all over.

This place is full of duplicates! The Keeper of Fortunes wasn't kidding when she told us we wouldn't have to fight over books. They repeat over and over in patterns, so it doesn't matter where we look—anywhere we go in the library, the answers will be right at our fingertips.

Eagerly, I climb back down and find a cozy corner between two bookshelves. I locate the three witch rune books and check the row underneath for anything on sirens.

One chocolate-brown book falls open to the author page, which shows an orc. "Oh, okay," I whisper, glancing at my piece of paper. I know that the last word in the phrase, *Sluewess*, is in the orcs' language. I shake the book, but nothing falls out, so I do the same to the ones around it. After several tries, a piece of parchment slips out of a deep purple volume:

Sluewess = Foul

I scribble it down and do a little dance. This challenge is fun! I feel like a historian hero in an epic fantasy. That's the kind of character I would want to be in a story—not a kick-butt one with a sword, but someone quieter, like a librarian with a magical book collection. A few days ago, I might have felt embarrassed about even thinking this, but now I just feel *inspired*.

"Good for you," someone whispers. "You look like you're having fun."

I peer through the bookshelves and see a familiar wrinkled face. "It's you again!" I say happily. "What are you doing here?"

"Oh, you know," the wizard says pleasantly, waving a hand. "Just taking in the sights and enjoying myself. Speaking of which, you look like *you're* enjoying yourself, too. Are you feeling more confident since the last time we talked?"

"Yeah, I think so," I say. "Having fun on the show

helps me do better at the challenges. And there's nothing wrong with that, is there?"

The old man beams. "So you're not worried about what anyone else thinks anymore?"

"I don't know about *not worried*. But I care a tiny bit less. It felt silly pretending to be in Pantaera at first, but . . . I'm here." I wave at the library around us. "Why not enjoy it?"

"How far you have come in your journey, young Sadie," the wizard says, grinning. "I'm proud of you. Now, I will leave you with one reminder: The coolest kids are the ones who are cool with themselves." He winks at me and puts a heavy book back on the shelf between us, blocking himself from view. I'm sure that if I ran over into that aisle, he would be gone.

I think about what he said for a second. It does make sense, and it's probably why Clip is so popular at school. No one's as cool with themselves as he is, and other kids seem to like that.

I turn my attention back to the shelves, and in a minute, I finally locate the siren books. I have to check six or seven volumes before I find a piece of parchment:

Buhcoco = Shines

I write down the translation, and then read over what I have so far. "Blank shines blank blank darkness blank foul," I whisper. "Three words down, four to go!"

CHAPTER TWENTY
JEREMY

WHEN CAPTAIN REDFERN LETS US LOOSE IN THE library, I just stand there and soak up the atmosphere for a minute. Being surrounded by the Grey Mages' wisdom is so amazing and inspiring. I feel like I'm breathing the whole history and magic of Pantaera right into my lungs. I imagine that the specks of dust floating in the sunlight are pieces of knowledge that the mages left behind, before the Great Betrayer ruined everything.

"I'm honored to be here," I whisper. "And I'll do whatever I can to help you guys."

I look down at my paper, where I've copied the magical phrase:

Urggle Buhcoco Lupinelle Querste Pexomera Incitafo
Sluewess

So far, this is what I know:

1. *Urggle* means *knowledge* in the language of the phoenixes.
2. I remember the witch word *Pexomera* from my graphic novel. It means *darkness*.
3. *Incitafo* is in the computer game. I don't know what the word means, exactly, but the warlocks used it to describe the ocean. Maybe *deep*?
4. I can't remember what *Buhcoco* means, but I know it's a siren word and it was in a puzzle inside the game. I think it has something to do with the sun, maybe.

I decide to double-check every single word, even if I feel sure I know what it means. I'm not going to disrespect the Grey Mages by rushing this task. I need to get them back into this abbey so they can keep doing good magic and fighting off the Great Betrayer's evil spells.

The library doesn't have signs to show how the books are shelved, but I think the mages would at least put similar ones together. Last summer, when I was helping Mom organize her home library, she said, "You don't have to alphabetize or use the Dewey decimal system, like public libraries do. But you should put books on the same topic together, so you can find them."

And that's what the mages seem to have done. When I check a random shelf, I find seven books on sirens in a row. I turn the pages gently as I look for *Buhcoco*. I want to be as careful with these books as I am with mine, which means no folding or dog-earing pages. Suddenly, a piece of parchment flutters out from one of the books:

Buhcoco = Shines

I scribble it down. "Knowledge shines something something darkness deep foul," I murmur. "Hmmm. Maybe darkness deep *and* foul? That makes more sense."

I'm sure *Querste* is in the ancient tongue of the dragons. I remember coming across it in the *War of Gods and Men* encyclopedia. I don't know the meaning, but I'm sure the answer is in the library somewhere. I smile at the books, knowing that they will always help me.

"I see you've been listening to me," someone says quietly, and I whirl to see the wizard. He's walking by with a tall stack of books, wearing the same periwinkle robe and flip-flops.

"Oh, hello!" I say.

He gives me a kindly wink. "You're feeding that fire inside of you, just as I advised."

I beam, feeling more like a fantasy hero than ever. After all, a wise old wizard *did* give me advice on my quest. "Yeah, I have. I feel great! Thanks for the tip. I appreciate it!"

"And you've finally started to believe that you belong here?"

"I mean, I'm still kind of shocked that I made it this far," I admit. "Like, top five in the competition is ridiculous. I didn't think I would last that long!"

"But you did," he points out.

"I did. And if I made it to the top five, then why not the top four?"

The wizard pumps his fist. "Good for you! That's the way you need to think. Well, I won't take up any more of your time, Jeremy. Just remember not to let that fire die out, okay?"

"Yes, sir!" I get the urge to salute, but that doesn't feel very epic fantasy–ish. So I bow instead, and when I look up, he's gone—probably off giving mysterious advice to the other kids.

I get back to the shelves, feeling even more excited, and my eyes land on three spines with stick figure–like symbols. "Dragonian Etchings!" I whisper, awed. I remember them from the video game. In the early days of Pantaera, the dragons used these symbols to communicate with other magical beings across the land. I scan the books, which are about dragon history, and the third one yields a scrap of parchment:

Querste = Even

That leaves only *Lupinelle* to translate. I know *lupus* means *wolf* in Latin, so I'm pretty sure it's a word in the werewolves' language. A lot of fantasy writers use old Latin to inspire the languages in their worlds, so I've picked up a bunch of it. Dad's so impressed, he thinks I should enroll in a beginner-level Latin class at the high school next summer!

I scan the bookcase for anything on wolves and finally spot a heavy volume edged in gold. The spine reads: *A Historian's Account of Hollybottom*. "Oh yeah!" I cheer under my breath. We were just there in that village for the challenge with the locked doors! My hands are shaking so much from anticipation that it takes a few tries before I find the translation:

Lupinelle = Through

I jump up and down silently with joy. The complete translated magical phrase reads:

Urggle Buhcoco Lupinelle Querste Pexomera Incitafo
Sluewess
Knowledge shines through even darkness deep and foul.

"Thank you," I whisper to the books, then hurry back to Captain Redfern. I try to be as quiet as possible, so I don't bother anyone else, but the others still notice as I pass.

George gapes at me. "You're done already, Jer?"

Clip, who is flipping through books with a panicked expression, glances up.

I just wave at them as I run by. Captain Redfern watches me approach with his arms crossed and a big smile on his face. He pats my shoulder, reads my translation silently, and then calls out loudly, so everyone can hear, "Jeremy is our first winner!"

There's a chorus of groans from various aisles, ladders, and corners.

"How did it go, Jeremy?" the captain asks in a lower voice.

"Great! I'm glad I read my encyclopedias over again so many times. I made spreadsheets, too, with everything

I knew. I think that helped a lot. Should I say the phrase out loud yet?"

He shakes his head. "Not yet. Let's wait until everyone else is done."

I plop onto a chair to catch my breath. I can't believe I made it through *another* challenge! I wonder what Mom and Dad will think. I hope they'll be proud.

After the second half of the Test of Intelligence, whatever that will be, we've only got the Test of Strength left. That makes me nervous, because weirdly enough . . . strength happens to be my weakness. But I'll cross that bridge when I get to it. And the wizard *did* just remind me that I have a fire burning inside.

"It's nice of the wizard to keep showing up and giving us advice," I say.

Captain Redfern is watching a sweaty, anxious Clip sprint across the library. He turns to me and says, "Sorry, what did you say?"

"The old wizard. He's so encouraging and always boosting our confidence. Not that *you* don't, sir," I add quickly. "I just like him a lot and I think he's cool."

The captain frowns. "What wizard? What are you talking about?"

Before I can respond, Lizard comes sprinting toward us. She shoves her translation into the captain's hand

and bends at the waist, panting. Right on her heels is a breathless Sadie, who hands in her own work before collapsing onto the chair next to mine.

"Well, I'm not in second place," Sadie says, gasping for air, "but at least I wasn't too far behind Liz. I probably spent more time talking to the wizard than I should have."

I beam. "I saw him, too! What did he say to you?"

"He said he's proud that I'm having fun and enjoying my challenges."

"I'm proud of you, too," I declare. "I'm glad you're owning your awesomeness!"

"Says the superstar who finished in first place!" she says, and we do a jellyfish fist bump.

"Can I get in on that, too?" Lizard asks, holding out her fist. We teach her how to wiggle her fingers like tentacles as she pulls away. "Guys! We're top three! Well, for this part of the test, at least. Will Clip or George have to go home after this?"

Captain Redfern shakes his head. "No. All five of you will stay for the second half."

"Oh, good!" Sadie says, looking relieved. She and Clip fight a lot sometimes, but I know she doesn't want him to get eliminated.

She doesn't have to worry, though, because Clip and George finish at the same time.

Captain Redfern checks their translations. "Nice job! You have successfully translated the phrase, and all that's left is for our winner to speak it out loud and help the mages return to their abbey." He smiles at me. "Please do the honors, Jeremy."

The other kids cheer as I stand up, smiling big. I feel like my entire life has led to this moment: standing in the library of the Grey Mages, surrounded by books and friends, getting ready to read a spell that will bring good magic back. "Hold on," I say, climbing on top of my chair. Somehow, it doesn't feel right to read something so special with my feet planted on the ground. The others form a half circle around my chair as I clear my throat. In my loudest, strongest voice, I cry: "Knowledge shines through even darkness deep and foul!"

At once, the gigantic tower bell starts swinging back and forth above us.

Bong! Bong! Bong!

Everyone jumps at the sound. Delicate harp music pipes up from somewhere, joined by a flute, and I recognize the "Elegy of the Grey Mages," this pretty music that plays whenever you level up in the game. A soft breeze rushes through the library, gently fluttering book pages. My eyes sting with happy tears as the melody plays on and the others look around in awe.

Finally, the bell goes still and the music stops.

A sudden loud rumbling shakes the floor, and we gasp as one of the bookcases slides backward into the wall, revealing a dark and secret doorway.

Captain Redfern whips out his sword. "Stay here while I go look."

"Are you sure you don't want backup, sir?" Clip asks.

"We got you," George adds.

Right at that moment, Princess Errin and the Keeper of Fortunes enter the library.

The Keeper might be a tiny ancient lady, but she's also really courageous, because she announces, "*I* will be the one to go," and marches toward the hidden room without fear. But she stops in the doorway, frowning, and holds her hands out like she can feel an invisible barrier. "There is a spell here that does not allow me to enter."

I look at Sadie in shock. She raises her eyebrows at me.

"Let me try," Captain Redfern and Princess Errin say together.

The captain frowns. "Your Highness, stay back. The king would never forgive me if anything happened to you." But when he tries to go in, he seems to bump into a wall we can't see.

Ignoring his protests, the princess pushes her way forward, but she can't enter, either.

"Here, let me try!" Lizard says, shoving her way

through the grown-ups. Her foot goes right over the threshold of the room, no problem. "Cool! The spell doesn't work on me!"

Clip walks over and waves his hand in the doorway. "I don't feel anything, either. Maybe it only blocks adults," he suggests.

"Wow, what kind of technology do you think it is?" George whispers to Sadie and me.

"I think the actors are just pretending they can't go in," Sadie murmurs back.

"Sadie! What happened to being immersed?" I exclaim, and she gives me a sheepish grin. "This has gotta be magic, that's what. The darkest magic!"

Captain Redfern pulls Lizard and Clip away from the secret room. "Hold on, this place might be dangerous," he says sternly. "Let's see what the Keeper detects inside it first."

The old woman stands in front of the room with her eyes closed and her hand stretched out, as though she is testing the air. "I sense that this is the secret library of a warlock," she says grimly. "I feel evil magic within. I think it was created by the Great Betrayer himself."

"This dude has a *library*?" George squawks.

The Keeper of Fortunes tilts her head, like she's listening to something that none of us can hear. "There is the sound of sand trickling through an hourglass inside, counting down to an event. Perhaps the self-destruction of this chamber."

We all gasp, looking at each other in horror.

"Why? To destroy the evidence inside?" Sadie asks.

The Keeper gives a grave nod. "I can feel the warlock's hatred for the Forgotten Queen. He thinks Pantaera should belong to *him*, and he will fight her for it. To keep his plans from falling into her hands, he has set up a spell to destroy that room if it is ever found and opened. We must gather all the information we can before that happens."

"Okay, so let's get in there!" Clip says fiercely. "The spell keeps grown-ups out, but it doesn't work on us. We need to check it out right away."

"But is . . . is the room going to blow up?" Lizard asks, looking pale.

The Keeper of Fortunes shakes her head. "My powers will keep the magic stable for fifteen minutes. You must go in, one by one. Each of you will have *one* minute to memorize everything you can, and then come back out and answer my questions. You will finish your Test of Intelligence by helping me confirm what I sense within that secret library." She pauses suddenly, closing her eyes again. "There is something else. I feel the presence of another Gem of Intelligence . . . perhaps the one that was given to the warlocks."

George gasps. "Inside the secret room?"

"Why did the gods give the warlocks a gem? Aren't they bad guys?" Sadie asks.

The Keeper opens her eyes. "Warlocks may practice dark magic, but not all of them want war and violence. And the gods wished to uphold balance, which is why they gave the jewels to every magical race in Pantaera." She studies the doorway. "I sense that the Great Betrayer stole the Gem of Intelligence for his own, and that it will reveal itself when the room self-destructs."

Sadie and I look at each other worriedly. We're both good at memory games, but can we do this under pressure, in an evil chamber that could fall apart at any minute? Can we collect enough information about the Great Betrayer to prevent him from taking over Pantaera?

"Jeremy," Captain Redfern says solemnly, "as the winner of the mages' challenge, you will go first."

I gulp.

Guess it's time to find out.

CHAPTER TWENTY-ONE
CLIP

SADIE SLAPS MY HAND AWAY FROM MY FACE. "CLIP, stop biting your nails!" she scolds me, sounding exactly like Grandma. "At this rate, you're just gonna have skin fingers. No nails."

"Gross," I say. Chewing my nails usually calms me down, but it hasn't helped since I set foot into this stupid library. I've been stressed the whole time.

"Stop freaking out."

"Haven't you learned not to say that to me?!" I exclaim.

She rolls her eyes. "Jer looked happy when he came back from his test, didn't he?"

"Yeah, 'cause he's got every fact about *War of Gods and Men* tattooed inside his brain." My hand flies back toward my mouth, but my sister's still watching, so I sigh and put it in my pocket. To distract myself, I check out what everybody else is doing.

Captain Redfern and Princess Errin are talking quietly near the closed door of the secret room, where Lizard is taking her turn. The Keeper of Fortunes is on the other side of the library, where she just finished quizzing Jeremy, and Jer is browsing through books while he waits for everyone else. George is pacing the aisles, looking tense and worried.

"The Test of Intelligence is not my favorite," I mutter to Sadie, who bounces nervously on her toes. "I came *this* close to getting last place when we were translating that phrase, and now we have to *remember* stuff? After spending only one minute in that room?"

"Everyone has challenges they're better at," she says in a sassy voice. "None of us are good at *everything*. Not even you."

I sink into a chair. "I know, I know. I'm bad at school. Bad at reading. Blah blah blah. Maybe you and Mom and Dad were right about me not being smart enough to design games."

Her smirk fades. "Wait, what? We never said that."

"Every time I bring it up, you guys don't seem to think I can do it," I say bleakly. "Maybe if I read books and got As like you, you'd believe in me more. But that's not me."

"Clip, are you for real right now?" she asks, putting her hands on her hips. "I think you'd be awesome at making video games. And so do Mom and Dad."

I squint at her suspiciously. "You do?"

"Yeah! Nobody plays more games than you do. And you have a feel for, like, stories and game worlds and stuff. School is . . . school." She shrugs. "Designing video games is about being creative and motivated. And you're creative, right?"

"Uh, I guess?"

Sadie kicks my foot. "Oh, come on! I heard you telling Iggy and Derek your ideas. And as for being motivated, you try hard at soccer and other things you like. You don't like school, but you like video games, so . . . there you go."

I sit up straighter. "So you think I *can* do it?"

She kicks my foot again. "Ugh, yes! Stop fishing for compliments!"

My shoulders feel a lot lighter all of a sudden. "I just feel like the big, loud, non-smart one in the family sometimes. Next to you."

"Well, you *are* big and loud. And you forgot obnoxious," Sadie says, dodging my shoe as I try to kick hers back. "But you're not non-smart. You're just not a bookworm, that's all."

I'm full-on smiling now. I've always believed in myself,

but it's nice to hear my family does, too. "Wow. Thanks, sis," I say.

"Any time!" she says, right as the door to the secret room opens and Lizard comes out.

"Go see the Keeper," Captain Redfern tells her. "Sadie, you're up next!"

My sister gulps. I hold my hand up and she gives me a high five before disappearing into the warlock's library. The door shuts behind her and Captain Redfern flips over a tiny hourglass.

George plops down beside me. "Who's going next? You or me?"

"Doesn't matter," I say, chewing my nails again since Sadie isn't watching. "I feel like I'm gonna suck at this challenge either way. My memory's horrible. I can't even remember my times tables. I get tripped up at eleven times eleven."

"A hundred twenty-one," he says immediately.

I narrow my eyes at him. "Or twelve times twelve."

"A hundred forty-four."

"So you're a math genius, too?" I groan.

George laughs. "Don't worry, the warlock probably doesn't care about multiplication. How big do you think the room is? If it's small, there won't be as much stuff to remember."

"I hope it's a closet, then," I grumble.

The door opens and Sadie comes out, her face flushed. The captain points her toward the Keeper, warning, "No giving clues or hints to the remaining competitors, please."

My mouth, which had opened to ask her what she saw, closes again.

The captain looks at me and George. "Which of you would like to go next?"

George shrugs. "Your call, Clip."

"Fine. I'll go," I decide. My mom always says anticipation is the worst part, and she's right. I *hate* waiting, whether it's for a shot at the doctor's office or that moment right before the teacher hands back a quiz you didn't study for. I'd rather just get things over with.

"You have one minute. Good luck," Captain Redfern tells me as I step into the room. It's pitch-black inside, but as soon as the door swings shut, it lights up.

The chamber isn't closet-sized, but it's not huge, either—probably the size of my room at home. Two walls have shelves with books and all kinds of weird stuff: jars of rats and frogs floating in liquid, skeleton limbs, glowing red spheres, and dusty vases full of poisonous-looking weeds. The walls that *don't* have shelves are covered in portraits of old bearded dudes.

"Looks like an evil man cave," I mumble.

In front of me is a table with a giant hourglass. There are only six inches of sand left to slip through it, so I jump into action, knowing the place might self-destruct soon.

I might not have Sadie's brain, but I'm not awful at remembering *some* things. Coach Katz says I have a sharp mind for game plans because I don't forget anything he tells us before a match, like who's playing what position and where we should move and when. So I pretend this task is like prepping my brain with details before I step onto the soccer field.

I do a quick turn around the room, adding things up in my head.

Number of paintings of old guys with beards: seventeen.

Number of jars full of weird pickled crap: seven.

Number of poisonous weeds in the biggest vase: five.

Number of books on Bookcase 1: twenty-two.

Number of books on Bookcase 2: fifteen.

Number of scrolls of parchment on the corner table: three.

I open the scrolls. One has a drawing of an ogre about to eat a cute baby goat. "Run, baby goat," I mutter. The second one has a recipe that looks like chicken soup . . . until I see that it calls for eyeballs. "What the heck? This Great Betrayer dude is wacky." The third scroll is blank.

Next to the scrolls is a globe, but the map printed on it doesn't have any countries I've ever seen. Nothing is labeled, either, but there are five sea monsters painted on one of the oceans.

The door swings open and the lights suddenly go out, throwing the room into total darkness, as Captain Redfern says, "Time's up, Clip. Come back out."

I hurry back into the mages' library, worrying about whether I might have wasted too much time counting stuff. What if the Keeper doesn't ask about any numbers at all? What if she asks about the colors of the books or the names on the paintings? A couple of the portraits had words inscribed into the frames . . . I think.

George nods at me, looking nervous and ready, while Princess Errin throws a smile my way. "Good luck answering the Keeper's questions, Clip!" she says.

I try not to grin at her too hard. Sadie, Jeremy, and Lizard sit at a table nearby and stare as I approach the Keeper of Fortunes. I shrink before her stern, serious gaze.

"Clip, I am going to ask you five questions about the warlock's hidden library," she says. "Answer them to the best of your ability, so that you can confirm what I sensed inside. We need to know as much as possible about his plans to take over Pantaera."

"Yes, ma'am," I say nervously.

"First, what was the biggest item on the bookshelves?"

Oh, boy. I was too busy counting stuff to notice . . . but I think one shelf had a giant glass jar that had a gross rat inside. "Umm, there was a pickled rat." I watch her carefully to see if I'm right, the way I watch my social studies teacher, Mr. Alles, when he's passing back tests, to see whether I bombed it or not. But like Mr. Alles, the Keeper maintains a neutral expression.

"How many warlocks' portraits were hanging on the wall?" she asks.

"Seventeen!" I can't help shouting. I *knew* counting them was a good idea!

I hear muffled giggles from Sadie, Jeremy, and Lizard's table.

The Keeper's mouth twitches. "What color were the robes of the warlock at the top?"

Oh, crap. I didn't think to look at the stupid robes. Warlocks don't usually wear bubblegum pink or orange, right? I would definitely remember that. "Uhhhh," I say, stalling for time. "He was wearing a dark color? Like black, maybe?"

"Is that a question?"

"No, ma'am. Black is my answer."

"What title was repeated again and again on the books?"

Crap, again. Crap squared. "How about I tell you how many books there were instead?" I ask, giving her my most brilliant, dazzling smile. But she only stares at me in silence. "Uhh, how about *A History of Pantaera*?" That sounds legit, right?

"What animal was drawn on one of the scrolls?"

I'm *so* glad I opened those scrolls! "A cute baby goat!" I yell, and I hear Sadie snicker.

"Thank you. You may go."

I join the others just as George strides past me toward the Keeper of Fortunes.

"Tell us what she asked you," Sadie demands, and we all share what the Keeper quizzed us on. None of us got the same questions. "How do we know what we got right or wrong, then?"

George comes over a second later, and then Captain Redfern, Princess Errin, and the Keeper talk quietly before approaching our table. My mouth goes dry. It's the moment of truth.

"The Keeper has deliberated over your answers and chosen a winner," the captain says.

"Jeremy wins both halves of the Test of Intelligence," the Keeper says, gesturing to him with an elegant hand. "Not only was he the first to translate the magical phrase, but he was also the only person to get five out of five questions correct. Congratulations."

Everyone cheers as Jeremy's hands fly up on either side of his face, making him look like the shocked emoji. He looks genuinely stunned. If I had his brains, I wouldn't be surprised, but I guess he's a lot like George that way—super humble. "I don't believe it!" he cries.

"Sadie is in second place, with four out of five correct," the Keeper goes on.

Sadie squeals, and she and Jeremy hug and jump up and down.

"Way to go!" I tell her, even as my heart sinks. I knew going into the Test of Intelligence that getting into the top three would be a long shot. But now that Jer and Sadie have snagged first and second place, and there are only two spots left, it feels terrifying. I cross my fingers for luck, even though I know luck doesn't matter now. How I performed is how I performed.

"Third place goes to George, who got three and a half questions right. You got the number of portraits incorrect, but you managed to recall three of the warlocks' names."

And then there's only one spot left in the competition.

Lizard and I look at each other, and it suddenly hits me that I could be the one leaving. I wasted so much time trying to translate that magical phrase and counting stuff in the secret room instead of paying attention to other details. I've messed up so many times on this show. I assumed being athletic would get me to the final, easy peasy. But it turns out being fast and strong aren't the only things that matter, and everyone understood that but me.

And now it's over. Goodbye, Clip Chu.

"Sorry, can you hold on a second?" I interrupt. "Could I say something real quick?"

The Keeper of Fortunes looks startled, but nods.

"Uh, like, I just want to thank everyone here. Every single one of you is a champ and you've taught me a lot." I look at Lizard. "You showed me that tough kids come in tiny packages sometimes. And, George," I say, turning to the guy I thought would be my biggest rival, "you're always so humble and hardworking. I'm going to try to be more like you."

Sadie pokes me. "Um, Clip? You don't have to do this yet. The Keeper hasn't—"

I hush her. "Jer, you're the smartest kid I know. You didn't think you would be up to these challenges, but you're rocking them." Finally, I turn to my sister. "And, Sadie, you always try to face your fears, and you've beaten me lots of times on this show. I'm not even embarrassed to say that, 'cause it's true and you deserve to be here. *All* of you do."

"Clip—"

I talk louder to drown her out. "You guys showed me, like, what goes into being a hero. You're all my heroes, no matter who wins, and I'm leaving with my head held high. No one can say Clip Chu isn't good at losing! So, uh, thanks. And okay, I'm done now."

The Keeper of Fortunes has an odd twinkle in her eye. "May I announce who is staying in the competition now? The person who will remain in the running for child hero of Pantaera is Clip, who got three out of five questions correct and is in fourth place in the Test of Intelligence."

I'm already halfway across the room. My feet are pointed out the door, and I'm ready to go back to the real world. "Okay, bye, everyone! I'm going to miss . . . wait, what did you say?"

Sadie groans. "Get back here, Clip! You're being so embarrassing!"

My brain slowly processes the Keeper's words. I turn to Lizard, who is staring at the old woman with her mouth open in shock and her eyes brimming with tears.

"Lizard got two answers right," the Keeper says. "She will be leaving the competition."

"Well done, Lizard," Captain Redfern says kindly, shaking her hand. She looks as dazed as I feel. "You've been a worthy contender. We are so grateful to have had you with us."

"Hear, hear!" George cries.

The other kids form a cluster around Lizard. I'm still frozen in place, so Sadie has to tug me into the group, saying, "Come *on*! Quit being strange!"

We do a big jumping group hug with Lizard in the middle. She wipes her eyes and manages a tiny smile, and all I can think of is: *I made it. I'm still in the game.*

"Since Clip took about half an hour to do his farewell speech—for absolutely no point at all—do you want to say anything, Liz?" Sadie asks, grinning.

"Umm, well, I agree with what Clip said. Thanks, guys, this was fun." Lizard takes a shaky breath and looks at the captain. "Okay. I'm ready to go. Where do I—"

Another low rumbling interrupts her. Everyone turns just in time to see lights flickering inside the warlock's secret library. Through the open door, we see a wall of sand cascading down from the ceiling, and the objects on the shelves crashing to the floor.

"Holy crap! It's happening!" Jeremy shouts, sounding *way* too excited about a room self-destructing just fifty feet away from us.

"Is it safe? Should we run?" George demands.

The portraits crumble to the floor, spraying cracked glass around the small room. We hear a deep, booming roar that sounds like a man yelling in fury as the door to the Great Betrayer's library cracks clean in half and the sheet of sand continues falling and falling. One of the jars plummets off the bookshelf and onto the ground, shattering to reveal a sparkling dark blue sapphire, which tumbles out the door toward us.

"Look! The warlocks' gem!" I yell.

Captain Redfern seizes it. "Let's get out of here!" he cries as he propels Lizard and Jeremy toward the exit, followed by the Keeper of Fortunes and George. Princess Errin grabs Sadie and me and hurries us after them, out the door and back down the stone steps.

Outside, everything is calm and quiet, with only the sound of the sea below the cliffs.

"What's going to happen to the building?" Jeremy asks, looking worriedly up at the abbey. "I hope the mages don't come back to find a huge mess."

"Don't worry. I expect that the secret room will collapse in on itself, and then the mages will wall it off securely." Captain Redfern turns to Lizard. "My knight will take you back to your own world now. Travel well, and take with you our good wishes."

A woman in a suit of armor leads two horses toward us. One of them is the big white horse that Lizard has been riding throughout the competition. The knight helps Lizard up, then gets on her own horse. They wave goodbye and ride off, and then Lizard's gone. Just like that.

Everybody's quiet for a moment, and I can tell that the others are as unsure as I am about whether to be sad that our friends are all gone, or happy that we've made it this far. Maybe both.

"That could have been me going home," I say, feeling numb. "I meant everything I said in there. You know? You guys deserve to be here."

"So do you," Sadie, Jeremy, and George all say together, and we laugh.

"I'm glad you told the cameras that I've beaten you a lot in this competition," Sadie says, grinning, and I blow a raspberry. "All right, Team Chu to the final challenge!"

Captain Redfern, the Keeper of Fortunes, and Princess Errin stand by the wagon, where the brass shield has reappeared, its six jewels glittering in the sunlight. The captain hands the warlocks' sapphire to the Keeper so that she holds both Gems of Intelligence, each shining a rich dark blue in her hands.

"The gods of Pantaera gave these Gems of Intelligence to the mages and the warlocks once upon a time," she says. "And today, it is my honor to present them to Jeremy, who excelled at both halves of the Test of Intelligence. Will you place them upon the shield?"

Jeremy steps forward, his face glowing, and snaps the jewels into place. There are only two empty spaces left on the shield, for the Gems of Strength. I make a silent promise to myself that I am going to do better and snag one of them for myself.

"All right, warriors. Now it is time to—" Captain Redfern begins.

The sound of thundering hoofbeats interrupts him, and for a second, I think Lizard's coming back. I imagine the Keeper of Fortunes saying, *Surprise! All of you are staying in the competition!* But instead of Lizard, it's a knight who turns the corner on his black horse.

"Captain Redfern, you're needed at once in the village of Larchmont!" he calls, looking frantic. "A dragon has been sighted. Please, sir, hurry! There's no time to lose."

"A dragon?" Jeremy and Sadie cry.

"A dragon!" George and I exclaim.

Books and hidden libraries and parchment—that stuff is Jeremy and Sadie's department. But fighting dragons? That's got Clip Chu written all over it.

For the first time today, I feel my old confidence coming back. A smile splits my face. "Well, what are we waiting for? Let's go!"

CHAPTER TWENTY-TWO

SADIE

ON THE RIDE THERE, I TURN TO JEREMY. "DO YOU think we'll have to fight a dragon for real?"

Clip and George watch him intently, waiting for his answer.

"I don't know. But it *is* our last task, so it'll probably be the most challenging." He looks as jittery as I feel. The Test of Intelligence might have favored the two of us, but this one won't.

"I wonder what weapons we'll get," Clip says. "Maybe a sword, like the captain?"

"Maybe a medieval slingshot?" George suggests.

"Dragons aren't always violent, guys. Some of them are good," Jeremy points out, but they're too busy discussing how to slay a gigantic flying beast to listen.

I look around the wagon. It feels so empty with only

four of us now . . . and I suddenly realize that I'm the only girl left in the competition. I'm not tough like Lizard or athletic like Caroline, so how am I going to survive? I stare at the fields passing by, which are full of tiny periwinkle-blue flowers. Their color reminds me of the mysterious wizard's robe, and that gets me thinking about what I told him in the library: that having fun helps me perform better.

Maybe that's all I need to do. Not worry about competing with George's strength, Clip's speed, and Jeremy's smarts; not think about winning or losing; not care about other people's opinions. I've made it all the way to the top four, and this is my chance to show the world that Sadie Chu is proud of everything about herself—even the part that loves to pretend she's in a fantasy world, fighting for justice. *Whatever comes next, I'll be ready for it*, I tell myself, feeling better.

Ten minutes later, we reach Larchmont and see people shouting and crying in the village square. We hop off the wagon and hurry toward them with Captain Redfern and his knights. The Keeper of Fortunes and Princess Errin, who rode over together on one horse, trail after us.

"What happened?" the captain demands. "Where did the dragon go? Tell us everything."

"It almost burned down a home!" an old lady shouts hysterically.

"It flew north." A tall red-haired man points to a river beyond the village. A stream of smoke rises from one of the cottages, which has a charred roof. "It must be on its way to the Desolate Peaks."

"I saved my children just in time," another man sobs, hugging two kids tightly.

Jeremy looks eagerly at them. "What did the dragon look like? That's important!"

"How can it be?" a woman asks, frowning. "What does that matter now? It nearly destroyed that family's house and now it's gone! Flown off somewhere!"

A short bearded man with dark skin, who introduces himself as Silas, speaks up. "The dragon was about fifty feet long," he tells Jeremy. "It was deep purple, with wings that made a curious whistling noise as it flew. The fire from its lungs was also dark purple."

"That's an Amaranthine Amberwing from the southern wilds of Pantaera," Jeremy says confidently. "If it wandered this far north, it must be escaping something. Maybe the orc wars, which have been tearing those lands apart for centuries. These dragons aren't usually violent, though. Why would it burn down a random home?"

The villagers, who were gaping in amazement at his knowledge, turn accusing stares on the tall red-haired man.

"I fired my crossbow at it," the man admits. "But I was

only trying to protect everyone! Also, do you know how much money those sparkling golden wings would fetch at market? No one in our village would ever go hungry again!"

Jeremy gasps. "Wait a sec. It had golden wings? Only the queen of the dragons is allowed to wear gold dust on her wings! It's how she marks herself as royal!"

"Then that must have been Lady Smolderheart, greatest of the dragons," the Keeper of Fortunes says in her low, deep voice. "She carries a Gem of Strength, but when I visited her in a dream to tell her about the prophecy of the child hero, she did not believe that a young human could ever be worthy of deserving the jewel."

"Surprise, surprise," George mutters.

"Even dragons doubt us," Clip grumbles.

Silas, the bearded man, speaks up again. "She dropped an egg at the edge of the river."

"Only *one*? Amaranthine Amberwings have been known to lay up to a dozen," Jeremy says thoughtfully. "I bet Lady Smolderheart lost this one by accident. She might be heading to the mountains to keep her eggs safe from the battles in the south."

"Oh no! It might come back for the egg, then!" the hysterical old woman cries. Her panic spreads to the other villagers, who all moan and wail. "And who knows how many houses it will burn this time?"

Captain Redfern shakes his head impatiently. "Stay calm. My warriors and I are here to help you. Right now, we just need someone to lead us to the egg."

Silas walks us to the river, which stretches to a forest on the other side. At the water's edge is an enormous egg lying on its side and giving off a ton of steam. It's about the size of a boulder, with a smooth purplish shell speckled with white.

"Why is it steaming like that?" I ask.

"Pantaera dragons keep their eggs hot to incubate them," Jeremy explains. "The babies find it comforting and it helps them grow and stay healthy. Be careful, sir!"

Captain Redfern yanks his hand back from the egg. "It's burning hot. But we've got to move it away from the village somehow, to keep the people safe when the dragon returns."

Realization dawns on George's face. "You mean get it to the other side of the river? Should we use those?" He points to three rowboats floating nearby.

Silas shakes his head. "The egg is too heavy. It will sink those boats, but we have tools and other items that might help." He points to a pile of ropes, wooden planks, and fishing nets.

The captain looks at the Keeper of Fortunes. "My lady, are you able to communicate with the dragon again? Tell her that we will move the egg across the water, so when she comes back for it, she will stay away from the villagers."

"I can try, but I must return to the castle right away," the Keeper answers.

"I'll take you on my horse," Princess Errin offers.

The old woman nods, then looks each of us in the eye. "Warriors, this is the first half of your Test of Strength. Each of you will be stationed at a different part of the river, and your job is to move this egg away from the village of Larchmont . . . without touching or breaking it. If you can do that safely, you will be in Lady Smolderheart's debt, and perhaps I can convince her that you are worthy of receiving the dragons' Gem of Strength after all. Good luck." She and Princess Errin hurry off together.

Jeremy and I exchange glances. The egg looks like it's heavier than either of us can lift. "Maybe it's lighter than it looks," I say weakly.

A hum of voices reaches our ears and we turn to see a large crowd of villagers spreading out along the river-bank. They whisper to each other, wringing their hands and staring at us.

"Looks like we've got an audience for this one," Clip mutters.

"Hey! There's the wizard!" I exclaim, grabbing my brother's arm.

Jeremy and George turn to look, too.

In the middle of the crowd, we see a tall pointy hat sticking straight up. The wizard is standing between a man with glasses and a tall, dark-skinned woman. Neither of them pays him any attention. He's looking around with a relaxed smile, like he's on vacation or something. As we watch, he takes a big bite out of a hot dog, getting a splotch of ketchup on his beard.

"Wow! They have hot dogs in Pantaera?" George asks, sounding like he wants one, too.

"You know, Captain Redfern had no idea who I was talking about when I mentioned the wizard to him," Jeremy says thoughtfully.

"He could have just been pretending," I suggest. "Maybe competitors are the only ones who are supposed to see the wizard."

"Wait a second. Doesn't that guy look familiar?" Clip points at the man in glasses to the left of the wizard. He has jet-black hair and a deep blue tunic, and even though he has a scarf hiding his face, he *does* look like someone I know. "And that lady . . ."

The crowd shifts, and I see that the tall lady next to the wizard is holding the leash of a dark gray dog with a happy wagging tail. They both look kind of familiar to me, too.

"I can't believe that dog isn't begging the wizard for his food. Tofu would be," I say to Clip. Our golden retriever, Tofu, is *obsessed* with hot dogs. But this dog doesn't seem to smell the wizard's snack or even *see* him, not even when the wizard reaches down to pet its head.

Come to think of it, not a single person notices the old man as he finishes his meal, catches our eye, and gives us a friendly wave. We wave back at him.

I poke Jeremy. "See that lady and her dog? Don't they look like—"

"Focus on me, please!" Captain Redfern interrupts, snapping his fingers for our attention. He's holding out a wooden quiver with four arrows. "Each of you take one of these. The length of your arrow decides what position you'll be in. Whoever gets the shortest arrow will go first, and so on." We do as he instructs, and Jeremy gulps when he sees that his arrow is shorter than any of ours. He'll tackle the egg first, then Clip, then me, and then George last.

"Clip, Sadie, and George, my knights will row you to

your stations and explain your tasks," Captain Redfern says, as three grown-ups climb into the boats. "Jeremy, you stay with me while we figure out how to get this egg going. Any last questions before we start?"

We shake our heads. Clip looks pale and George seems anxious, too. I'm glad Jeremy and I aren't the only ones who are nervous about this challenge.

I hop into a rowboat with a knight who introduces herself as Evelyn. She gives me a reassuring smile and says, "I'm glad a girl is still in the running! You're going to do great."

"Thanks," I say weakly. "I hope so. I'm not very strong."

She waves my comment away. "There's more than one kind of strength."

Several feet away, I watch Clip climb out of his boat and onto a small wooden dock on the river. He picks up a big fishing net and stares at a dozen giant logs floating in the water, and I realize what he has to do: After Jeremy gets the egg to him, Clip will have to trap the egg in his net and move it across those logs. I swallow hard. Hopefully my task won't be as tricky.

Evelyn pulls up to the next dock, which is about twenty feet from Clip's. My dock has some kind of machine that's four feet tall, with a wide wooden shelf attached to a long, sturdy neck. It looks like those cherry pickers that electrical workers use to fix cables up high. I run my hand over the shelf with a sinking feeling. This reminds me *way* too much of a catapult.

"You ever use a trebuchet before?" Evelyn asks, watching me.

"A treb what?"

"A trebuchet," she repeats. "Treb-yoo-shay."

I shake my head, feeling queasy. The machine is on a round platform that can swivel from side to side and be

aimed in any direction. It also has a big hand crank, and when I turn it, the neck lowers until the shelf lies flat on the dock. "Oh, okay," I say, chewing on my lip as I think. "So I try to roll the egg onto this shelf somehow. And then what?"

Evelyn doesn't say anything; she probably isn't supposed to help me.

I notice a button under the hand crank. I push it and the neck of the trebuchet snaps up with a loud *crack*! If the egg had been on the shelf, it would have been flung right over the water toward George. Stretched across his dock, I see a big, soft-looking net, ready to catch the egg. That's my task: to aim the machine right at that net and launch the dragon's egg safely over there. "No sweat, right?" I joke, feeling queasier than ever.

"The Test of Strength has begun," Evelyn says.

I look back at the riverbank, where Jeremy is holding two planks of wood and using them to maneuver the egg

across a short bridge. He seems to be struggling a little, as though the bridge has holes he needs to avoid or bumps he has to carefully move the egg over.

"You can do it, Jer!" I call, as Clip and George shout their support, too. "So this is a kind of relay race. We have to work together to get the egg safely across the river."

Evelyn nods. "Exactly."

I hold my breath as Jeremy continues to struggle. It's not that the egg seems *heavy*—in fact, I see it bounce a little, which means it doesn't weigh as much as it looks. What's tough is that the surface is round and smooth, making it hard for Jer to grip it with the planks of wood.

I don't know what I want more: for Jer to hurry up, succeed, and pass the egg on to Clip, or to slow down so it'll take longer for the egg to get to me.

My stomach churns as I kneel down to study my mini cherry picker. Evelyn called it a treb . . . a trebu . . . some French word. Jeremy would know. I see a small pile of stones next to the machine, which must be for practice. Quickly, I turn the hand crank to lower the neck back down and place a stone onto the shelf. I try to aim at George's net, and then I push the button.

FFFFFFLPTTTTTT!

The neck of the machine snaps up into the air, propelling the stone about a foot too far left from George's net. I gulp and try again after I adjust the aim. Finally, after a few tries, I've got what I *think* is the perfect angle. I turn the hand crank, lowering the shelf all the way down to the dock again so it's ready to receive the egg.

I hear a shout of triumph and turn to see Clip receiving the egg from Jeremy. "Nice job, Jer!" I scream, and watch as my brother swings his net like a cowboy lassoing a pony. After a few attempts, he whoops with triumph as the egg gets snagged. He gingerly steps onto the floating logs, which bob under his weight, and slowly tugs the egg along, trying not to fall.

"Go, Clip!" I cheer. I'm *so* glad I didn't get his task, because I would have had a hard time keeping my balance. Clip makes it look easy, though, moving with grace and speed. I hate to admit it, but sometimes I can see a good reason for my brother's bigheadedness.

In pretty much no time at all (and with a few scary moments where he almost fell or dropped the egg) he's rolling it onto my dock, panting and sweaty. "Go for it, Sadie!"

Here it is. The moment of truth.

"You can do this, Sadie," Evelyn says encouragingly from the rowboat.

I exhale. Mom always says that if something feels too tough or overwhelming for me, I should break it down into steps. "Step one: Remove the egg from the net," I say, and it's harder than it looks because Clip *really* got the egg tight in there. I have to fiddle with it carefully so that 1) I don't touch the egg, 2) the egg doesn't roll off my dock, and 3) there's still enough net beneath the egg so I can drag it onto the cherry picker shelf.

What makes it worse is knowing how many people are watching, from Evelyn and the captain to the other kids and knights and the crowd of villagers on the riverbank. I wonder if the wizard is still there. *Enjoy the task and have fun*, I remind myself, trying to think of this as a game. Finally, I manage to drag the egg onto the wide wooden shelf, breathing hard at the effort.

"Step two: Secure the egg," I mutter, making sure it's safe in the middle of the shelf.

Simple pimple, right?

I wipe sweat off my face. "Step three: Launch the egg across twenty feet of water and into the goal," I say, looking at the expanse of river between my dock and George's. I try not to imagine what will happen if the egg drowns instead. "Here goes nothing."

I press the big button.

FFFFFFLPTTTTTT!

The neck of the cherry picker flies upward, flinging the egg into George's cheesecloth net. It lands safe and sound. "Got it, Sadie!" George yells, waving.

"Oh my god," I say faintly. "I did it. I used a treb . . . yoo . . ."

Evelyn grins. "Trebuchet. Nice job!"

George's task is similar to the one Jeremy had, except he's got two bowl-shaped objects to lift the egg across a path of flat stones. Luckily, he's just as graceful as Clip and manages to move it onto the opposite riverbank, where he rolls it carefully away from the water and onto a patch of grass. The villagers erupt into cheers and applause, and I hear the dog barking excitedly.

Evelyn rows me over to George, where we're joined by Clip and Jeremy, and we all do a relieved group hug, all laughing and talking at once.

"Did you see how close I got to dropping that stupid thing?" Clip yells.

"I almost wiped out five times!" George exclaims.

"I was terrified that cherry picker was gonna launch the egg right in the water!" I add.

"I was nervous about everyone watching me, but I haven't given up once in Pantaera and I wasn't about to start now!" Jeremy says cheerfully.

I hug him again. "That's the spirit, Jer!"

The knights row back to the village, then return with the captain and a bunch of supplies.

George points at the tents and sleeping bags. "Are we camping out or something, sir?"

"We are," Captain Redfern says. "We have to stay and make sure the egg is safe until the dragon comes back.

If anyone steals it, she might blame the villagers and get angry at them."

"People steal dragon eggs?" Clip asks.

"Bad people in Pantaera raise dragons and make them fight for money, like evil humans do in our world with dogs. It makes the dragons scared and aggressive, even though they don't want to be." Jeremy sounds sad, and I know he's thinking about Chickpea. It hurts his feelings when people avoid her at the park because they think all pit bulls are mean and scary.

I put an arm around him. "Chickpea's the nicest dog I ever met, besides my own dog."

"Chickpea's the *nicest* dog," Clip agrees. "People suck."

"And I'm glad we're going to protect this dragon," George adds.

Jeremy brightens. "Me too. Camping out here tonight will be fun!"

I shrug. "Let's go pitch these tents, I guess!"

CHAPTER TWENTY-THREE
JEREMY

"THIS IS PERFECT," I SAY HAPPILY, AS WE SIT IN front of the fire after dinner. "The only way it could get *more* perfect is if we had Hershey's chocolate and graham crackers."

"Don't forget giant marshmallows, Jer!" Sadie reminds me.

I rub my stomach, even though we've just eaten our weight in cheese sandwiches and roast turkey. The knights brought a boatload of food but didn't include s'mores—since those don't exist in Pantaera. "S'mores will be the first thing I eat when I get home," I decide. "I'll have you guys over to roast them in my dad's firepit. You're invited, too, George!"

"I'll fly in from Philly just for the occasion," George promises.

The makeshift campground is peaceful. The captain and his knights are sitting nearby, talking quietly. Earlier, we pitched four tents near the river's edge: two for the captain and his knights, one for Clip and George and me to share, and a tiny one that Sadie gets to herself.

I glance at the dragon's egg, which is keeping warm by the fire. That's the reason I can't *completely* relax, knowing the mama dragon could be coming back at any time.

Clip follows my gaze. "You think she'll be back tonight?"

"Maybe," I say. "Amaranthine Amberwings are very protective of their eggs. I just hope Lady Smolderheart knows we're keeping her baby safe and not hurting it or anything."

"I'm sure she knows, Jer," George reassures me. He pats his stomach. "That turkey was good. But ever since we saw the wizard today, I've been wanting a hot dog with extra ketchup."

"Oh yeah, I've been craving one, too," Clip says.

"I still think it's weird how the dog didn't even notice him," Sadie says thoughtfully.

Her brother nods. "Tofu would have smelled that hot dog a mile away. The wizard's robes would have been like a towel on beach day. Soaked with drool!"

"Gross!" George says, laughing.

"It's true, though," Sadie says. "At home, Tofu could

be watching a movie with Clip and me in the basement. And Dad could be in his bedroom, two floors up, and he wouldn't be able to open a bag of popcorn without Tofu knowing."

"Tofu *does* love popcorn," Clip agrees.

"And the dog didn't even notice when the wizard petted it," George adds. "I get why Captain Redfern and the villagers pretend not to see or know about him, if contestants are the only ones who are supposed to. It makes sense. But dogs can't pretend like that."

Jeremy nods. "I kept thinking that dog looked like Chickpea. It was too far away to tell, but if it *was* her, we trained her to have good manners and not beg for human food. She would at least have been staring at the wizard and watching him eat, though."

"Exactly," Sadie says. "It's weird. Almost like he didn't exist."

"But that's impossible . . . right?" George asks.

We sit for a moment in silence, thinking. And then Clip stretches his arms, yawns loudly, and says, "I hope we get to sleep before our next task."

Captain Redfern overhears him. "Get some rest, everyone. I'll watch over the egg."

We get up, grateful, and Clip glances at Sadie. "Are you going to be okay alone?"

"Oh yeah, I'll be fine," she says. "I'll scream if the dragon tries to take me away."

"Don't even joke about that!" I say anxiously. "You don't want to be captured by an Amberwing. They're not violent, but they don't look on humans with a friendly eye."

Within fifteen minutes, everyone is cozy in their sleeping bags. Usually, it takes forever to fall asleep because we're busy talking about everything that's happened. But tonight, we're all so tired that the second we climb into our warm cocoons, everyone is down for the count.

I feel like I've barely fallen asleep before someone roughly shakes me awake. "Get up right away! Come out of the tent!" a man says in a harsh voice.

I blink my bleary eyes and see Clip's and George's confused faces as two tall figures move across our tent. "Captain Redfern?" I ask. "Is that you?"

"Be quiet!" one of the men barks.

I'm alert at once. That didn't sound like the captain, and now that I look closely at the figures, they don't *look* like him, either. They're slender and dressed in light silver cloaks. One of them practically throws Clip out of the tent, followed by George and me. I'm surprised to see a pale light in the sky, which means we've been sleeping for five or six hours. On the ground in front of the dead fire are Captain Redfern and Sadie, their hands bound tightly with rope.

"Sadie! Are you okay?" Clip asks, panicking.

"Silence!" one of our captors growls, as they tie us up and throw us beside her. "You are now the prisoners of the King of Elvenhame! And it will be our honor to bring you before him."

"The King of Elvenhame?" I screech. "The legendary dark elf of Pantaera?"

They freeze. They look almost identical, with white skin, ice-blue eyes, and silver hair. The only difference is that one is a head taller than the other, and he's wearing a fancy tiara with a single large diamond in the center.

"You know of His Majesty?" the shorter elf asks me in disbelief.

"Of course!" I exclaim. "He and his followers betrayed the High Elf King after the Elven Rebellion of 1111. They created a new kingdom, called Elvenhame, deep in the Forgetful Forests. And they joined evil orcs and warlocks to try to take over the Kingdom of Celadon."

The elves' jaws drop.

I keep going, because I'm like a faucet when it comes to *War of Gods and Men*. You turn the handle, and it all comes gushing out. "The King of Elvenhame is also famous for creating a fashionable silver dye that doubles as a poison. It comes from the edelmeyer plant, which only grows during warm winters. That's how he killed all of his enemies at a birthday feast."

Despite our dire situation, Sadie grins at how shocked the elves look.

"So!" Captain Redfern says angrily. "Your false king is going *against* the forces of good. And now you've captured my warriors and me to bring back as trophies? Some wise ruler you have! Arrogant and weak, with no integrity whatsoever!"

"Hush your disrespectful mouth or I will shut it for you!" the tall, crowned elf says furiously. "Man or elf, no one is allowed to speak of my father that way!"

I gasp. "Father? You're the king's son?"

"Yes. I am Prince Endymion of Elvenhame," he says in a haughty voice, looking us all up and down. "And *you* are the child warriors from another world. As soon as I heard of the prophecy of the Pantaereon, I was curious to see you. You don't look like much, do you?"

Clip rolls his eyes. "Why did you tie us up, then?"

"Yeah!" George says. "Why did you? It's like you're afraid of us or something."

"Afraid?" Prince Endymion scoffs. "Of a bunch of babies? The Keeper of Fortunes is a silly old bird if she thinks you can stand against me, let alone save Pantaera from war. But then again, stranger prophecies have come true and my father can't take any chances. How proud he will be when I drag you four back to him! Dead or alive . . . I suppose it doesn't matter."

"No! You'll have to take me first!" Captain Redfern yells, struggling against his ropes.

But the shorter elf is gazing at Clip, George, Sadie, and me with an odd, almost guilty expression. "We are to bring your father any prisoners of war alive and unhurt, Endymion. Let's just put them in the wagon and go." He sighs. "Truth be told, this feels wrong to me. Taking the captain hostage is one thing, but these innocent children, too?"

Doubt crosses Prince Endymion's face, but it disappears quickly. "You and your soft heart, Lysandan. We just have to do it. Think of the riches His Majesty will pour upon you! And I will finally be the true heir to Elvenhame, favored above all of my brothers and sisters for the throne, when we bring my father the child hero!"

Lysandan paces in front of us. "That's why I hesitate. If one of these children has such a great destiny, it's not our place to stop them from fulfilling it. The prophecy—"

"—is a fairy tale, that's all." Endymion sneers, but there's uncertainty in his expression again. "But we have to make sure it doesn't come true, just the same. These babies' so-called destiny is to stop the war . . . a war that would give my father even more power than he has now. The Forgotten Queen promised it would."

"You know we can't trust her promises," Lysandan says flatly. "And you don't want war any more than I do. You're different from your father, no matter what you say. If the Forgotten Queen seizes Pantaera, do you think she'll recognize his right to rule? Or yours? No. She would take Elvenhame for her own. She would burn the forests down!"

Endymion is quiet for a long moment. "You don't know that for certain."

"We need to discuss this further," Lysandan insists, and they move away, still arguing.

That's when I notice that the dragon's egg is gone. "Captain Redfern!" I say urgently.

"Hush, Jeremy," the captain says in a low voice. "The elves didn't notice the egg. My knights hid it in those trees over there, safe and sound." He struggles, trying to loosen the ropes around his wrists, but they're too tight. "Those elves seem unsure about capturing us."

George nods. "They're chickening out."

"I think maybe their plan *sounded* good," Sadie agrees, "but the reality of it is too much."

Captain Redfern looks around at each of us. "Perhaps,"

he says significantly, "they can be persuaded to set us free. That shorter elf, Lysandan, seems like he could be swayed."

"And that prince guy doesn't seem too sure about kidnapping us, either," Clip adds.

"Let's try!" I declare. "Let's get them to see the error of their ways!"

"After all, you are undergoing the Test of Strength, and strength isn't just about physical might. It can also mean winning over others with the argument of good." The captain gives a decisive nod. "It will take all of you to make this work. I want you to reason with those elves and tell them not to go through with this!"

My chest swells with confidence. Even though evil elves are trying to capture us, and we have to save not just ourselves, but all of Pantaera, from darkness . . . I don't feel nervous. I feel *ready*. The wizard told me to keep the fire burning inside of me, and that's what I plan to do. "Excuse me!" I call to the bickering elves. "Can you guys come back, please?"

They approach us, looking wary.

"So, uh, listen," I say. "It sounds like you two don't want war. I bet you were pressured into pretending you do. Prince Endymion, maybe your dad's dangling the throne in front of you to get you to do his dirty work.

And, Lysandan, maybe he threatened your family or something. But it doesn't have to be like this. You don't have to make this choice. You don't have to fit into how other people want to define you. I know all about that."

The elves are silent.

"I came to Pantaera thinking I wasn't warrior material," I go on. "Mostly because heroes tend to look a certain way and, like, are strong and stuff. But then I survived an orc castle, a sirens' marsh, and a vampire maze, and I never gave up. I kept going because it was the right thing to do, and I want to keep doing the right thing, no matter how hard it is."

"What does this have to do with us?" Prince Endymion asks gruffly.

I take a deep breath. "Gandalf the Grey once said that we decide what to do with the time we have. I choose to fight for good with my time. Will *you* decide to let me?"

The prince's eyes shine with tears. He doesn't speak for a long moment. "So young, and yet so full of honesty and courage," he whispers. "Do you truly mean all of that?"

I look him right in the eye. "I do."

Without warning, he whips out a long, sharp silver dagger from his belt.

"Whoa, whoa, whoa! Back it up!" Clip yells.

"Put that away!" George shouts.

"I'm not going to hurt you," the elf prince says calmly, looking at me. "I'm going to set you free. That is, if you promise that you *will* fight for good."

I stare back at him, hardly daring to breathe. "I promise. You have my word."

"Your Highness, are you sure about this?" Lysandan asks quietly.

"No, I'm not," Prince Endymion admits. "But our king . . . my *father* wants the opposite of everything I stand for. Perhaps it's time I realized that." He kneels down and cuts my ropes, freeing my hands.

"Thank you," I tell him. "You are a true prince. Will you let my friends go, too?"

"Let's hear what they have to say first," he replies.

Sadie speaks up. "I didn't think I was warrior material, either. I was ashamed to be here and I worried what kids at school would think about me pretending." She pauses. "But I'm not pretending anymore. I *am* a warrior. And all the things we've been tested for, like being brave and smart and determined . . . I know I have all of that now. That's who I am. And if that makes me a geek, then I'm glad, 'cause I get to be like my best friend, Jeremy."

As soon as Prince Endymion frees Sadie, I hug her. She's grown so much since we came on this show, and she's finally learned that she's as awesome as I think she is.

"I'm a warrior, too!" George bursts out. "Uh, I don't live in Pantaera. But I still came to fight for you guys and everyone else who lives here. Because like Jeremy said, it's the right thing to do. So, um . . . yeah. Please let me go so I can keep helping you. Cool?"

The elves don't look convinced. They turn their attention to Clip, who looks flustered.

"I'm, like, a total warrior," Clip says, looking around frantically like he's searching for a teleprompter to feed him a speech. "And, like, I want to fight for good, too. And for everyone who lives here. I have to do the right thing, or whatever. Um, I don't live in Pantaera, but . . ." He stops when he realizes he's saying pretty much everything George just said.

Sadie covers her eyes and shakes her head.

"Oh! I thought of something else I wanna say!" George says. "Every one of us is a hero. Every person who entered this competition, even though they were nervous or scared. So I'm also here to support my teammates, 'cause that's what they are. Teammates, not rivals. We fight together and I'm proud to be with them, no matter who ends up being the child hero."

The elf prince bends down and sets him free.

Clip lets out a long breath. He knows he just lost the competition. "Well, that's that," he says, shrugging and smiling. "Awesome speeches, you guys." It looks as though Sadie isn't the only Chu who's grown a ton on this show. The minute Clip's ropes are cut, he shakes George's hand and hugs Sadie and me. "Congrats. You all deserve to keep going."

"I'm sorry, Clip," I say sadly, as Sadie wails, "I don't want you to go!"

But he only laughs. "Don't worry. I did my best! I'm bummed to lose that trip to LA, but I'm happy for whichever one of you gets to go."

"You're a hero through and through, Chu," George tells him. "And we're gonna keep hanging out. We'll play *War of Gods and Men* online. That's a promise."

"Oh, and by the way, when we get home? I'm gonna make us do a movie marathon so you learn how to make a *good* epic fantasy speech," I add, and Clip gives me a sheepish grin.

"This isn't right," Sadie says, upset. "You should be going to the final task, too."

Clip waves her words away. "Nah. You're the one who showed up and did the work. You and Jer and George. So you go and represent Team Chu, sis!"

Captain Redfern, who has also been freed, looks at the

elves. "Thank you for doing the right thing. It is noble of you to help these young people stop the war."

"It truly is noble!" I declare. "And the books, stories, and songs will remember you."

A giggle escapes Lysandan, but he quickly recovers. "I suppose we ought to forget this ever happened," he says. "We will return to our king and not mention any of this."

Prince Endymion takes off his silver tiara. "This diamond is a Gem of Strength, bestowed upon the elves long ago. I have been its bearer all these long years, but now I think it should go to someone who is more worthy of it." He plucks off the sparkling jewel in the center and holds it out to me, and I'm so shocked, I can't even move. Sadie and Clip have to push me forward and lift my hand for me so the prince can drop the diamond in it. He smiles at George, Sadie, and me. "Continue your journey. With the three of you fighting for Pantaera, I will dare to hope for peace. Goodbye, and good luck."

We watch as they vanish into the forest, and then I look down at the beautiful gem in my palm. It's cool and heavy against my skin, and as clear as water.

"You go, Jeremy!" Clip exclaims.

"Another gem for the gem *master*!" George shouts, as Sadie gives me a jellyfish fist bump.

Captain Redfern surveys us with fierce pride. "You

have proved your heroism to me. All *four* of you. It is time to go: Clip to his own world, and you three back to Winterhearth House."

"Will your knights stay with the dragon egg, sir?" I ask anxiously.

He nods. "They will, Jeremy. They'll see it safely returned to its mother."

When we row back to the other side of the river, the villagers cheer and thank us for protecting their homes. The Keeper of Fortunes is waiting by our wagon with the brass shield. Her ancient face creases into a bright smile at the sight of us and the diamond I'm holding. "My young heroes," she says warmly. "I told Lady Smolderheart of your great deed in relocating the precious egg that she lost and will return to claim. She is astonished by your strength in doing so safely . . . and she is grateful, too. Here is the Gem of Strength that she has carried ever since it was gifted long ago to the dragons. She asked me to pass it on to you." She holds up a diamond that's identical to the one in my hand.

Clip nods at George and Sadie. "This one's definitely for you two!"

"Why just us?" George protests. "We all worked as a team on that relay race."

"Yeah! Clip did a really good job, too!" Sadie tells the

Keeper of Fortunes. "Can't he help George and me put the diamond on the shield?"

The old woman laughs. "I was hoping all four of you would do the honors together."

"Here, George!" I say happily, holding out my jewel. "You can help me put the elves' gem on, and Clip and Sadie can add the dragons' gem together."

The Chu siblings carry their diamond over to the brass shield together and snap it in place, and George and I do the same with our jewel. We stand back, admiring our work. Ten glittering gemstones, all representing the courage, determination, humility, intelligence, and strength we've shown this week.

"You four have accomplished so much in your short time here," says the Keeper. "Only the final challenge remains now, and tomorrow, our three remaining competitors will prove their right to claim the title of child hero." She turns to Clip. "We wish you a safe journey. Thank you for all you've done for Pantaera."

"Thank *you*, my lady." Clip bows to her, as a knight approaches, leading a cinnamon-colored horse. "Guess that's my ride back. One last trip for old times' sake, eh, Teddy Bear?"

Teddy Bear gives a loud snuffle in response.

"Yes, thank you, Clip," Captain Redfern says. "Pantaera will never forget you."

"Thank you, sir. And good luck, you guys! See you on the other side!" Clip climbs into the saddle with the help of the knight, and with one last wave, they ride off into the distance.

"He wanted to win so bad," Sadie says, sighing. "But I'm glad *we're* still here."

I grin from ear to ear. "Can you believe it? Us in the finals!"

"I believe it," George says, slinging his arms over both of us. "You two have proved what I've said all along: Heroes aren't just big, muscly guys with swords. They're people like you."

"They're people like you, too!" Sadie tells him.

"I'm glad it's the three of us," I add contentedly.

We climb back on the wagon, heading back to Winterhearth House for some good food, long hot showers, and lots of sleep . . . before whatever faces us next.

CHAPTER TWENTY-FOUR

SADIE

"I DIDN'T KNOW THEY HAD WAFFLES IN PANTAERA," George says at breakfast the next morning.

"Well, we *did* see the wizard eating a hot dog," Jeremy points out.

"That's true."

The table in the common room looks enormous now that there's only George, Jeremy, and me eating there. Kathryne lays down golden-brown waffles with butter and maple syrup, fried ham, and a pitcher of fresh-squeezed orange juice before going back into the kitchen to cut some fresh fruit for us.

"I feel like they're feeding us *especially* well today, and giving us all the food we like. I wonder why," I say suspiciously.

George pretends to look terrified. "Maybe this will be

our last meal ever! They don't think we'll survive our final challenge: fighting a balrog!"

"First of all," Jeremy says brightly, pouring syrup over his waffles, "balrogs belong to the Lord of the Rings and there's gotta be some kind of copyright on them. Second of all, I'm pretty sure we won't be fighting demons of the old world for our last test."

I pour myself some orange juice. "But what, then? The captain didn't give us a single hint about what we're doing today. He was so secretive when we asked him."

"He probably just doesn't want us to know too much," George says, his mouth full of ham. "You guys know what's weird, though? I don't feel nervous at all."

"Me, neither," Jeremy says, looking surprised. "Like I told those elves yesterday, I didn't think I would make it this far. So if this is where my journey ends, and one of you becomes the child hero, I'm cool with that. You know what I mean?"

George nods. "I know what you mean. I'd feel the same way about you or Sadie winning. No matter what, the champion is going to be the best hero Pantaera's ever seen."

"Agreed! We should just have fun today," I say. The boys cheer and we clink our glasses of orange juice together. "I have a feeling the final challenge will be a little of everything we've done so far. Solving puzzles, putting things together, and going through a maze or an obstacle course. That's my guess anyway."

"I think so, too, Sadie," Jeremy agrees. "They might test our courage and strength and all of those virtues again, to make sure whoever's the child hero *definitely* has them."

George looks around at the empty chairs. "It'll be fun, but I wish the others were still here, too. It would be nice if all ten of us did the last challenge together."

I nod. I miss Clip, even though he's only been gone for one night. But I know he'll be watching and cheering me on somewhere with Mom, Dad, Grandpa, and Grandma.

After breakfast, we go outside to meet Captain Redfern and his knights, who are waiting with our horses. "Today, we are headed to the fields and woods behind the Castle of the North Wind," he tells us. "You will need your horses for the first task, so climb on and let's go."

We do as he asks and start riding. I'm so busy thinking about what our task might be that I don't even notice that Captain Redfern has led us on a detour through town until sudden loud cheering makes me jump. A huge crowd starts whooping, hollering, and waving at us the second we come into view. Some of them bellow, "Jere-MY!

Jere-MY!" while others yell, "Go, Sadie; Go, Sadie; GO!" and another group chants, "George is the MAN! George is the MAN!"

George, Jeremy, and I burst into laughter.

"This is amazing!" Jeremy shouts.

The townspeople believe in us. They *believe* in us.

Grinning, Captain Redfern looks over his shoulder to see our reactions.

I scan the crowd eagerly, feeling sure that the two Larchmont villagers and the dog who caught my eye yesterday were Red Nguyen, Jeremy's mom, and his dog, Chickpea. Our families were probably all there in disguise and I'm sure they're here today, too, to watch the final task. Among the many happy faces, I spy three familiar ones: a tall gray-haired woman, a shorter blond woman, and a thin, feathery-haired boy.

Jeremy sees them, too. "Sadie, look! It's the Blackwoods!"

We wave, and they wave back. Mardella and her sister, Luellen, created the laser tag game that got us on this show, and Mardella's son, Tom, became our friend over the summer. They're part of the reason we get to be in Pantaera, and I feel a rush of gladness that they're here, too.

The producers must have hired more extras, because the teeming crowd spreads all the way up to the castle. The drawbridge is packed with fans cheering like we've brought home the World Cup (if they *had* a World Cup in Pantaera). It's like we've already won the whole show.

Jeremy wipes away happy tears, and George and I beam at each other.

King Rothbart and Princess Errin are there, too, cheering and waving. And then Captain Redfern leads us to the back of the castle, where we get our first glimpse of what lies ahead: an obstacle course in a large open field, which reminds me of our first day in Pantaera. I see knights waiting for us in the course with jousting poles, bows, and arrows.

"Hey!" George cries, pointing. "Look, it's Lizard!"

"And Molly and Kris!" Jeremy adds.

All three girls jump up and down at the sight of us, and I wave frantically at them. They wave back at me with just as much excitement, especially Molly, who gives me two thumbs-up and mouths, *You got this, Sadie!* I give my new friend two thumbs-up right back.

Captain Redfern signals for us to stop. "Today, the three of you will undergo a series of mini-challenges that will again test the five qualities you've shown during the competition," he explains, and George, Jeremy, and I exchange excited glances. We guessed right! "The first mini-challenge you will face is the Test of

Determination. Lizard, Molly, and Kris are going to demonstrate what you have to do. Watch them closely."

The girls mount their horses, and each takes a jousting pole. Lizard points to the tip of hers, which is sharper than the other end, and then the three of them leap into action.

The obstacle course has three entrances. Each rider plunges down her own lane, swerving and jumping over bales of hay placed as roadblocks. Even though they're just showing us what to do, George and Jeremy and I scream and cheer like they're competing for real. The girls are not only avoiding obstacles, but also dodging arrows fired from machines hidden throughout the hay. One arrow bounces harmlessly off Molly's back, leaving a splotch of red paint on her tunic.

Jeremy gasps. "Whoa! It's like playing paintball!"

As we watch, Lizard deftly avoids an arrow and spears something on the ground with her jousting pole. She lifts it, showing us a piece of paper attached to the pointy end, and then the three of them finish the course and pull their horses off to one side.

"As you all saw," Captain Redfern says, "the object is to avoid obstacles and arrows, find the instructions for your next mini-challenge, and make it to the other side. If you get hit with a painted arrow three times, you will have to start the obstacle course over again. Understood?"

"Yes, sir!" we shout, lining up at the entrance to the course.

"On your mark, get set, go!" Captain Redfern calls.

I tear down my lane, with George and Jeremy on either side of me. I direct Sugarplum, my horse, around three hay bales as the painted arrows start to fly. One whizzes over my head and I duck. They're harmless, but I don't want to get splattered with paint and have to start over.

The task is tougher than it looks because our focus gets pulled every which way: There's the cheering from the three girls, the captain, and knights; there are the arrows flying out from all directions; there are the hay bales blocking our path; and then we also have to hold on tightly to our jousting poles *and* look for the paper with our instructions.

I tighten my hands on the reins as Sugarplum jumps over a hay bale. Something cold and wet slicks across the back of my neck. "Ugh! I got hit!" I groan. My exit is twenty feet away, but I haven't found my instructions yet. I'm starting to worry about having to go back when I see them tucked against a hay bale. I aim my jousting pole and spear the paper neatly, right as a second arrow smacks me on the leg. One more arrow and I'll have to start over.

On my right, Jeremy screeches as he avoids a rain of three paint-dipped arrows.

"Okay, Sugarplum," I say. "As Clip would say: time to go big or go home!"

I dig my heels into my horse's sides, urging her into a canter, and duck low as we plunge through the exit to safety. Lizard, Kris, and Molly dance and cheer as I cross the finish line.

"I made it!" I say in disbelief. "I'm done with the first mini-challenge!"

CHAPTER TWENTY-FIVE
JEREMY

SADIE FINISHES THE OBSTACLE COURSE FIRST, AND then George is done a minute later. I try not to panic. My horse, Pinocchio, and I have been going super slow because I don't want to get hit by any arrows. We just passed through a section where they were raining down, but when I do a quick scan of my body, I realize that none of them got me!

"Phew!" I say, gripping my jousting pole with the instructions attached to it. I got lucky and found them near the start, but it's been tricky to hold on to them while riding, swerving, and jumping, not to mention my hand is gross and slippery with sweat. Finally, I make it to the exit.

"Yeah! Goooo, Jeremy!" Lizard, Kris, and Molly shout.

A knight helps me off my horse. "Read your instructions before your next mini-challenge, which will be the Test of Strength," he advises me.

"Oh no," I mumble. Getting that dragon egg across the river was hard enough, and now I'm going to be tested on strength *again*. But I'm in too deep now. I didn't make it this far just to make it this far, and—most important of all—Pantaera needs me.

My instructions turn out to be in the form of a poem:

> *In times of great need, a hero appears*
> *To fight for what's right, in spite of their fears*
> *The Cairn of Destiny tests your power*
> *You've only a quarter of an hour*
> *To climb to the top and prove your might*
> *Be wary of paths: Some are wrong, some right*
> *More instructions await you at the peak*
> *So hurry! A way down is what you seek.*

That's when I notice the mountain in front of me. Well, it's more like a very tall, steep hill made of big gray rocks. "That's it. The Cairn of Destiny," I say weakly, shading my eyes to look at the top. It must be about sixty feet above the ground. I don't see stairs or an elevator, so there's only one way to reach the peak and fifteen minutes to do it, according to the poem.

There's no time to hesitate.

I hurry toward the base of the cairn and start climbing. The rocks slip and slide under my feet, making it tricky to keep my balance. Some spots are so steep, I have to use my hands to pull myself higher. Within three minutes, I'm already sweating buckets. There are red flags here and there to mark different paths that we can take. I come to a fork where one route skirts low around the side of the cairn, while the other leads straight up, with a knotted rope dangling down.

"I think I know which one I like better," I say, heading for the lower path.

But right at that second, George is jogging back up it toward me. "No good," he pants. "That one's a dead end, Jer. It leads to the bottom."

My heart sinks. "Okay, thanks. Have you seen Sadie?"

George points up. "She's way ahead of me," he says, then grabs the knotted rope and heaves himself up. He makes it look so easy. When he reaches the next level of the cairn, he waves at me and disappears, and it's my turn to grab the rope.

I'm getting flashbacks of gym class and the other kids laughing at me again.

And then a stone clatters down near my feet.

I look up, thinking maybe George stayed to make sure I'm okay, but it's not him. It's the old wizard, his face crinkled in a smile. In his arms is a big, shiny black cat with bright amber eyes—Tuba! The wizard winks at me, then turns and leaves without saying a word. He doesn't need to. Seeing him is reminder enough to keep that fire burning inside me.

"Because that's what heroes do!" I declare.

I wipe my sweaty palms on my pants. And then I push my embarrassing memories of gym class far away, grab the rope again, and climb.

What's weird is it doesn't feel *that* hard. The knots give my hands a good place to hold on to while my feet scrabble up the rocks. "One knot at a time," I whisper, trying not to worry about going too slow or wonder what will happen if I don't reach the peak within fifteen minutes. After all, I climbed the wall at Hollybottom, and if I did that, I can do this, too.

My muscles shake as I reach the top and swing my leg onto the next level. I did it!

"Arrrrrrrgggghhhhhhh!" shrieks an orc with purplish-gray skin and bulging yellow eyes.

"Oh nooooo!" I moan, stumbling to my feet as the orc chases me.

I run up the winding path, which splits into three branches. Two are less steep and the third is another vertical climb, but this time, it's up a rope ladder. "What do I do?" I mutter, trying not to panic. If I pick a dead end, the orc will catch me. But the only path I'm *sure* isn't a dead end is that rope ladder, because I can see it going directly to the next level up.

There's no more time to think.

I throw myself onto the ladder. Even though it's a *tiny* bit easier than the knotted rope, it's still tricky because it swings back and forth as I climb. The orc stands at the foot of the ladder, growling at me, but it doesn't try to follow. I guess it hates climbing, too. "Here we go," I pant as I reach the top. My whole body is shaking so hard at this point that it's hard to stand, and I give myself a few precious seconds to lean against the wall of stones and catch my breath. I don't see any enemies here, thank goodness.

Suddenly, a rain of pebbles falls over me. I yelp, cover my head, and run up the path, not waiting to see if another orc or some other bad guy caused it. It turns out this walkway leads right to *another* knotted rope going straight up, and it's *twice* as long as the first.

"Whyyyyyyyy!" I scream, shaking my fists at the sky. I know this is the Test of Strength, but my muscles and I would like to file a complaint.

But I've made it this far. And I know the wizard and Tuba are rooting for me, and so are my friends, and Captain Redfern, and the Keeper of Fortunes. Lots of people believe in me. I need to push through to the end. I grab the rope with a groan and focus on moving my hands up one knot at a time, making my slow, painstaking way up the side of the hill.

"Keep going, Jeremy!" someone says. I see two knights stationed at the top, watching as I struggle. "You've got this! Come on, you're doing great! Almost there!"

And then, amazingly . . . I'm *there*, collapsed at their feet.

They help me up, asking, "Are you okay?"

"If there aren't any more ropes to climb, then yeah, I'm great," I say weakly.

The knights crack up. "No more ropes to climb, we promise," one of them says with a grin. "You have reached the very top!"

The other knight hands me a piece of paper. "Here are your instructions for the Test of Intelligence, which will take place in that field." He points far below us, where I can see nine or ten different stations set up across the grass. "Take this slide down and keep your arms and legs close to your body, okay?"

"Okay! Thanks!" I scramble onto the long slide that's been built onto the side of the cairn, feeling grateful I don't have to climb down the rocks. I slide and whoop all the way to the bottom. The breeze feels amazing on my sweaty face.

The next mini-challenge reminds me of circuits in gym class, where we do push-ups at one station until the whistle blows, then work on the balance beam, then do sit-ups on the mats, and so on. I actually like circuits because they break the time up and make it feel shorter.

My new instructions are made up of three poems. The first one reads:

STATION #7

To start, untie those ugly knots
To free your second clue
Go slow and move from east to west
Or it'll be tough to do.

I see George standing in front of what looks like a vertical puzzle, moving circular blocks of wood to form a pattern. Meanwhile, Sadie's on a giant checkerboard, lifting big black and red pieces to different squares. I've caught up to them both!

I jog through the numbered stations and laugh when

I find #7, because it's a giant tangle of thick ropes. I can't get away from ropes today! "At least I don't have to climb these," I say cheerfully. I grab one of the tangles and start working, but then I realize I'm not following directions. The poem said to "move from east to west," which means from right to left.

So I scoot to the right side and patiently loosen knots one at a time. It's slow going, but it isn't hard. As I work, I realize that if I *had* ignored the instructions, I would have made an even bigger mess of the ropes. Since I listened, though, other knots farther down the line unravel by themselves as I continue. In ten minutes, I've loosened almost the whole thing. Underneath the tangle, I see my prize: an empty quiver for carrying arrows.

"Bet these are for the next task," I say, slinging the quiver onto my back. I go back to my to-do list. The next item says:

STATION #2

Find the trunk with letters on top
Name the Warlock of Krest
This shall unlock what is inside
And help you on your quest.

I jog past George, who is now working on what looks like a medieval chemistry set. He's standing at a table of glass vials with different colored liquids inside, which he pours and mixes. As I watch, he combines a blue liquid and a red liquid, and then pours the purple mixture into a vial with a clear liquid. It foams and bubbles for a minute, and then turns muddy brown. George groans, dumps it onto the ground, and starts over.

I'm so busy watching him that I almost forget I'm supposed to be searching for Station #2. I scurry across the field and find a wooden trunk. The lid is flat, with shallow grooves on it, and there's a pile of stones etched with alphabet letters nearby. I lift a few and realize that they're different weights. Some of the smaller ones are actually heavier than the bigger ones. If I spell the warlock's name right and put the correct stones into the correct grooves, I bet the trunk will open. I clap my hands in excitement, because this is just the kind of word puzzle I love.

The only problem is, the Warlock of Krest has a zillion names. He's known all over Pantaera, and different lands know him by different nicknames.

"Okey dokey, let's see what we're working with here," I say in a low voice. Whenever Sadie and I play a word game called Bananagrams, I always like to organize my letters first. So I do the same thing here: I put the vowels on one side and the consonants on the other to help me figure out which name the trunk requires.

I spot the letters S, D, B, and R.

Right away, Shadowbringer pops into my head. It's what the Warlock of Krest is called in western Pantaera, because of his ability to control darkness and light. Another name I can think of is Starbrooder, which is what the people of Yellowdale call him because he studied astronomy when he lived among them in the Fourth Age of Pantaera.

And then I spot two Os. "Aha! Starbrooder it is!"

This would be a little trickier for anyone who didn't know *War of Gods and Men* well, but they could always look at it as a word scramble or move the stones around randomly. I'm glad I *do* know the game well, though, because as soon as I lay the stones down, the latch pops open to reveal a ring of silver keys that are all different shapes and sizes.

"Woo-hoo!" I put them in my pocket, then move on to my final task.

Once again, Sadie and George have finished before me and vanished. I remind myself not to panic and to keep my eyes on my own paper, so I focus on my last poem:

STATION #9

Four wooden buckets lie ahead
Fill them with bags of sand
Until they all weigh just the same
You'll need the tools that land.

I hustle to the edge of the field, where the forest begins. Hanging from a branch a few feet off the ground are four empty buckets. Underneath them are ten bags of sand.

"Okay, so this is like the phoenix feather puzzle." I pick up the bags, and again I find that some of the smaller ones are heavier than the bigger ones. It feels like there are stones inside to help weigh them down more. I organize them by weight and then start the task by putting the lightest bag into the first bucket, which drops about three inches. Next, I try to even out the rest by putting in a single bag or a combination of bags.

It takes a ton of trial and error. My mind keeps going back to Sadie and George as I work, wondering how far ahead they are. I hope they're doing okay, especially Sadie. It would be so cool if she won and became the child hero of Pantaera!

Finally, I manage to even out all of the buckets and

hear a *click!* as something drops from the treetops: a bow and a pair of leather archery gloves. I want to sag against a tree and take a celebratory break, but there's no time.

I put on the gloves, grab my bow, and hurry into the woods, crossing my fingers that I can at least catch up to my friends.

CHAPTER TWENTY-SIX

SADIE

I'M THE FIRST ONE DONE WITH THE TEST OF Intelligence! George and Jeremy are still doing their puzzles as I run into the trees, hoping to get a good head start on whatever's next.

I come to a small clearing with a platform about thirty feet high. The only way to get on it is to climb a ladder—which is trapped inside of a wooden cage. In front of the cage are three targets: big, medium, and small. "Oh, boy," I mutter. Archery definitely isn't my strength.

A knight greets me. "Welcome to your fourth mini-challenge, the Test of Humility. The object of this task is to find the arrows to fire at those targets, which will free the ladder."

"Okay," I say nervously. "I've got a bow, gloves, and a quiver. Where do I find arrows?"

He points to some objects on the ground. I see cloth sacks, wooden chests of different sizes, and metal canisters. I can feel arrows inside the sacks, and *hear* them inside the chests and canisters when I shake them, but I have no idea how to get them out. The sacks are sealed and have no openings, the chests are locked, and the canisters have been welded shut.

And then it hits me. "Duh!" I say, clapping a hand over my forehead. I forgot about the dagger I got from doing the puzzles! I pull it out just as George sprints into the clearing, listens to the knight (who gives him the same instructions), and says, "Hey, Sadie! How goes it?"

"Um, okay, I think. I can cut the arrows out of the sacks with my dagger, but I don't know how to open any of this other stuff. I don't have any other tools—"

"I do!" George says, holding up a pair of metal pliers. "I got this from completing my puzzles. I can use these to pry the lids off those metal canisters."

"Nice! But what about the wooden chests? Do you have any keys?"

"Nope. I bet you anything Jeremy does, though." He scratches his chin. "Weird how the puzzles gave us all different tools, huh?"

A light bulb turns on in my brain. "Well, this is the final

Test of Humility, right? And part of being humble is asking for help. I think it's better if we work together, 'cause we'll find more arrows that way. I bet some kids would try to do it alone, though, to get ahead," I add, chuckling as I think of good ol' Clip . . . though my brother *has* learned to be a lot humbler lately.

George nods. "Agreed, let's work together and wait for Jer."

I start hacking apart the cloth sacks. My dagger isn't sharp, so it takes some muscle to cut through the tough material. By the time I've collected a total of five arrows, George has gotten most of the metal canisters open with his pliers.

When Jeremy arrives a minute later, we bring him up to speed. He holds up a bunch of keys on a ring, his eyes shining. "I can take care of opening the wooden chests!" he says.

Soon, between the three of us, we've uncovered fifteen arrows.

"Five for Sadie," George says, handing some to me. "Five for Jer, and five for me. Since there are three targets, should we each take one? Which ones do you guys want?"

"Do you mind if I take the big one?" I ask sheepishly. "I'm not great at archery."

The boys agree, and George takes the medium

target and Jeremy the smallest one. We stand on Xs made of red tape and put our gloves on. I take deep breaths to calm the butterflies in my stomach before nocking my first arrow and aiming for the center of the big target.

THWFFFFPPP!

"Ughhhh," I groan, as my arrow lands right at the very edge of the target.

George hits his bull's-eye on the second try. "Woo!" he cheers.

Jeremy takes his time adjusting his feet and his bow. When he shoots his arrow, it hits dead center on the small target, first try. "Yay!" he says. "Go, Sadie, you got this!"

The boys give me their unused arrows and back away. Jer knows I can't focus with people hovering, but knowing they're watching makes me nervous all the same. I miss the bull's-eye again on my second arrow, so I nock my third, trying to breathe and aim carefully.

Third arrow: bounces off.

Fourth arrow: hits the very edge again.

Fifth arrow: bounces off.

"Agggggghhhhh!" I feel silly struggling when this was so easy for George and Jer.

A sudden movement catches my eye from the

platform above. I glance up, surprised to see the wizard smiling down at me and holding a familiar black cat, the one who was obsessed with Iggy. The cat blinks its amber eyes and meows at me in an encouraging way. Seeing the two of them reminds me of my promise to just have fun at these tasks.

So I roll my shoulders back. I relax my arms, take a few more deep breaths, and then nock my sixth arrow and take my time aiming it.

THWFFFFPPP!

The arrow pierces the bull's-eye on the big target.

CREAK!

Ropes lift the wooden cage into the air, where it hangs above the now-free ladder.

"Yaaaaaaaaassssss!" George and Jer yell.

"I knew you could do it, Sadie!" Jer exclaims.

"Well done," the knight says, grinning. "Climb the ladder to face your next task. Someone will be there to give you instructions."

"The wizard, right?" I say happily.

"That must be why he's waiting for us up on the platform with Tuba," Jeremy says, and George nods in agreement.

The knight looks puzzled. "Wizard? No, I meant other knights, like me."

I exchange amused glances with Jeremy and George. I guess we were right: All of the actors have to pretend that only kids can see the wizard. Maybe it adds to the magic.

One by one, we climb onto the wide platform to find two knights waiting for us, and also Derek and Caroline Marshall. "Hey!" I cry, hugging the twins. "What are you guys doing here?"

"We're going to demonstrate this next puzzle for you!" Caroline says.

George and Jeremy hug them, too. Jeremy scans the platform, asking, "Wait, where's the wizard? He was up here with you a second ago."

"No, he wasn't. He was with *you* guys." Derek points at the ground far below us. "Caroline and I saw him cheering you on down there."

"No, he was up here," George, Jeremy, and I say at the same time.

The twins exchange confused glances, and one of the knights interrupts, saying, "Okay, everyone, let's get started on this next puzzle. Time is ticking!"

"Right," Caroline says quickly. "So, since you guys decided to work together on the Test of Humility, this puzzle is designed to split you up again. You have to do it alone."

Derek points out three metal seesaws, which look like ones on any playground, and then points out a random collection of stones, bricks, boxes, and branches. "You each get a seesaw and a bunch of objects, all of which have different weights. You have to figure out how to place every single object on your seesaw so that the two sides even out perfectly."

"Once the seesaw balances out, it'll activate the zip line," Caroline adds.

"A zip line?" Jeremy squeaks.

The platform ends just beyond the seesaws. There's only empty air, and a thick web of ropes and metal chains stretching so far into the trees, I can't see where they end. I look up and notice three safety harnesses dangling above us.

"Don't worry, it'll be fun!" Derek says. "The zip line will be your fifth and final mini-challenge. It's the Test of Courage for today."

I gulp. Flying through the trees in a harness, high above the ground, will definitely test my bravery today. But first, I have to focus on the puzzle at hand.

Jer gets on his hands and knees to sort out his objects, while George goes for a different technique: putting random items at random spots on the seesaw. I remember he did the same thing with the phoenix feather puzzle and really struggled—tasks like this must not be his strength, like they are for Jer and me. This could be our chance to pull ahead of George.

I sort my items, too, by weight. My heaviest objects are a brick, a rock, and a tree branch, and the lightest are a copper mug, a sack of grain, a small hammer, and a wooden box full of dirt. I start placing them, feeling fairly confident . . . until I realize how sensitive the seesaws are to the slightest ounce. Mine keeps shifting just when I think I've got it.

There's a moment when the two sides are *exactly* even and my heart jumps . . . but the harness doesn't drop, and I realize I forgot to include the sack of grain, which means I have to start over. It makes me feel a tiny bit better to see George having to start over, too.

Jer, meanwhile, looks like a scientist working on important research. His brow furrows as he positions each object, waits to see how the seesaw will react, and then adds another item.

I try to do the same, holding my breath as my seesaw tips back and forth.

Suddenly, it levels out beautifully! But the harness *still* doesn't drop. "What the heck am I missing?!" I ask, and one of the knights gives me a sympathetic smile and points behind me. I follow her finger and realize I've forgotten an item *again*—this time, the copper mug.

"Arrrrrrrrgghhhhh!" I groan.

Back to square one.

CHAPTER TWENTY-SEVEN
JEREMY

I FEEL AWFUL WHEN I HEAR SADIE'S CRY OF FRUS-tration . . . because I've figured out the puzzle. This challenge is a lot like my task with the wooden buckets. It takes trial and error, but the seesaw is harder because it matters *where* you put the items, too. Placing heavier stuff near the edge has a bigger effect than setting them close to the center. I've lined everything up, and now all I have is a rusty old helmet, which doesn't weigh much. Gently, I put it near the middle and wait.

The seesaw evens out in a perfect line, straight across. *THWIPPPPP!*

My leather safety harness drops onto the platform.

"YES, JEREMY!" the Marshall twins shout.

Sadie and George stop working and cheer, too, looking genuinely happy for me.

A knight helps slip the harness over my head. It has a thick leather strap under each arm, three straps across my chest and waist, and a wide part to sit on, like a swing at the playground. Two chains link the harness to the ropes and pulleys that plunge into the trees. It feels safe and secure . . . but still, I break out into a cold sweat as the knight leads me to the edge of the platform. I can't even look down because I know it will make me dizzy.

"I hate heights," I confess.

"You're going to be fine," the knight says kindly. "Keep your arms and legs close to your body. The zip line goes about a hundred feet, and it's designed to slow down before you reach the next platform. You'll see two knights waiting to help you once you're there. Got it?"

"Got it," I say weakly, clutching the straps on my shoulders.

"As mentioned, this is your Test of Courage," the knight says. "And to start, I have a question for you. Do you want me to push you, or do you want to jump off by yourself?"

Something in his voice tells me this is part of the test. I glance at Derek and Caroline, who give me an encouraging thumbs-up. Sadie and George are still working, but she gives me a huge smile and George calls, "You're the man, Jer!" My friends all believe in me. They think I'm a hero, and part of being a hero is being brave—something I never dreamed I could be.

I've always thought of myself as scared and slow and weak. I'm the one who can't run a mile, the one who gets picked last in gym class, the one who falls on his butt a lot, the one who only knows what it's like to be courageous when he's playing a video game.

But then I came to Pantaera. And I showed everyone, including myself, that I am made of way stronger stuff than I appear.

"I'll jump!" I declare, and the knight nods and backs away.

"Yeah, you will!" George and Derek yell supportively, as Caroline claps.

"Woo! I'm proud of you, Jer!" Sadie shouts.

I move closer to the edge of the platform. The zip line is thirty feet off the ground, which doesn't seem like a *lot* . . . but there won't be anything around me except empty air, which is sort of terrifying. There's nothing else to do, though, except close my eyes and bellow, at the top of my lungs, "FOR PANTAERAAAAAAA!"

I jump and immediately slice through the air, with the harness holding me securely. The zip line cables tilt slightly downward, so I feel myself speeding up and open one eye to peek at the trees zooming by. My stomach does this exhilarating swoop, kind of like when you're on a plane that's taking off. I try to scream, but the wind has been snatched from my lungs and no sound comes out. It's the wildest experience, zipping through the sun-dappled woods with my arms and legs dangling into nothingness. This is what it must feel like to fly.

And then, *way* too soon, I reach another wooden platform. The zip line rises up to slow me down, and I coast gently toward two knights who pull me to a stop. "You okay?" one asks.

"Yeah! That was so fun!" I shout, and they both laugh.

"You're not done yet." The knight pulls me and my harness over to the opposite side of the platform, then holds up a dark blue cloth eye-mask. "You've got about five hundred more feet to go, and this time . . . you're going to be zip-lining with a blindfold on."

My stomach does a nervous little flip-flop, but it's weird: I don't feel that afraid anymore. I guess that's the funny thing about facing your fears . . . they don't seem as scary once you've already gone through them. So I say, "No problem! And I'll jump again this time."

"Sure." She puts the mask over my eyes, which lets in only faint sunlight. "Okay, hold on to my hand and I'll lead you to the edge. Feel your toes hanging off? You can jump any time."

I hesitate, my knees wobbling. And then, out of nowhere, I hear the wizard's cheerful voice in my ear. "Keep that fire burning, young man!" he says, and Tuba meows in agreement. I gasp, because I *know* there's no one else on this platform except the two knights and me. How could a wizard and a cat climb up here that fast without anyone seeing them?

For a second, I think that maybe, just *maybe*, the grown-ups haven't been pretending. Maybe this is one epic fantasy where only we can see the wizard, because it's meant to be. Because we are the warriors of Pantaera, and we are the chosen ones.

"Are you okay, Jeremy?" the knight asks, concerned.

"Oh yeah!" I say, grinning. "I'm more than okay!"

And then I jump.

The wind whooshes past my ears and birds sing in the trees as I fly. My mouth is still wide-open in a grin, which I know isn't a good idea 'cause I don't want to swallow bugs, but I can't help it. In the fantasy books that I read, the main character always finds their destiny, and I know now that this experience in Pantaera is mine.

"I'm a herooooooooooo!" I scream, my voice echoing through the forest.

The zip line starts to tilt downward and I feel myself speeding up. Finally, it lifts and I hear someone call,

"Okay, we're going to catch you! You're approaching the last platform!"

I nod in the direction of the voice, and a moment later, I feel two sets of hands pull me to a stop. Someone takes off my blindfold and I see another pair of knights. They help me out of my harness, and I stop and catch my breath for a second. This platform is a lot smaller, with a hole in the middle and a fireman's pole leading straight down.

I peek through the hole and see Clip Chu and Iggy Morales beaming at me on the ground. "Hey, Jeremy!" they cry, waving. "Come down!"

"Wh-what? Am I done?" I ask, shocked.

"Not yet," Clip calls. "You've got one more challenge to get through."

I hook my arms and legs around the metal pole and slide onto the grass, my knees more wobbly than ever as I land. Clip and Iggy catch me before I collapse to the ground, and we all hug. "What are you guys doing here?" I ask breathlessly.

"We're here to give you instructions," Iggy says, pointing. "Get a load of *that*."

I see three big plywood boards, each standing about six feet high. The outline of a giant map of Pantaera has been painted onto all of them, looking like if you combined South America and Australia. In front of each board are seven pieces of wood that have been whittled into the shape of some of the different lands and kingdoms of Pantaera.

A smile forms on my face.

"It looks like you already know what to do," Iggy says, chuckling. "But we'll tell you anyway: You have to attach those wooden pieces where they belong on the map."

"If you do it right, the puzzle pieces will spell out the path you need to take." Clip points to what looks like a hedge maze with three entrances, looming beyond the map. "Take the correct path to the end and you will be named . . ."

"The child hero of Pantaera, final member of the Pantaereon!" they say together.

I start dancing in place. "Can I start now?!"

Clip throws his hands up. "Yes!"

"Go, go, go!" Iggy yells.

I fling myself at the map. Someone who doesn't know the geography of Pantaera could look at this as a classic puzzle and figure out where the pieces fit. As for me, though? I know the map by heart. Mom bought me a juice glass printed with it for my birthday, and when Dad and I were at Comic Con, I got a rug of the

Pantaera map for my room. How many times have I sat on that rug doing homework and drinking juice from that glass?

The pieces of wood have magnets on the back and are labeled, and I realize that they're all the places we've been to in Pantaera. There's Frostthorn Castle, where the orcs were making dangerous Crystals of Crestfall. I spot Glimmervale Marsh, where the sirens lurked with riddles and songs. I see Hollybottom, the village of the werewolves, and also Shadowheart Manor with the vampires' maze of mirrors. There's the Abbey of the Grey Mages and the riverside village of Larchmont, where we moved the dragon egg and encountered the elves. And of course, there's King Rothbart's castle and next to it, Winterhearth House, where we've been living.

My eyes get teary because it reminds me of *The Return of the King*, the final movie in the Lord of the Rings trilogy. At the end of the film, the camera pans across the map of Middle-Earth to show you how far the characters have come. Like them, my friends and I have been through so much together. We've endured countless dangers to prove ourselves and fight for Pantaera, and it feels perfect that our very last challenge is to put this map together.

I put King Rothbart's castle near the center of my board, knowing that his land is a crossroads between kingdoms. Frostthorn Castle goes to the southwest, and I smile as I remember how we ran around looking for devil dust and dragon's blood. I place Glimmervale Marsh, home of the sirens, to the east and Hollybottom toward the southern region of the map.

The vampires live up north since the sun isn't as strong there, so I stick Shadowheart Manor above everything else. I position the Abbey of the Grey Mages along the western coast, near the sea. Finally, I put Larchmont below the Desolate Peaks, where that poor dragon was trying to take her eggs. I hope she's been reunited with the one she dropped.

I'm so into the task, just trying to get everything right, that it takes me a second to notice I've spelled out a message. Each puzzle piece has a letter carved onto it, and when I stand back and look at the whole map, a word appears: M-I-D-D-L-E.

I'm so stunned, I just stare at it for a minute.

"You did it! You're done!" Clip squawks. "Go, Jer! What are you waiting for?"

"Hurry! Someone's coming!" Iggy shouts.

A pair of sneakers hits the wooden platform above us. George or Sadie just got off the zip line and finished the

Test of Courage . . . but I don't even wait to see which of them it is.

I hustle down the middle path between the hedges, gasping through a stitch in my chest. In minutes, I burst into a grassy field on the other side of the forest.

Everywhere I look, there are people, horses, and royal banners, and the second they see me, everyone explodes into thunderous applause and cheering. I nearly fall down at the sudden noise. Drums and trumpets sound out, and firecrackers go off. The spectators shout my name and wave flags, and I spy Lizard, Molly, Kris, Derek, and Caroline, who must have run out here after demonstrating the earlier tasks. I see the Blackwoods standing near King Rothbart, Princess Errin, Captain Redfern, the Keeper of Fortunes, and a ton of knights, courtiers, and servants, all applauding.

I see cameras and microphones and equipment everywhere, no longer hiding, as the crew surrounds me and films my reaction. They tried to dress in medieval clothes to fit in, but they still look out of place because some of them are in sunglasses and baseball caps.

I focus on a big group that looks even *more* out of place, seeing as they're all in jeans and T-shirts. I see Clip and Sadie's parents and grandparents, Iggy's dad, the Marshalls' dad, and the families of the other competitors.

And then everyone else seems to fade into the background when I see two people and a cute gray-and-white pit bull who is barking and wagging her tail. Mom and Dad hold out their arms, eyes shining, and Chickpea goes crazy with joy at the sight of me. This entire journey, there hasn't been a moment that feels more heroic than seeing how proud my family is of me.

I burst into tears and run right into their hug.

Dad is crying as hard as I am. "I love you, Jer Bear. I'm so proud of you, son."

"You are a certified, grade-A hero," Mom says, wrapping her arms tight around me.

Chickpea soaks my pants with excited drool, then jumps up on her back paws to join our hug. She leans her head lovingly against my stomach, her eyes soft.

Pantaera was fun. But this?

This is home.

CHAPTER TWENTY-EIGHT
SADIE

THAT NIGHT, EVERYONE GATHERS INSIDE THE CASTLE
of the North Wind. King Rothbart and Princess Errin sit
on thrones in the Great Hall, with the Keeper of Fortunes
and Captain Redfern standing nearby. All of the actors
are in full costume and makeup and cameras swivel
everywhere as the crew hurries around with equipment,
capturing every detail. I spy Red Nguyen and the other
producers, checking their phones and tablets and direct-
ing the workers.

"Isn't this cool, Sadie?" Dad asks, putting an arm
around me. "I can't believe you and Clip got to *live* this
for an entire week! I'm so jealous!"

"Me too," Mom agrees. "They said there's a show for
grown-up contestants, right?"

"They already filmed that season," Clip reminds her,

from where he stands wrapped in Grandma's tight hug. "Why? You weren't thinking about auditioning, were you?"

Mom wiggles her eyebrows playfully. "Why not? What you kids did looked *so* fun."

Our parents told us they had been watching us all week, hiding out with the other families in strategic positions in the castles, forests, and other locations. Most of the time, they were tucked away somewhere, enjoying the action from a TV screen. But other times, they were right on set with us, just hidden away really well. And we were so focused, we didn't notice them—except of course when I spotted Red, Dr. Thomas, and Chickpea among the Larchmont villagers.

"You made the top three, Sadie!" Grandpa says proudly. "You even beat Clip!"

I nod in disbelief. "I know. I didn't think I was going to last that long."

Grandma clicks her tongue. "Why do you think this? Didn't I tell you? You are a girl who can do anything," she says, hugging me next.

"You made Team Chu proud, sis," Clip tells me. "I'm still jealous you rode a zip line!"

I laugh. Flying through the trees was one of my favorite parts of the show, even if I only got to the final platform in time to see Jeremy win . . . and I wouldn't have it any other way.

"And I'm jealous of Jeremy's grand prize! Getting to hang out on the movie set," my brother adds, sighing. "He deserves it. He's a bigger *War of Gods and Men* fan than I am, and anyway, maybe I can give him some of my video game ideas to share with Red."

Red comes up behind him, eyes twinkling behind his glasses. "Video game ideas, huh?"

Clip whirls, his jaw dropping at the sight of his hero. I can see his entire vocabulary disappearing from his head. "Ummmm . . . uhhhhh . . . you . . ." is all he manages to say.

I roll my eyes. "Clip's biggest dream is to become a video game designer someday," I inform Red. "He's got some great ideas already, and he wanted to win this whole show so he could pitch them to you when he went to LA."

"Hmmm, I'm always excited to talk about ideas, especially with a young Vietnamese American designer! How about you and I video-chat sometime, Clip? That is, if it's okay with your parents," Red adds, looking at Mom and Dad, whose mouths have fallen open, too.

"Of course it's okay!" Dad says, at the same time Mom replies, "Thank you so much!"

Red hands Clip a business card. "Shoot me an email and we'll set something up, okay?" he says, patting my stunned brother on the shoulder. "You folks enjoy the celebrations!"

Clip watches him walk away, then looks down at the card like it's made out of solid gold. "I-I can't believe it. I get to talk to him about my ideas!" he sputters.

"*I* believe it. You're a talented guy . . . and humble, too. We saw the footage in the vampire castle," Mom adds, chuckling, as she kisses the side of his head.

Clip breaks into a huge grin. "Red is gonna freak out when he hears my *awesome* ideas!"

"What were you saying about him being humble, Mom?" I joke.

Suddenly, a familiar face appears in front of us. "Well, well, well. Looks like Team Chu wasn't just a one-hit wonder after that laser tag win!" Tom Blackwood declares.

"Tom!" Clip and I cry. I hug him, and Clip gives him a high ten.

"I was watching you guys with your families the whole time!" Tom says. "Mom and Aunt Lu were there, too. You did such an awesome job on the challenges!"

We introduce Tom to our family, and Grandma says good-naturedly, "So *your* family's the one who's been taking all of Clip and Sadie's money for laser tag games this summer."

Everyone laughs as Derek, Caroline, Iggy, and their dads make their way toward us.

"Hey, hey, Team Chu's all here!" Derek says. "But wait, where's Jeremy?"

"I checked with his parents earlier." I point at the Thomases across the room, who are surrounded by a swarm of villager kids all petting and hugging Chickpea. The dog sits calmly, licking their faces and enjoying the attention. "They told me the producers pulled him aside earlier. They've got something big planned for him!"

"Maybe he'll have to make a speech or something," Caroline suggests.

"We all know he's expert level at those," Iggy says.

Derek laughs. "Way above expert level."

The other competitors aren't far away, either. I see George, Lizard, and their families near the Thomases, and Kris and Molly and their parents are standing near the thrones. Molly catches my eye, and we smile. On the field earlier, when all the kids reunited to celebrate Jer's epic victory, we agreed to exchange numbers and keep in touch once we get our phones back.

"By the way, Iggy," I say, suddenly remembering. "Jer

and George and I kept seeing the wizard during our final challenge, and he had Tuba with him."

Iggy's eyes widen. "Oh yeah? I've been looking for that cat everywhere! I haven't seen him in a couple of days. I guess he really *does* belong to the wizard after all," he adds, sighing.

"Cheer up, Igster," Clip says. "Maybe you guys will get to say goodbye."

"Yeah! I bet the wizard will show up tonight." I stand on tiptoe to peer around the Great Hall. "The show's over, so the grown-ups won't have to pretend they can't see him anymore."

"Here's our chance to ask," Derek says, as Red and his coproducers, Andy and Bess, walk back over to us. "Hey, Red! Is the wizard gonna be here tonight?"

Red looks up from his phone. "Sorry, who?"

"You know, the weird old guy," Derek continues. "The wizard with the black cat. He was nice, and we just wanted to say thank-you to him."

"I don't know who you mean," Red says, startled. He looks at Andy and Bess, who shrug and shake their heads. "I specifically made sure not to write a wizard character into the show."

I watch the grown-ups carefully. Their confusion looks real, which means either they're good actors themselves . . . or they truly have no idea who we're talking about.

"But there was definitely a wizard," Iggy insists. "His cat followed me around part of the time. Ask Captain Redfern. He saw the cat!"

Red nods. "I remember the random stray cat. Andy and Bess and I debated whether to edit him out of the show, but he was so cute with you that I think we'll keep him."

"But you *must* have caught the wizard on camera," Clip argues. "He appeared to all of us at some point. He was in the orc castle and the vampire manor. He was chilling in the sirens' marsh. He even talked to my sister at Winterhearth House!"

"We *all* saw him," I agree.

"Look, maybe it was another actor you saw. A knight or a villager." Red can clearly sense us getting frustrated, because his tone is low and soothing. "Don't get me wrong. I love a good wizard! But when I was writing the *War of Gods and Men* show, I wanted to avoid that cliché 'cause so many fantasy movies have a character like that."

Bess looks at us thoughtfully. "You know what, though, Red? Didn't the adult and teen contestants say something similar when we were filming their seasons?"

"Yeah, come to think of it, I seem to remember some-one mentioning an old man on set who was in costume," Andy adds.

Red frowns. "No one said anything about that to *me*. That's odd. Maybe we have some kind of cosplaying superfan sneaking in to watch the filming?"

"We keep security pretty tight around here," Bess says doubtfully. "But it's possible."

"You're not listening to us!" Iggy says in a loud voice, and his dad puts a hand on his shoulder to calm him down. "This dude was a straight-up wizard! He looked exactly like one, with a beard and a pointy hat. And he was wise and encouraging and stuff. He gave us advice."

"Yeah!" Caroline, Clip, and I say together.

Andy's headpiece buzzes. He presses a finger to his ear, listening to whoever's on the other end, and taps Red on the shoulder. "We gotta get going, Red. Ten min-utes to showtime."

"Right." Red looks around at us. "I'm sorry, guys, let's talk about this later, okay? I need you to go out to the main entrance right now. You're going to be part of the grand procession, along with the Pantaereon and the other warriors. They're waiting for you in the hall. Bess, Andy, let's split up and get the other kids." The producers take off.

"Ooooh, a grand procession!" Mr. Marshall says.

"This is going to be epic," Dad says, looking impressed.

"Have fun, you guys!" Mom adds.

Grandma elbows Grandpa. "Get your camera ready! This sounds big!"

"I wonder why Red is still pretending that the wizard doesn't exist," Caroline says, after we say goodbye to our families and Tom and start heading toward the castle's main entrance. "I mean, the competition is over. We don't need to be immersed anymore."

"I dunno if he was pretending," Clip says thoughtfully. "He seemed confused for real."

"But why act like we were lying, then?" Iggy asks.

"I don't think he thought we were lying," Derek points out. "Just mistaken."

"Bess and Andy said some of the contestants from the other seasons saw the wizard, too," I remind everyone. "Maybe we can ask them in the hall."

Iggy brightens. "Good idea, Sadie."

But as soon as we enter the corridor outside the Great Hall, all thoughts of the wizard go right out of our heads. The place is *packed* with workers, cameras, lights, and microphones, and I can see why: It looks as though the producers have invited all ten adults from

Season 1 and all ten teenagers from Season 2 to come back for this grand finale. The grown-ups are wearing flowing green velvet cloaks and the teens are in billowing blue velvet ones. They all look tall and confident and athletic, and I feel glad I wasn't competing against them.

"Hey, here are our child warriors!" says a cameraperson, who grabs a pile of red velvet cloaks from a nearby table and holds them out to us. "Can you guys please put these on?"

"Wow, cool!" Derek says, draping the rich fabric around his shoulders.

"Look how epic we are!" Clip brags, moving over to admire himself in one of the big bronze mirrors on the wall.

Caroline and I help each other fasten our cloaks, beaming the whole time. "Now I *really* feel like a hero of Pantaera," she says, and I nod in agreement. The weight of the velvet feels comforting and powerful, and as I look at myself in the mirror, I chuckle at how far I've come. I'm not one bit ashamed to be wearing this costume. Instead, I'm totally enjoying it.

The workers hurry back into the Great Hall to prep their equipment and set up lights and speakers, leaving the competitors alone in the corridor.

"Hey, hey, child heroes!" says an adult contestant. "You guys did awesome!"

"We were watching you compete," another grown-up agrees. "That sirens' marsh was the *best*! When Clip and Derek and George got stuck in that trap . . ."

"How about Jeremy answering that *Labyrinth* riddle correctly, eh?" says another adult, shaking her head in amazement. "Who would've thought kids today would have even *heard* of that old movie. I had such a huge crush on David Bowie!"

"My favorite part was the vampire manor," a teen contestant pipes up. "Phew! When that guy with the top hat went after Sadie and Molly, I thought it was all over for them."

Molly comes toward us with George, Kris, and Lizard just in time to hear this. "They're talking about us like we're their favorite characters or something!" she tells me, looking stunned.

I laugh. "I think that's pretty cool."

"Hey! Look, guys!" someone calls. "It's the Pantaereon!"

Three people have just walked through the main doors of the Castle of the North Wind, their golden velvet cloaks fluttering behind them. The first person is a short woman in her forties with long red hair and cool tattoos all over her arms. The second person is a guy who looks like a seventeen-year-old version of Clip, with spiky black hair, olive skin, and an athletic build. And the third person is my best friend in the whole world.

Jeremy is grinning so hard we can see all his teeth. "Guys! Isn't this amazing?" he calls.

The energy in the room is incredible, with thirty warriors of Pantaera all introducing themselves and swapping stories about the show and laughing. Somehow, though, the sound of a single person clapping manages to cut through the noise. The conversations die down at once.

A man stands alone in the doorway of the castle, wearing a periwinkle-blue robe, a pointy hat, white tube socks, and beat-up flip-flops. His eyes twinkle above his big gray beard, and wrapped around his shoulders like a fluffy black scarf is none other than . . .

"Tuba!" Iggy cries, and the cat meows back at him affectionately.

"The wizard!" a grown-up and a teen both say.

Another adult contestant pumps her fists. "Yes! I wondered if he'd show up!"

"All of you can see him, too?" Clip asks, stunned, as everyone around us nods.

"Oh yeah," a teen says. "He kept popping up in

random places during filming to give us advice and encouragement. It was great!"

"I thought he was part of the show, but the producers had no clue who I was talking about when I mentioned him," an adult competitor says, and several other people nod in agreement.

George scratches his head. "There goes our theory about him only appearing to kids."

"Maybe all of the contestants can see him, and no one else," Lizard suggests.

"How is that possible, though?" I ask. "They must have caught him on camera, right?"

A man shakes his head. "I got that producer, Andy, to show me some of the footage 'cause it was bothering me so much. But we couldn't find any of the parts where the wizard had conversations with the competitors. It was a little creepy, actually. Either someone went in and took the trouble of cutting out *just* those scenes, every single one of them, or . . ." He trails off with a shrug, and we exchange puzzled glances.

The wizard strides into the hall, bumping knuckles and high-fiving competitors along the way. When he passes me, he pats my shoulder and says, "Hello there, Sadie!" and I know this guy is *real*. I can feel the warmth of his long bony fingers and his robes swish against my legs as he walks past to say hi to the other kids. There's no way all of us, all *thirty* contestants, could have imagined him up together. Right?

"Well done, all of you," the wizard says to the whole group. "I am proud of your hard work, and I am especially pleased with our ten child warriors. You deserve this magnificent celebration. But there's a quick word I need to have with one of you . . ." He scans our faces, stroking his long gray beard, until he finds Iggy. "Aha! You, young man! Please come here."

Iggy gapes at him, frozen. Clip and Derek have to push him forward.

"I have a gift to bequeath upon you," the wizard says grandly.

"Uh . . . thanks . . . that's great," Iggy stammers. "Wh-why me?"

"Because the gift has chosen you." And with that, the old wizard lifts Tuba off his shoulders and holds him out to Iggy. "I think my small friend here has found a new home. His time in Pantaera has come to an end, and soon—like all of you here—he must leave this world for another. I think he will be very happy with you."

Iggy takes Tuba in disbelief and hugs him tightly, his eyes full of tears as the cat purrs contentedly against his chest. "Th-thank you. I'll take really good care of him. I promise."

"What about your dad, though?" Clip asks him. "He said he didn't want another cat."

"Well, he won't be happy," Iggy says, looking lovingly down at his new pet. "But he can't say no, not when a wizard has bequeathed Tuba to me. I guess we'll have to do paperwork or something before I adopt you and fly you home, huh?" The cat's purring gets even louder.

"Okay, heroes!" Red says, hurrying into the corridor, his hands full with a phone and a tablet and a clipboard. His eyes are glued to his phone. "Here's the plan. First, we're going to—" His words die in his throat the second he looks up and his eyes find the wizard. His mouth falls open. The clipboard slips from his hand and clatters onto the floor, and one of the teens picks it up and holds it out to him, but he doesn't notice. He's staring at the wizard in total shock, taking in everything from the top of the man's pointy periwinkle hat to his socks and flip-flops.

I seize Clip's arm. "He sees him! He can see him, too!" I hiss.

"See? We weren't lying," Iggy says smugly.

"Uh, Red?" says the teen holding the clipboard. He pokes Red with it. "You okay?"

But Red can't seem to speak a word. It's like he's turned into a statue or something.

"Well, hello there, Red," the wizard says in a gentle voice, his eyes glittering with amusement. "How are you this fine evening?"

Red swallows hard. "This . . . this is impossible," he croaks. "Wh-who are you?"

"You know who I am."

"No, I don't." Red takes off his glasses, wipes them, and puts them back on. His voice is almost afraid. "Who are you and how did you get onto the set of this show?"

The wizard shrugs. "I am Zanzyfyr the Wise, and you are the one who brought me here."

I raise my eyebrows at Jeremy. I don't know who Zanzyfyr the Wise is, but then again, I don't play the video game like everyone else does. The other kids look just as confused as I do, though, and Jeremy's face is blank as he shakes his head at us. He knows more about *War of Gods and Men* than anyone here, yet he's never heard of this wizard, either.

Red looks like he's about to faint.

One of the adult contestants, a big, brown-skinned man with a crew cut and a kind face, takes Red's elbow, clearly afraid he'll crumple right to the floor. "Hey, are you all right, man?" he asks. "This is just an actor who was hired to play a part. That's all."

"No, he's not," Red says emphatically. He hasn't taken his eyes off the wizard once. "Who are you? How can you possibly know who Zanzyfyr the Wise is? How can *anyone* know? It's a character I made up inside my head when I was ten years old! I drew him in an old spiral-bound notebook with a number two pencil. I wrote his character sheet on my dad's giant IBM computer in the basement and saved it on a floppy disk! I still *have* that floppy disk!"

"What the heck is a floppy disk?" Molly whispers, and we all shrug cluelessly at her.

"I have never, *ever* shared that character with a single living soul," Red continues, running a shaking hand through his hair. There are tears in his eyes. "He was kooky and fun, and even then, I didn't want to do what other fantasy writers were doing. I didn't want a typical wizard. So I drew him with socks and flip-flops and I gave him a weakness for hot dogs and coffee, because I thought that was weird and cool. There is no possible way *anyone* could have known about this character or what he looked like."

A chill runs up and down my spine. "So this wizard is, like, imaginary?" I gasp.

"He just exists in your old notebook? And your . . . flurry disk?" Jeremy adds, stunned.

"Floppy disk," one of the adults corrects him.

A tear runs down Red's face. "He was someone I created just for me when I first thought up the world of Pantaera. I was a lonely kid. I was bullied at school for being quiet and drawing weird things, and I didn't have any friends, and my parents were getting a divorce and . . . I made Zanzyfyr up because I wanted someone kind. Someone wise. Someone to help me be brave and make me feel like a warrior—" He chokes up.

"Oh, poor Red," Caroline whispers. She and Iggy have tears in their eyes, too.

Another grown-up competitor, a motherly looking woman with pale skin and short blond hair, comes over and gives Red a hug. Two of the teen contestants pat him on the back.

"How is this possible?" Red whispers.

The wizard holds out his hands, and after a long moment, Red takes them. "*You* made it possible, Red," Zanzyfyr tells him. "You. A boy with a gift and a boundless imagination, who grew up to create an entire world that has made so many people happy. You've helped them feel brave and strong and heroic."

"For real!" one of the teens says. "I was bullied at school, too, and *War of Gods and Men* gave me something to look forward to every day."

"I made *so* many friends because of the video game," another teenager declares.

"Me too," several other people chorus.

"Being on this show has changed my life," says the woman with the red hair and tattoos, the adult hero of the Pantaereon. "It gave me courage and confidence."

"Me too!" I call, and all around the corridor, everyone joins in.

"You brought me to life." Zanzyfyr smiles at Red, then looks around at the competitors. "All of you did. Your imagination, your passion, and your dedication lifted me right out of the pages of a lonely child's notebook. That kind of energy is a powerful force for good. It's a sort of magic, don't you see? You manifested me, all of you. Together."

The clear, silvery sound of trumpets suddenly ring out back in the Great Hall, playing a majestic fanfare and making us all jump. Both Red's phone and tablet start chiming at once—probably texts or calls from the other producers, telling him to get a move on, because he wipes his wet face and straightens. "Um, okay," he says, flustered. "The . . . the show . . ."

"Must go on," Zanzyfyr finishes, grinning. "And so must I."

"Will I see you again?" Red asks, his hands trembling.

"Of course. If you really want to," the wizard promises. He gives Red a kindly wink, then turns in a slow circle, nodding and waving at us all. We wave back, dazed. And then, right before our very eyes, Zanzyfyr disappears into thin air. One second, he was standing there in his weird outfit, and then a blink of an eye later, there's nothing but empty space.

My friends and I look at each other. "Yeah . . . he does that," we all say at the exact same time, and everyone in the corridor bursts out laughing.

Bess and Andy hurry out of the Great Hall. "Red, come on! What's happening? We have to get a move on," Bess says impatiently, tapping her watch.

"Are you . . . are you all right?" Andy asks, seeing Red wipe tears off his face.

"Yeah. I'm awesome!" Red gives them a huge, watery grin, and then clears his throat loudly. "Okay, everyone, you're going to march into the Great Hall in groups. The adults go first, two by two. Ursula? Where is my adult hero . . . ah! Ursula, you will lead the adult group. And Patrick, my teen hero, you will lead the teenagers in pairs and follow the adults. Finally, we'll have the kids, led by

Jeremy. Please march slowly to the thrones, bow to the king and princess, and then move off to the side. Captain Redfern will show you where to stand."

We pair off: Kris and Molly, Clip and Derek, Caroline and Iggy, and George and Lizard.

Jeremy looks at me, his eyes shining. "You're going to lead the procession with me!"

"Me?" I squeak.

"Yes, you, Sadie Chu! No one else!" he says, and we do our jellyfish fist bump.

Red waves his hands for our attention. "Ursula, Patrick, and Jeremy, my three heroes of the Pantaereon: When you come up to the Keeper of Fortunes, she will give each of you one magical artifact. Ursula will get the sword, Patrick will get the armor, and Jeremy, you'll have the shield. Hang on to those until my signal, okay? Everybody ready?"

The trumpets blast louder than ever as the adult contestants march into the Great Hall, two by two. Loud cheers, applause, and stamping feet greet them.

My stomach feels like I've eaten a bowl of wriggling worms. I'm excited and nervous, but there's no place I would rather be than standing with my best friend and all of our fellow competitors. We might have known some of them for only a week, but after this whole intense experience, I feel like we've been bonded together for life.

The teenagers march in next, led by their hero Patrick in his flowing gold cape.

"Child warriors, you're up next," Red says. He seems like he's recovered from seeing the wizard. His eyes are still red, but they're shining with happiness now, too.

"Hey, Red? Thanks for everything," Jeremy says. "I think Zanzyfyr is really, really cool. And I think maybe he should be in the movie."

Red laughs. "I think you're right, Jer. Okay, child heroes! Go on in!"

As our group starts walking, I hear Bess whisper to Andy, "Who's Zanzyfyr?"

"Here we go!" I say to Jeremy.

My best friend grins, then switches into epic fantasy hero mode. His eyes are bright, his chin is lifted, and he walks tall and proud with his shoulders back. Slowly, we march into the Great Hall on a long, plush crimson carpet lined with gold, and are greeted by loud cheers and applause. I spy Mom, Dad, Grandpa, and Grandma all smiling and waving at us, and all of the other contestants' families are beaming proudly, too.

We reach King Rothbart and Princess Errin, who have

gotten to their feet to greet us. Everyone bows, and then Captain Redfern waves us over to one side. The Keeper of Fortunes, looking ancient and beautiful in silvery robes, hands Jeremy the shield, which sparkles in the light. We all look proudly at it. We earned every single gem and put them on, *together*.

When the music ends, King Rothbart lifts his arms and silence falls over the room. "Good evening, my friends, and welcome to the Castle of the North Wind! Over the past week, these ten young warriors have shown us what it means to be a hero. They endured many dangers and surpassed all expectations to prove their courage, determination, humility, intelligence, and strength. I know I also speak for Captain Redfern and the Keeper of Fortunes when I say that we could not have chosen better or braver warriors to fight for Pantaera."

The room explodes into applause again, and two servants appear beside the king with about a dozen shining brass medals attached to thick purple velvet ribbons.

"Whoa!" Caroline exclaims. "I didn't know we were gonna get anything!"

"Me, neither," Kris agrees.

King Rothbart takes one of the medals. "George Quinn Jr., please step forward," he says, and when

George obeys, he drapes the ribbon over his neck. "Lizard Baker."

One by one, he calls our names and puts the medal on us.

When he gets to "Sadie Chu," I'm so excited, I almost trip in front of all those cameras. When the medal goes around my neck, it's all I can focus on. The velvet ribbon feels warm on my skin and the round brass pendant is pleasantly heavy. I study the shape of Pantaera etched onto the front, and when I flip it over, I gasp—my name has been inscribed into the metal!

"Mine says Lizard! Not Elizabeth!" Lizard says happily. She shows off her pendant to me and I show off mine to her, both of us overjoyed to have gotten actual medals for being here. But then I think, *Why not? We're heroes of Pantaera, right?* It's so different from what I would have thought at the beginning of this show that it makes me want to cry happy tears.

Finally, when everyone's got a medal, the musicians pick up their trumpets again and start playing a slow, grand song that echoes up and down the hall.

I spy Red standing alone at the entrance, his arms crossed, a big smile on his face as he looks around at this world he's created and brought us to. I think about what Zanzyfyr the Wise said: that believing is a sort of magic.

And as Captain Redfern signals for the Pantaereon to step forward, it's so easy to believe that all of this is real. The three heroes stand at the foot of the thrones and face the crowd, and right at that moment, the light of the setting sun comes through the windows of the Great Hall. The golden rays land on each of the magical artifacts they hold, making them glow, and an impressed "Oooooohhh!" echoes throughout the room. Jeremy looks happier and prouder than I have ever seen him, and when I peek at his parents, I see both of them tearing up. Jer didn't just prove to himself that he's a hero—he's proved it to everyone, and I know that means the world to him . . . even if he was just competing for fun.

"Long ago, the gods of Pantaera created these relics to protect our land. And now, thanks to our heroes . . . *all* of our heroes," King Rothbart adds, looking significantly at the contestants outside of the Pantaereon, to include us, "the artifacts have been reunited. And what's more, all of the gemstones of power have been collected. Pantaera has been saved!"

A wind rushes through the room, lifting everyone's hair and cloaks.

The magical relics glow more brightly than ever, and I realize now that it's more than just the light of the setting sun—there are skillfully placed spotlights shining right on them. The brightness gets more and more intense until I have to shield my eyes, and then we see ripples of golden light all over the ceiling, walls, and floor of the room. An invisible choir of angelic voices bursts out from somewhere, singing in a different language, and the trumpets pick up the melody.

I get full body shivers, and glancing at the other kids, I see that most of them have tears in their eyes, moved by how amazing and magical this moment feels.

When the music ends, thunderous applause rocks the room. The three heroes of the Pantaereon bow, grinning and waving at the crowd, and then King Rothbart steps down and lifts Jeremy's right hand in the air. "The child hero of Pantaera!" he cries.

If I thought the room had been loud before, it's *nothing* compared to now. The cheers are deafening, and I clap until my hands hurt, sobbing with joy for my friend.

After a solid five minutes of noise, King Rothbart waves his arms again for silence. "Our child hero has a few words he would like to say," he says.

Jeremy doesn't even look nervous to be speaking to so many people. His shoulders are still thrown back and his head is high. He looks like a hero. He *is* a hero. The whole room is quiet, eager to listen to him. And, being Jeremy Thomas, he does not disappoint.

"Greetings," he says, in his fanciest, most epic voice. "I'm honored to be your child hero and to join these two cool people who are already in the Pantaereon. I do not hail from Pantaera, but I have loved the beauty, magic, and majesty of your world for years. The inhabitants of this realm represent everything I have ever wanted to be: brave, strong, and true, and not afraid of fighting for good." He looks right at Red, who smiles and thumps his fist over his heart.

I'm not the only one who sniffles loudly. If there's a dry eye in this room, I can't see it.

"I came here feeling small and unimportant. I kept thinking about how much bigger, stronger, faster, and smarter the others were compared to me. When most people think of a hero, they picture the physical qualities." Jeremy puts a hand over his heart. "But what I learned this week is I've got a fire here. We all do. Being a hero is about keeping that fire burning, no matter what. Being a hero is about pushing through fear and doubt, and never losing hope even when you think you can't do something . . . because you *can*. That fire is inside of you for a reason."

Clip wipes his face, and Iggy blows his nose loudly on his sleeve.

"He's *so* good," Kris whispers, and Molly and I nod in agreement.

"And I just want to say, to anyone out there who doubts themselves: Keep that fire burning," Jeremy goes on. "And this day doesn't belong to one man alone. It belongs to all."

"Okay, he stole that from the Lord of the Rings, but I don't even mind," Derek whispers.

Jeremy suddenly seems to realize how many eyes are on him. He looks overwhelmed by the moment and the pressure of finding a good ending to his speech. "And, um . . . I just want to say thank-you? And I wanna dedicate this victory to my fellow warriors, especially my best friend, Sadie Chu! And also my mom, my dad, and my dog, Chickpea. Thanks!"

Cheers and applause rock the room once more as all of the kids rush toward Jeremy and we do another jumping, hugging huddle. Everyone is crying and talking at once.

Through the crush of flailing, yelling, excited kids, Jeremy's eyes find mine and Clip's. His mouth moves as he tries to say something to us.

Clip cups a hand over his ear. "What?" he screams.

"This victory," Jeremy bellows, "is for Team Chu!"

"Team Chuuuuuu!" Clip and I yell.

Everyone takes up the cry, even George, Lizard, Molly, and Kris, who *aren't* on Team Chu, but have definitely become honorary members for life.

"Team Chu! Team Chu!" we all chant, raising Jer's arms above his head.

It's an epic fantasy ending to remember.

ACKNOWLEDGMENTS

I laughed through writing most of *Team Chu and the Epic Hero Quest*, which seems to be a theme with this whole series! These books are so fun to write, and much of my joy comes from the amazing people who helped me through the process from beginning to end.

The first thanks is for my family and friends, who surprise me at book events, buy multiple copies of everything I write, and cheer me on through every high and low. This epic publishing adventure is less daunting with you guys on my side, telling me I have your swords. (I can't even get through my acknowledgments without a reference to Lord of the Rings, but I'm sure none of you will mind since you love it as much as I do!)

To Tamar Rydzinski, the wise and all-knowing wizard leading me through the fog to my destiny: I'm grateful to call you not only my agent, but also my friend. Can you believe this is already the *sixth* published book in which I have thanked you? My gratitude only increases with each one. May there be many more books and many more thanks in our future!

To Trisha de Guzman, editor extraordinaire: Thank you for always knowing which thread of the magical tapestry to pull (or cut!) to make the actual book match the sparkly version inside my head. I'm glad we finally got to meet in person and show the world our formidable Virgo powers combined. Also, thank you for laughing at all the right places in my manuscripts!

To everyone at FSG and Macmillan Children's, including Eleonore Fisher, Brittany Pearlman, Molly Ellis, Leigh Ann Higgins, Melissa Zar, Elysse Villalobos, Mary Van Akin, Trisha Previte, Aurora Parlagreco, John Nora, and Allyson Floridia: It has been an honor and a delight to work with such a dedicated, fun, and kind group of people. The Team Chu series couldn't be in better hands, and I am grateful to you all!

To the phenomenally talented Chi Ngo: Thank you for the cover art and illustrations for this series. It's been surreal to see my characters and settings come to life under your skillful hands! Thank you to Monica Rodriguez, my social media and TikTok oracle, for helping me promote and launch my books. You and your wisdom are so appreciated! Thank you to my wise friends Dhonielle Clayton and Naima Dennis for your valuable insight on the cover art, and to Angela Tran and Richard Nguyen for portraying Sadie and Clip so beautifully on the audiobook!

I'm very grateful to the authors who blurbed my first Team Chu book: Samira Ahmed, E. L. Shen, Akemi Dawn Bowman, Scott Reintgen, and Adrianna Cuevas. I admire and respect each and every one of you and I cherish your kind words!

Thank you to Katherine Arden for doing my launch party with me and to all of the lovely Phoenix Books staff, including Beth, Tod, and Katie, for your wonderful support for everything I've ever written. No matter where I am, you'll always be my hometown indie!

A huge, heartfelt thanks to the educators, librarians, and booksellers who help get my stories into young readers' hands. I've said it many times before: I am an author today because of folks like you who encouraged me to read and write in my childhood. I know there will be many books in existence, as the years go on, that might never have come to be if it hadn't been for you!

Thank you to every single reader who has ever picked up one of my stories. Without you guys, I would just be a weird lady writing stories for herself in her pajamas, so thank you for letting me write for you, too! I hope I get to thank many more of you in person on my travels.

And finally, this book's for every kid who has ever wanted to see themselves as an epic fantasy hero. You *are* one, and now you're a member of Team Chu, too, and I am so excited for you to join Sadie, Clip, and friends on even more daring adventures!